PRAISE FOR ANN DÁVII

WE NEED NO WINGS

"Ann Dávila Cardinal's *We Need No Wings* beautifully articulates an older woman's life, her grief over the loss of her husband, her frustration with the sexism and racism in her professional life, her need to reinvent herself—the landscape so many of us aging boomers are traveling in our lives or will travel. Cardinal magically weaves pilgrimage, levitation, a sixteenth-century mystic, [and] a journey to heal and recover into an elegantly structured novel. *We Need No Wings* is a twenty-first-century older woman's quest that will inspire readers to consider what lies at the latter end of their lives. Spoiler alert: possibility, hope, and love. We need more novels that deepen our understanding of these later stages of a woman's life and put wings of hope on our hearts. The book soars, her best so far, a transcendent read."
—Julia Alvarez, international bestselling and award-winning author

"From the very first sentence, you know that Ann Dávila Cardinal's *We Need No Wings* is a story for the ages. Tere Sánchez is a grieving widow, a loving mother, a brilliant professor and, oh yeah, she levitates. This novel explores the inexorable pull of blood ties, the power of ancestral homecomings, and one woman's transcendent journey into selfhood. Sassy, smart, humorous, and deeply affecting, this book will make you want to fly."
—Connie May Fowler, author of *Before Women Had Wings*

"There is a wonderfully compelling authority on each and every page here, one borne from hard-earned wisdom, the kind that can only bloom from hardship and loss. But Ann Dávila Cardinal is able to capture all of this with humor and life-loving passion and poetic grace. Cardinal is the real deal, and once again, her fine writing soars."

—André Dubus III, *New York Times* bestselling author of *House of Sand and Fog*

"An unflinching examination of grief through the eyes of an extraordinary woman. With humor and sensitivity, Ann Dávila Cardinal weaves a potent narrative that demonstrates the resilience of women who are more than their roles in the family—and that the third act of life can be a vibrant new beginning."

—Dawn Kurtagich, author of *The Madness*

"Ann Dávila Cardinal expands the reach of the beloved Santa Teresa de Ávila with this exquisite novel about a woman who learns that all journeys lead back to the broken heart. *We Need No Wings* is masterful storytelling—tender, funny, original, and sharp."

—Rigoberto González, author and literary critic

"Poignant, witty, and downright refreshing, *We Need No Wings* will crack open your mind and heart to show you how grief can help us live, doubt can make us trust, and change can bring us back to our true selves. I cried, I laughed, I desperately wanted to visit Spain with Tere Sánchez. This novel is pure magic."

—Eden Robins, author of *Remember You Will Die*

THE STORYTELLER'S DEATH

"In Ann Dávila Cardinal's *The Storyteller's Death*, nothing can stop the cuentistas in the Sánchez family from telling their stories, not even death. I found myself captivated by the young Isla Sánchez and enthralled by the secrets of Isla's ancestors. Like the Sánchez family, Cardinal is a gifted cuentista, and *The Storyteller's Death* is a welcome addition to Puerto Rican storytelling."

—Marisel Vera, author of *The Taste of Sugar*

"Ann Dávila Cardinal is back to captivate us with *The Storyteller's Death*, a striking novel about secrets so restless they're dangerous. Isla, the book's spirited protagonist, will endear herself to all of those who have stumbled upon those terrible truths that make our beloved families that much more complicated, flawed, and human."

—Rigoberto González, author and literary critic

"Ann Dávila Cardinal writes with the razored clarity of a surgeon, the spare and evocative beauty of a poet, and the immensely compelling passion of a natural-born storyteller. I will gratefully read anything she writes!"

—Andre Dubus III, *New York Times* bestselling author of *House of Sand and Fog*

"A stunning, magic-infused tale of family ties and secrets… Cardinal's storytelling prowess shines in this beautifully imagined and multi-layered story, as do her fully developed characters. Fans of sweeping family sagas will enjoy every page."

—*Publishers Weekly*, Starred Review

WE
NEED
A NOVEL
NO
WINGS

Ann Dávila Cardinal

sourcebooks
landmark

Copyright © 2024 by Ann Dávila Cardinal
Cover and internal design © 2024 by Sourcebooks
Cover design by Sara Wood
Cover images © Hein Nouwens/Getty Images

Sourcebooks and the colophon are registered trademarks of Sourcebooks.

The characters and events portrayed in this book are fictitious or
are used fictitiously. Any similarity to real persons, living or dead,
is purely coincidental and not intended by the author.

All brand names and product names used in this book are trademarks,
registered trademarks, or trade names of their respective holders.
Sourcebooks is not associated with any product or vendor in this book.

Published by Sourcebooks Landmark, an imprint of Sourcebooks
P.O. Box 4410, Naperville, Illinois 60567-4410
(630) 961-3900
sourcebooks.com

Cataloging-in-Publication Data is on file with the Library of Congress.

Printed and bound in the United States of America.
SB 10 9 8 7 6 5 4 3 2 1

For my beloved tía, Georgina Dávila Altieri,
who inspired me to go to Ávila and connect with our ancestors.

"The soul here resembles someone on a journey who enters a quagmire or swamp and thus cannot move onward. And, in order to advance, a soul must not only walk but fly."

—Santa Teresa de Ávila,
The Book of Her Foundations

CHAPTER ONE

The first time Tere Sánchez levitated, she was in the garden.

She aimed the hose in an arc over the lush peony bushes, the stream of falling water glinting like diamonds in the sunlight. The blooms were releasing their clean, sweet scent in clouds, and she closed her eyes and inhaled deeply, her mind and body slowing. Her husband had planted them for her since she found the scent of the many-petaled flowers intoxicating. She remembered the day she'd come home early from the university to find his muddy but fine jean-covered ass sticking out from between three young bushes. He was so excited for her to see the new additions to his immaculately manicured garden. The man wasn't effusive, rarely expressing his emotions or complimenting her, but he demonstrated his affection in more tangible ways, in ways that lasted. They'd made love right there on the grass, next to the newly patted-down earth that still held imprints of his big-knuckled hands.

Now, ten years later, the peonies were wild and unrestrained, their bloom-laden branches breaching the careful mulch boundaries he'd laid for them, and in this state, the bushes were more like her. As she inhaled, a feeling of lightness spread through her body, not the dizziness that sometimes plagued her, no. More like the restraints of her day-to-day life released their hold, and Tere felt as if she had slipped outside her body, outside time, place. She let out an audible sigh in that moment of near ecstasy, then slowly opened her eyes to see the pink flowers getting farther away, the stream of water lengthening like a bartender lifting the bottle as he poured. She looked down and saw her green-stained sneakers hovering a foot above the grass.

"What the actual fuck?"

The familiar electric heat of panic flooded her body in a wave, and suddenly she no longer felt weightless but rather unbalanced, out of control. She pinwheeled her arms and kicked her legs, but all this did was upend her in the air, until she was horizontal to the ground, frantically swimming with her limbs and getting nowhere. She held tight to the bright green hose, the only thing tethering her to the earth. Her stomach lurched, and she wondered if she was going to vomit; meanwhile, all she could do was impotently flail about like a fish on a dock.

Then, ever so slowly, she lowered to the ground, until she lay grabbing at the grass with her fists, breathing heavily, her pulse racing. She tried to take mindful breaths in through her nose and out through her mouth, then flipped over onto her back putting her hands to her chest. She let go of the hose, and now it whipped around like a cobra, occasionally spraying cold water into her side and across her stomach, soaking her well-worn Ramones T-shirt.

Tere lay there, looking at the cloudless blue Vermont sky, occasionally glittering with drops of hose water, wondering what the hell had just happened.

Or if anything *had* happened.

Had she finally lost her mind?

It wasn't the first time she'd questioned her sanity, though everyone else in her life thought her overly capable. She'd been told she came across as infinitely competent: always stayed organized, never missed an appointment, with all needed materials in hand. But there had been times over the past year, hours spent sitting in a chair staring off into space, wondering what the purpose of it all was—times when she felt as if the silence of the empty house had weight, like a pile of cinder blocks that pressed down on her.

But this? No, this was on an entirely new level, and she had to admit she was scared shitless. She was afraid to move, afraid she would float up again. She could picture grabbing on to the branches of the bushes, being left with fistfuls of scented petals as she floated off into oblivion. In the moment, though, before she'd opened her eyes and reality had come crashing back, she'd felt good. More than good. Better and freer than she'd ever felt. And with that realization came a crushing wave of guilt. She was a woman in mourning. There was no joy to be had in that.

Even more disturbing, there was something achingly familiar about the…experience. She couldn't call it what it was in those first moments, not even in her mind. But familiar to what? She struggled to remember, but in the past decade, the card catalog of her brain had grown disordered, inaccessible, rusty. Unlike the brains of her young colleagues, it did not respond with the cerebral equivalent of a Google search; instead she was often left groping blindly for a term or memory in the cobwebbed corners of her mind. Was that why she hadn't gone back yet from bereavement leave? That she felt inadequate? Old?

She had to admit that for much of the year since Carl's death, Tere felt as if it were she who haunted their home, walking around aimlessly, as if she had lost something but didn't remember what it was. But in the past few months, she'd started to feel a stirring in her chest, at her core. Almost like when she'd felt that first butterfly-wing

flutter of a baby in her womb. Was the new stirring related to the…
incident she'd just experienced?

She couldn't have *actually* done that, she told herself. *People don't
hover above the ground.* Everything looked the same. How could
everything be the same? With shaking hands, she wrangled the hose
and twisted the tip to turn it off, then got to her feet to find she
was exhausted, like just-finished-a-marathon exhausted. She stood,
adjusted to being upright, and started walking back to the house. She
had to step over a rake and then accidentally kicked an empty pot
onto its side. She could almost hear Carl's bitching from beyond: the
abandoned yard implements scattered about the lawn would have
made him insane. He liked everything in his garden just so, in its
proper place. As she closed the sliding glass door, she looked back
at the long green snake of a hose and the puddles of water around
the peonies, then shrugged. She missed him desperately, but part of
her appreciated this small rebellion even though there was no one to
notice.

Now safe inside, she was suddenly so very tired, but still the anxiety wasn't receding. It felt as though a swarm of bees were buzzing
around inside her head, their furry bodies bashing against the inside
of her skull in panic and impotence. "No," she said aloud. She would
not freak out. Tere would handle this as she did any other problem;
she was a scholar after all. She walked over to the desk and sat in front
of her sleeping laptop. As she faced the blinking cursor of the search
engine, she typed out the word "levitation" for the first time, though
seeing it on the screen in black and white disturbed her. She scanned
through the initial results that included a music festival, magnetic
fields, and architectural projects. It was just too broad a subject; she
had to focus the query.

Before she could type a new search, her leg started buzzing, and she leapt in the chair, almost upending it. "Christ, get ahold of yourself, Tere!" Hands shaking again, she pulled her phone from her pocket, and water dripped off it. She did a cursory wipe on her pants and saw the handsome bearded face of her son, Rowan.

She whipped up what she hoped was a smile and pressed Connect. "Good morning, honey! You're up early for a Sunday!"

He paused at that, his eyes narrowed. "Mom, it's Tuesday."

Her hand went to her throat in an old-lady gesture her mother used to do, reminiscent of ancestral pearl clutching. "Oh, it is?" She forced a laugh. "Yes, of course it is!" There was nothing convincing about her response, nothing at all.

He stared at her through the glowing rectangular screen. "You're really starting to worry me."

She waved her hand in dismissal. "Oh, I'm fine, Rowan. How are the kids?"

"They're fine, and you're changing the subject." He regarded her for a beat more. "You feeling okay? You haven't had any more of those dizziness episodes, have you?"

Tere could see that she had actually scared him. She'd been looking at that face for thirty-two years, and she could read it like a book. Hell, she was scaring herself that morning, but *Son, I levitated in the garden* was not something you dropped on someone over FaceTime. "No, no, nothing like that. I'm really fine. It's just, when you don't go to an office every day, weekday, weekends, they become all the same. It's a good thing, right?" Her falsely cheery voice was fooling no one.

"I guess…but you are checking in with the doctor regularly, right? Uncle Richard said that fainting spell when you were hiking really freaked him out."

She waved her hand in dismissal. "I did not faint! And Richard gets freaked out when they're out of his favorite brand of kombucha."

"Still…someone has to watch out for you."

She sighed. "Honey, I appreciate the concern, but trust me, I can take care of myself just fine."

Rowan let it go. "Doesn't that summer course you're teaching start in a few weeks?"

Tere froze. Why did the question feel like a punch in the gut? She missed teaching, the give-and-take with the students, connecting with her colleagues…didn't she? "Right. Yeah."

"Well, what have you been up to?"

"Oh, I was just doing some gardening."

"Ha! You? With the gangrene thumbs of death?"

Though she and Rowan had always had a teasing relationship, she was actually kind of hurt at that. "I'm trying! Besides, I like spending time in your father's garden."

"Yours."

"What?"

"It's your garden now, isn't it?"

"No. It will always be your father's."

"Look, Mom, I miss him too. More than I can possibly express, but don't you think it's time you, you know, start moving on?"

"You working today?"

A long sigh. "Yeah, I was about to log on but thought I'd check in with you."

"About something in particular?"

"No, I just worry about you, Ma. All by yourself in the house. Uncle Richard told me he never sees you anymore."

So all this anxiety was being fed by Richard. Damn him. He was not actually Rowan's uncle but rather her friend and colleague at the university, but since Carl had died, he and her son had been bonding. She was glad Rowan had the male mentorship but hated that they talked about her as if she were some grieving old lady. Well, she kind of was, but she still didn't appreciate it. "Well, Richard can be a lot to take on a *good* day."

He laughed at that. She loved his laugh; it was deep and reached down to his belly, much as his father's had. "Speaking of the old blowhard, didn't you have some kind of presentation to give to Richard's class this afternoon?"

Tere looked at her watch and read the date and time. "Holy shit! I'm supposed to be there in forty minutes to give a guest lecture!"

"See? This is what I'm worried about. It's so unlike you, I—"

"Gotta go, honey! Love you!"

"Indeed, I confess that in me it produced great fear—at first a
    terrible fear.
One sees one's body being lifted up from the ground;
and although the spirit draws it after itself,
and if no resistance is offered does so very gently,
one does not lose consciousness..."

—Santa Teresa de Ávila,
The Life of Saint Teresa of Ávila by Herself

CHAPTER TWO

She rushed to the bedroom, threw on somewhat-presentable clothes over her still-damp skin, hastily tried to arrange her half-gray, half-black hair, shoved her laptop into her backpack, and tore out of the driveway in less than ten minutes. She was baffled. She'd gone out to water the garden just after ten o'clock, and suddenly it was one thirty. Over three hours lost. Not to mention that she hadn't even known what day it was. This piece really upended her, as Tere had always prided herself on having an impeccable internal clock.

Maybe Rowan was right to be concerned: What *was* happening to her?

She pulled into the faculty parking lot and turned off the engine, then just sat there for a few moments, her mind still spinning. Where had she gone when she was in the garden? Tere pictured a hovering invisible holding cell, where time slowed or quickened while the world rushed ahead outside the four transparent walls.

Lost time.

Levitation.

She had a lot to process and no time to do it, and this after a year of nothing but time. Why had she even agreed to guest lecture? Because Richard had been relentless, that was why. Well, maybe after the lecture she would tell him about the experience. He'd helped her resolve countless things in their twenty plus years of friendship, and she usually processed everything with him. But the more she thought about it, the more it seemed like a terrible idea. He was a pure linear thinker, and this…well, this was the opposite of that. She was wasting time, and she knew it but was surprised to realize she was as nervous as when she'd stepped in front of her first class in graduate school. "This is ridiculous—you can't sit in the car all day!" Tere chastised herself, climbed out of the car, and made her way along the familiar route.

It felt weird when she stepped onto the curb and was officially "back on campus." She'd taught there for twenty-eight years and had been gone for only one, but it seemed like an eternity since Carl's death, when everything had changed all at once. In many ways, she was a different person since she'd last been there. Tere had been a vibrant teacher, performative and outgoing, but in the last year, she'd turned inward, spent hours reading and thinking about aging, death, and her place in the world. She was no longer a wife, her kid was grown, and she hadn't been teaching. All her identities had been taken from her.

Several students called out greetings to her as she made her way down the walk to the psychology sciences building, and she waved and smiled. The pink crab apple trees along the path were in full bloom, the nearby fountain was bubbling, and Tere had to admit it felt good to be there. It had been her second home for almost half her life.

Before going into the building, she breathed deeply, pulled down her cotton motorcycle jacket, and adjusted her bright red glasses in an attempt to feel more put together.

She strode through the doors and made her way to Richard's classroom.

It was unexpected that she was nervous; she had given this lecture so many times, she barely needed notes. But it was weird to be walking into a classroom again. When she opened the door, the room went silent, all those undergraduate eyes staring at her.

"Well, this isn't awkward at all," she quipped.

A pause. Then the room broke into laughter—tension released.

"Class, this is Dr. Sánchez, though she clearly needs no introduction," Richard said with a huge smile. He pulled Tere into a fierce hug, and there were a few high school–level snickers among the students. When he released her, he read a short version of her bio (always boring, but she was proud of all she'd done), then added, "So, since this class is about psychology in the arts, and this unit is about issues related to diversity and underrepresented voices, I wanted you to hear from an actual literature professor." He looked over at Tere. "And one of the best."

And with that, he gave her the floor, the nerves fell away, and she did what she did best, launching into a lecture about the "Latin American Boom novelists and their role in the creation of the doctrine of magical realism." Though she had shared this work before, it felt new each time, the faces of the students attentive. It was a gift she had: the ability to present information in a way that engaged. She always felt as if she were weaving some kind of spell when she taught. Near the end, when she asked if there were any questions, a young man with a tumble of blond hair raised his hand immediately.

She pointed to him. "Yes, go ahead."

He crossed his arms on the desk, and Tere didn't miss his cocky posture. Oh, to have the confidence of an undergraduate student again. "Yeah, Professor, I still don't understand why you wouldn't consider Neil Gaiman's work magical realism. He writes about everyday working-class people too, and all his books have magic in them."

Tere paused and took a slow breath. She loved situations like this, talking about a subject she felt strongly about and staying oh so calm when students challenged her. "Well, actually—" There was a titter from the girls at her using the stereotypical mansplaining opening. "What's your name, Son?"

"Justin." He seemed a bit ticked by the laughter.

"Justin. I love Gaiman's work. All of it. He's a brilliant writer. And have you ever listened to his audiobooks? The man could read me the phone book, and I'd be enthralled. But he is British, and by all definitions—especially from an American viewpoint, I might add—England is a colonizing country, while the authors I spoke of, the founders of magical realism, were all from South American countries that have been overtaken, conquered, and colonized. Now, I can only speak personally from a Puerto Rican perspective, an island that is the longest-lasting colony in the *history of the world*." She let that hang in the air for a moment, then started walking among the rows of desks. "You see, down there, magic is in the air, riding on the sweet scent of night-blooming jasmine and accompanied by the two-note song of the tiny coqui frogs. It's infused in the hatched palm trunks and the glowing blue water of the bioluminescent bay. When you're there, you can believe anything is possible. That feeling is also present in these works. Take Garcia Marquez's town where it rains for four years, eleven months, and two days, the piano that plays with the cover down, and the levitating—"

Tere stopped short and froze for a second.

Then she looked around at the expectant faces and continued, "Priest. The people of these countries *know* ghosts exist, but here, when you tell someone you believe in ghosts, they think you're off your meds." Laughter. "Marquez wrote those works while his country was in the midst of a bloody war in which two hundred thousand people would die. It was the magic in his stories that gave hope to the powerless."

She stood by Justin's desk and put her hand on his shoulder. "So, to sum up a very long answer to your question, Justin, magical realism is about giving a glimmer of hope to those who politically and socially do not own their own destiny. And I'm fairly certain that Neil Gaiman of Hampshire, England, brilliant as he is, does not fit that definition."

After she finished, a wave of awe spread through the room, even from Justin, and Tere felt a familiar rush run through her body. It was meaningful to be good at your job. And she was really good. So why wasn't she looking forward to getting back to it?

Richard stepped in front of the class. "Thank you, Doctor Sánchez. That was so enlightening and amazing. These guys don't know how lucky they are. Have your essays done by next class, no extensions—that means you, Justin."

The students stood in a cacophony of scraping metal chair legs, and Tere watched them flood toward the exit. As she started to pack up to leave, a young woman hesitantly approached Tere. The girl had fierce eyes and wild hair. Just from looking at her, Tere could see the student's focus was on her studies more than the social aspects of college life.

"Dr. Sánchez? My name is Constanza Flores. May I ask you a question?"

Tere liked that she didn't begin with flattery, the way so many did. She got right to the point, something the teacher in Tere respected. "Of course, ask away."

"I appreciated your definition of magical realism as the literary movement of the colonized, rather than just a story with magic in it. It sucks that people water down the movement, treating it as if it were merely a trope and not a political statement. But how can it possibly represent the voices of the colonized when there were no woman writers in its foundation?"

"Well, Allende—"

"Yes, but Allende is post-Boom, as you indicated. Is it fair to say it's a true literary form without full representation that transcends gender and color lines?"

Tere liked this student. Saw a bit of her younger self in her. "You're correct, Constanza. However, since women were rarely published nor encouraged in the literary arts at that time, there were no women whose voices could be added to the canon until later."

The student's face twisted like she had smelled something foul. "Yeah, I'm not buying that. I'm determined to find some women writers from those periods who were underpublished, translate their work, and have the canon updated."

Tere paused and looked at her, impressed. She was about to respond, when her scalp started to tingle and a weird yet familiar swooning feeling built in her chest.

Oh shit!

No…not here…

The student was staring at her, waiting as Tere looked around, desperate to hide what she was certain was about to happen. She noticed the few inches of space at the bottom of Richard's big ancient wooden desk and shoved her feet underneath, hooking her toes on the lip as she rose. It wasn't enough. She grasped the edge of the wide desk with both hands, holding on until her muscles flexed and her knuckles went white. *This is* not *happening*, she said over and over in her mind while she imagined floating up to the high industrial ceiling like some kind of sideshow act while everyone gaped at her from below. Her life and career would be over.

"Professor? Are you all right?" The girl's eyes were concerned. Like Rowan's.

Tere's heart was banging on the inside of her ribs so hard, she was surprised the girl couldn't hear it. "Yes, yes." She did a quick rewind, trying to remember what Constanza had said. *Women writers. Updated canon. Right.* "I think that's a brilliant idea. Please email me if I can support you in any way."

The girl beamed. "Thank you." She went to leave, and Tere let out a long breath. But then Constanza turned back around. "When are you coming back to teach, Professor? I didn't get to take your classes before you went on leave, and that lecture was amazing."

Tere stood as upright as she could while still holding on to the desk with her hands and her feet. "Thank you, Ms. Flores. The honest answer is…I don't know." *Yeah, can't exactly teach when you're hovering below the ceiling.*

Disappointed, the student nodded, thanked her, and went to step away.

Tere regretted that she'd let the air out of the girl's sails, so she called out, "But, Constanza? Regardless of who you end up studying with, don't stop asking these questions. Ever. We need voices like yours in the scholarship. Promise?"

The young woman smiled, nodded again, and walked out with a bit more bounce to her step.

Tere wanted to put her head on the desk, but she didn't dare call any more attention to herself. Several more students thanked her as they walked by and told her they'd really enjoyed the lecture, and she smiled back, while the out-of-body and outside-of-time feeling hummed through her, her eyes threatening to roll back in her head, as she fought the feeling of ecstasy. Slowly, her feet lowered to the linoleum. She was covered in sweat and totally exhausted, but at least her feet were on the floor.

"I get so embarrassed that I want to hide, anyplace at all. I pray wholeheartedly to God to stop making this happen to me in public, and you will have to pray too, because it's a real nuisance, and it doesn't seem to help me at all in prayer. Lately I've been seeming almost as if I were drunk."

—Santa Teresa de Ávila, *Progress of a Soul*,
"Letter to Her Brother Lorenzo"

CHAPTER THREE

Tere stood there breathing hard, her elbows on the desk, until most of the students had left. This was all in her mind... It had to be. Some manifestation of post-traumatic stress or something. She distracted herself by watching a group of young women encircle Richard. He had been the source of thousands of student crushes over the years, and as a young blond woman gave him her best shy flirtatious smile, Tere tried to see him as they did. Full head of salt-and-pepper hair, deep-blue eyes, and trimmed scholarly beard. He always wore jeans that were modern and stylish, not dad jeans like so many of their colleagues, and they fit his lean body like a glove. Yeah, he was a looker all right, and brilliant, but she knew him way too well to find him attractive in that way. Plus, she had been friends with many of his exes and knew where his relationship skeletons were buried. But still, she understood why the students buzzed around him like honeybees.

Once the room was empty and Tere was finally breathing normally, Richard came and stood next to her, grinning. "Well, look who's still got it? I haven't seen those fuckers so engaged in months."

Tere laughed, primarily from relief after having to tense everything to keep her feet on the floor. *Just act normal,* she instructed herself, as if she still had command of her body and its gravity. "Yeah, but I'm a diversion from the everyday. Did you ever consider that maybe it was less about me being engaging and more about you boring them to tears week after week?"

"Ouch. Somehow, I didn't miss that sharp wit." But he was smiling. This was their relationship, throwing barbs and jabs like siblings. "Do you have time to grab a coffee?"

Tere almost automatically said no—she clearly couldn't control this…situation she was in, and she was beyond exhausted—but then she thought of Rowan's comment about her not going out and knew she needed to act normal despite what was going on, so she said, "Sure."

After procuring their coffees at the campus café, they settled into a corner booth, the sun painting the tops of the industrial tables in golden stripes. Tere could have curled into a corner of the leather-covered bench and fallen asleep right there.

Richard was smiling at her. "So? How did it feel?"

Had he seen her as she talked to Constanza? Did he know? "How did *what* feel?"

"Being back in the saddle again, of course!"

Tere laughed with relief. "Well, I don't know about getting into any saddle, but it was fun. Seems like you've got a good group this semester." She took a sip of her coffee, starting to feel like herself again.

"I do, for the most part. But hopefully you will too this summer." He was watching her over the lip of his double espresso.

She stared at him for a moment. "Wait, was that what this was about? Trying to remind me of what I'm missing or something? I wondered how this lecture fit in with your syllabus."

"What? It fits in beautifully! We were talking about how literature provides a psychological balm in colonized societies."

She folded her arms across her chest and stared at him.

He put his hands up in surrender. "Okay, fine! It was a stretch. But can you blame me? You're one of the best minds in higher education. Do you know they gave Pearson all your classes this semester? Pearson! He has the IQ of a ferret."

"Well, ferrets are actually rather intelligent."

Richard ignored her. "It's just a waste of talent, T, that's all." He went to take another sip of his espresso but seemed to change his mind. "I mean, look at Constanza. She's barely said a word all semester. Excellent work but never engages with me."

Tere stared at the tabletop. Damn him. Richard had known her long enough that he knew just where the tender spots were. It was exhausting, but on some level, she had to admit she needed the truth telling. She took a long sip of the overly milky latte. After a pause, she looked up at Richard. "Pearson, huh?"

He nodded, and they sat in silence for a minute. Then Tere snort-laughed, and they both broke down, laughing until tears ran from their eyes.

When Tere could finally breathe again, she said, "I don't know, Richard. I think you're overestimating him *and* insulting ferrets." They laughed again, and it felt good. Like old times. Times when this coffee date was a twice-weekly occurrence, a time to discuss their classes, colleagues, and set goals for their coming sabbaticals. Normal things. Unlike today.

"God, I miss you, T," Richard said with a sigh.

"What, you're not seeing me now?" She put her hand over his. "Oh my God, Richard! Have you lost your sight, and you're just now telling me?" Tere said with exaggerated concern.

He smiled and gave her the finger.

"How old are you, Professor Walsh?" Tere stuck her tongue out at him, and when he responded in kind, she noticed the new network of lines spreading out from either side of his eyes. When had those appeared? "I miss you too." It came out automatically, but then she wondered: *Did* she miss him? She loved Richard as a friend, but she just wasn't sure if she truly missed seeing him as a colleague each and every weekday.

"Tere, I seriously want to talk about it."

"'It' what?" She hoped against hope it wasn't about his wanting more from their friendship. It had been the elephant in the room the last few months to the point that she avoided seeing him. She'd left that little detail out of the morning's conversation with Rowan.

"'It' as in, are you actually coming back to the university this summer? You love teaching and you know it."

She stared at her friend. This was also a well-trod subject, but something was off. His smile didn't quite reach his eyes. There was something he wasn't telling her. "What's this really about, Richard?"

He sighed, and even the partial smile slipped away. "Dean Hammerston said if you don't come back to teach that Iberian lit class this summer, they're going to revoke your tenure for neglect of duty."

Tere gaped at him. "You have got to be fucking kidding me! My husband died. They're not even paying me right now, for God's sake."

"I know, but that was a year ago, Tere! Requirement for family leave is three months tops. He feels they've been more than generous."

Tere snorted. "Yeah, generous."

"I'm afraid that's not all. There's talk that he's going to appoint Pearson as the chair of your department."

Tere felt that one like a blow to the stomach. In the fifteen years since she earned full professorship, she had applied to become chair of the English department whenever the position became available, but no matter how many classes she taught, grants she got, or papers she published, Hammerston had never seen fit to give it to her. The roiling in her stomach made her wonder if *that* wasn't a part of why she hadn't returned from bereavement leave. A barista dropped a glass behind the counter, and Tere jolted, coming back into the moment. She coughed. "Well, I wish him luck, but they'll probably eat him alive."

Richard stared at her. "Luck? Tere, you've been the best candidate for that job for over a decade!"

When she brought her coffee to her mouth, she noticed a slight tremble in her hand. No, she hadn't been looking forward to coming back, but she'd worked her ass off for that tenure.

He ran his hand through his still-thick hair. "I mean, we all thought you'd be back by now. Even you, right? I just think it's time, you know? It would be good for you. Carl's been dead almost a year, and—"

She didn't let him finish. She stood up abruptly. "Thanks for asking me to guest lecture, Richard. It was fun. But I'd better get home." She slipped out of her chair, grabbed her backpack, and made for the door.

He was taken by surprise and knocked over his half-full coffee cup while getting out of his chair to follow her. "Oh, c'mon, Tere! Don't leave!"

She walked briskly toward the front door of the café. She could hear him calling her name as she passed the tables scattered here and there, the faces of the patrons seeming to lean in toward her, forming a tunnel that was narrowing as she went. She tried to walk faster, but it was as if her feet were stuck in deep mud as she pulled and lifted her legs, hoping to break free. When she finally burst outside into the cool late-spring air and the door closed behind her, she took large, gulping breaths, letting them out with a whoosh as she rushed to her car.

Once she reached the parking lot, Tere took a few stumbling steps forward. She looked up at the blue sky and just breathed. The air felt good in her lungs, but her head was spinning, much like it did when she had one of her dizzy spells. She stayed stock-still, waiting for the feeling to pass.

Tere heard footsteps running up to her from behind.

She didn't turn around, but she felt Richard take her hand as he had so many times in the past: when her first book got published, when he saw baby Rowan for the first time, and a year ago, when she thought the sadness would slowly kill her. She did wonder for a moment what their standing there holding hands looked like to other people, but in truth, she no longer cared.

They'd never slept together, Richard and Tere, even though half the department thought they had. But there had always been an attraction there, a meeting of the minds. She could tell he was interested—he had been hinting at it for some time—but she wasn't. Tere wondered if that part of her had died with her husband.

"I'm sorry. I shouldn't have pushed so hard." His voice was gravelly after a day of teaching.

"Apology accepted."

Richard was quiet for a moment. Then his voice brightened. "I know. Can we try this again? A do-over? Let's have coffee again tomorrow. My last class ends at three."

Tere shook her head. "Can't. I have a tattoo appointment."

WE NEED NO WINGS

Richard chuckled. "Another one? Do you even have any skin left that isn't covered? Not to mention you're sixty years old!"

She put her free hand to her chest in mock horror. "Wait...am I? Am I really...sixty?"

He snorted. "Yes, and 'sarcasm is the lowest form of wit.'"

"'But the highest form of intelligence.' I can quote Wilde too, Professor. And I won't be done until my skin is too wrinkly to tattoo."

Tere was sad to realize she was finding their usual banter wearying. She just wanted to be home, sitting in her overstuffed chair, surrounded by their things...her things. She pointed in the direction of her car. "I really have to get going."

He put his hands on her upper arms and stared into her eyes as if searching for something. "T., what's really going on?"

And there it was. Tere had wondered if she'd be able to keep the day's bizarre experiences out of her demeanor, but clearly, she hadn't been successful. It was just too big. But she kept trying. "What do you mean?"

He narrowed his eyes. "C'mon. We've known each other for decades. I know something's up. Is it the dizziness again?"

She threw her hands up, "No! Why does everyone keep bringing that up? I was dehydrated!" Come to think of it, she was feeling a little dehydrated right then. The afternoon sun had been beating on the asphalt of the parking lot, and the hot-oil smell made her stomach turn just a little. Or maybe it was the conversation. She sighed. "I don't know, Richard. Everything is different after this past year."

"Hell yes, it is! You turned sixty, lost your husband of thirty-four years, and took a year leave from your job. Pretty sure that covers three of the top five life changes."

Tere shook her head. "No, it's not just that." She knew she

couldn't articulate it. She had spent the past year in a kind of stasis, having as little to do with the outside world as possible, barely getting dressed, leaving the house only to water Carl's garden. But over the previous few weeks, even before today's events, something else had begun to stir in her chest, a quickening, but not of the body. There was no way to explain it to others when she didn't understand it herself, and this frustrated her. She enjoyed working through queries like knots in yarn, poking and pulling until they untangled and broke free. This not knowing? This she was not accustomed to. She didn't elaborate.

Richard lifted her chin, so she had to look at him. "I'm worried about you." He was standing close, close enough that Tere could feel the heat from his body in the cooling air, could smell the roasted-nut scent of espresso on his breath.

"Look, I appreciate your concern, but there's nothing to worry about." Her voice sounded convincing, though she didn't believe it for a second and didn't imagine he would either. She worked to sell it, crossing her chest and holding up two fingers like a Girl Scout. "Promise."

He looked at her for a minute longer with squinted eyes. More gray had appeared on his temples over the past year too, but it suited him. When she'd started growing her gray out after Carl's passing, people had asked if she was feeling okay. Men? They just looked distinguished. Richard deflated a bit in resignation. "Okay. But I still think something's changed. And I'm talking since I saw you at the food co-op last week."

Tere's mind spun a little at this, like a tire skidding over ice, lots of furious movement but no traction. Once again, she considered telling him—hell, she'd almost floated in his classroom. But no. This was something she needed to keep to herself. These days she felt she didn't know much, but she knew that. "Nothing's changed, Richard. Every day, every hour is the same." Her eyes started to fill.

He put his hands on her shoulders. "Then come back to work! We miss you. I miss you."

"Thank you. Truly. And I'll decide definitively by the first of the month. I'm just...struggling a bit."

"Okay, well, what about talking to someone? Are you still seeing that therapist at the Stroke Center? The one that you started seeing when Carl had his?"

Her heart tightened at another mention of Carl, and a memory ran behind her eyes, unbidden: She was sitting at the foot of his hospital bed during a moment of calm between stroke incidents, watching the stubble of a gray beard on his strong jaw that twitched slightly as he slept. She laid her head on his blanket-covered legs, the muscles of his calves still so strong, and she wept. He was the one grounded to the earth, his feet firmly planted. He reminded her to live outside her head. As she lay across him, she found herself praying that when he had the next stroke, which was sure to be his last, that he would take her with him when he went.

She shook her head to try and clear the memory. "Maybe I'll give her a call."

Richard gave her a sad smile. "Okay. I'll take that. I better get back for my next class." He kissed her forehead, turned, and started walking back with his hands in his jeans pockets.

As she walked to the car, their friendship played out in her mind. All the late nights at conference bars, laughing until they cried or arguing a point until one of them stormed off. Dinners with both families thrown together, Rowan laughing as he and Richard's numerous dogs chased each other in the backyard. Creative risks encouraged and supported. Personal secrets shared and harbored.

She got behind the wheel of her car, fastened her seat belt, and sat for a bit, thinking about the whole bizarre day. The hours in Carl's garden. Levitating. Giving the lecture. Connecting with Constanza. Then levitating again. What was the link between these events? She sighed, pressed the ignition button, and put the car into reverse. Almost immediately she felt her body lift as she had twice before, this time straining against the seat belt, her thighs hitting the bottom of the steering wheel, her feet lifting slightly above the pedals. She was hovering, her butt an inch above the seat, the belt the only thing stopping her from floating up to the ceiling of her SUV. Sweat broke out on her forehead, and the hair on her arms stood at attention.

No. Not again.

"It's just your imagination. Get ahold of yourself." Tere's voice shook. She yanked the seat belt tighter with shaking hands, then stretched out her foot to reach the gas pedal. The car lurched backward, and the loud *brap* of a horn made her jolt and stomp on the brakes. She looked back and saw a woman in a minivan glaring at her and shaking her head with disgust.

"Sorry!" Tere yelled out the partially open window, then worked on slowing her breathing as the van took off behind her with an angry roar of acceleration. She closed her eyes, tears leaking out from the corners. When she opened them again, she looked down and saw she was firmly seated, her legs pressed to the leather seat, her feet solidly on the carpet.

No.

Enough.

She'd almost gotten hurt this time, and worse, she'd almost hurt someone else.

Tere needed to figure out what the hell was going on. But first, she needed to get home in one piece. She let out a long breath, looked both ways, and slowly backed out of the parking space, everything shaking now.

"This experience has been so traumatic for me that many times I tried with all my might to resist it. I have been especially reluctant to yield to it when it happened to me in public, and yet when I have been alone, I have been afraid that I might be suffering from delusions."

—Santa Teresa de Ávila,
The Life of Saint Teresa of Ávila by Herself

CHAPTER FOUR

Tere was still reeling when she got home. She pulled off her lecture clothes as soon as she walked into the house, threw on some sweats, and put water on for tea. She stood at the counter in bare feet, waiting for the kettle to boil, going over the entirety of the weirdest day of her life. It had started like any other: she'd had her usual nut-butter toast, mango juice, and coffee, and had gotten the mail. After, she had watered Carl's garden: that's when it had all gone cattywampus.

Not to mention they were going to take away her tenure. She still couldn't believe it. Three decades of her life, she'd given to that institution. Well, the solution was simple: she would have to go back to teaching, ready or not. Then she pictured herself writing on the whiteboard, the dry-erase pen sliding upward as she levitated in a room full of twenty-year-olds—or worse, careening down Interstate 89, unable to reach the damn brake pedal, then crashing into a van full of orphans and nuns. She buried her face in her hands.

The whistle of the teakettle made her jump. "Lord, you're losing it, Sánchez." She grabbed a mug, put a hibiscus tea bag and a teaspoon of Vermont honey into it, and drowned them with boiling water. The normal daily ritual was comforting; the hiss of the kettle, the gentle sound of tumbling water, the scented steam of the citrusy flower were so familiar and safe. But when she walked into the living room and caught sight of the peonies through the sliding glass door, she stopped short, her red tea splashing on the hardwood floor. The silence became weighted then, hanging around like a storm through the empty house.

No. She needed to act and now.

Tere went straight over to her desk and woke up the laptop. She typed in "levitation as sign of mental illness," though she didn't really want to see the results.

Man with schizophrenia has out-of-body experience in lab came up, and *Understanding Delusions*, and *Disassociation and Psychotic Symptoms*.

Tere swallowed hard. "Yeah, maybe this isn't the best idea." She pressed the Delete button until all the remained was the single-word search from earlier in the day: "levitation." For the sake of the research, she would proceed with the assumption that she was indeed levitating, as the other hypothesis was proving to be much scarier. "So I need to narrow the search. But how?" She tapped her teeth with her fingernail for a second, then typed in "how to stop levitating." *Might as well start there.* A series of posts about how to stop the priest character from levitating in a role-playing game called *World of Warcraft* came up. It had been a long shot.

What did she even know about levitation? Mysticism. It was often associated with mysticism and religion. She went back to her original query on levitation and added the word "mystic," hit Search once more, and scanned the results. Halfway down the page, under the heading of "mystical levitation in Christianity," she saw it: Saint Teresa of Ávila. It was as if a tropical breeze passed across her skin, and she was thrown back to summer Sundays at her abuela's house in Bayamón, Puerto Rico.

She could almost hear the squeak of the rocking chairs, the birds calling from among the bright orange blooms on the flamboyán trees beside the house. The heavy feeling of an after-church pot roast brunch sitting in her belly as the old women talked in their slow melodic voices. It was there, on that veranda, that Tere had listened to tales of sinners and saints and her aunt Nivea had first talked about the mystical branch of their family tree.

Her family tree.

Tere would go right to the root of that tree. She stood, grabbed her cell phone off the coffee table, and perched on the couch. Her aunt Nivea answered on the fourth ring. The line crackled the way it used to over landlines when she'd been a kid, the calls to the island always sounding as if they traveled through an electrical storm.

"Halo?" Her aunt managed to make the word sound somewhere between English and Spanish, as if wishing to cover both bases. A symptom of the colonized, Tere supposed.

"Titi, it's Tere," She always spoke too loudly when she called Nivea, though the eighty-two-year-old woman could hear better than people half her age.

"Yes, I know dear. The cell phone tells me who is calling."

"Right. Sorry." Tere pictured her aunt in the sitting room, perched on the antique dark wood furniture from Spain, the ceiling fan spinning lazily overhead as golden light filtered in through the windows.

"What's wrong, Tere?"

"Why does there have to be something wrong? Can't I call my aunt and see how she's doing?"

"M'ija, you only call when something's wrong. Or you're coming to visit, and you only come in the winter because it's 'too damn hot' for you down here the rest of the year. Also, I can tell by your voice.

Your mother used to sound the same way, like someone was standing on her trachea."

"Well, *that's* an image."

"So, tell me, joven, what's going on?"

"Titi, I was just thinking about a family legend you used to talk about."

"Ha! Which one? There are too many to count."

Tere took a deep breath. "The one that we're descended from Saint Teresa of Ávila?"

"Legend? M'ija, that's fact. You've been in academia too long; you are losing your faith."

"So, you believe it?"

"No! I'm certain of it. Before the founding of Puerto Rico, our family goes back to Ávila, Spain, and our roots trace back to the Sánchez family, her paternal line."

Tere paused. "And you're certain of that?"

"Ay, Madre de Dios." She could imagine her aunt making the sign of the cross, her eyes darting up to the omnipresent crucifix over the piano, Jesus with his bleeding feet and hands, his eyes raised up to the Lord as if he too found Tere frustrating. "Your cousin Arturo researched it all the way back. And he's an academic too. If you don't believe it, you can go check it yourself. Sign on to one of those ancestry programs."

"And Saint Teresa levitated, right?" It was the real question hiding behind the others.

"Yes, she had many mystical experiences, including visions of angels, the devil, even Jesus Christ himself. She also reformed the Carmelite Order and founded many convents and monasteries. And she wrote three of the most important books in Spanish literature. But I'm sure you'd find out more from Google, no?"

"Tía, you're better than Google. Wait, I think I took a class in undergrad where we studied her…I have to have that notebook somewhere…" Tere could see her scribble-covered journal and the worn paperback cover of the saint's autobiography in her mind. She glanced over at the bookshelves that lined the far wall, but nothing jumped out.

"You'd know all this if you'd joined us on that trip to Ávila in 2017. It is our motherland, m'ija."

Tere considered Puerto Rico her motherland, despite the family's colonizer roots, but with the day's rather unorthodox events, a spark of interest in the Spanish branch of the family swelled in her. Could the propensity to float above the floor be…genetic? A family curse, perhaps? It was an insane thought and not exactly something that was tracked by 23andMe. Still, it was the only lead she had. "Do we have any relatives there?"

"Yes. A cousin of mine and your mother's. Isabella. But I haven't talked to her in…oh, about five years now. Don't even know if she's still alive." A pause. "Why the sudden interest in Ávila and Santa Teresa?"

"No reason, just curious." Tere knew her aunt wasn't going to buy that. They were too much alike, but since the woman had been trying to get her back to the Catholic Church, perhaps Nivea would think it was a good thing. The truth was, Tere had never considered herself a Catholic. She couldn't support a faith that excluded people for who they were or loved, but let her aunt believe whatever she wanted.

"Bueno." Then a sigh. Why were people sighing so much around Tere lately? "So, when do you go back to the university?"

Tere jumped up, ran to the front door on tiptoes, opened it quietly, and rang the doorbell. "Whoops! Someone's at the door, Titi!"

"Tere, I heard you run and open the door before it rang. What is—?"

"Gotta go! Love you!" She pressed End, closed the door, and walked over to the bookshelves.

Finding the notebook from that particular undergraduate class would be a challenge since there were built-in bookshelves on every wall of the living room. Carl had built a section for her each Valentine's Day, and it was the most romantic thing anyone had ever done for her. He'd understood that her heart was held aloft by books.

It took some time, but she found it on a bottom shelf in the farthest corner, shoved between a copy of the Columbia catalog for 1985 that featured her as a big-haired punky senior perched at the base of the famous *Alma Mater* statue, book in hand. Wasn't Saint Teresa always depicted with a book in hand? But the girl in that photo seemed to be from lifetimes ago, worried about exams and maintaining her 4.0 average, wondering if the misanthropic guy in her Don Quixote class would finally ask her out. Tere carried the notebook to the couch and settled in. She smiled at her handwriting, familiar yet way more legible than it had become later in life.

Santa Teresa de Ávila
Born in 1515 in Ávila, Spain, to a large noble family.

Tere remembered that, according to her aunt, their family was descended from one of the saint's ten siblings, though she had no idea which one.

Her father was Jewish and converted to Catholicism to avoid expulsion or even execution.

She'd forgotten that detail. It wasn't surprising that her relatives never mentioned the Judaism in their history when they waxed

rhapsodic about the family's saintly roots. Tere was enjoying this ret-
rospective trip; there were so many details she did not remember.
She also felt like she was in conversation with her twenty-year-old
self, especially when she saw, scribbled on the margins, boys' names
surrounded with bulbous hearts pierced by arrows.

From childhood Teresa was obsessed with the lives of the saints
and at age 7 ran away with her younger brother to...seek martyrdom?! Hoping to be beheaded? (UGH!) At age 20 she was sent to a
convent, like a lot of noble girls back then. But she was outgoing
and popular, and she got wrapped up into the social aspects of
monasterial life. After a vision of Christ, she devoted her life to
the church, but became frustrated with the laxness of the order.
She didn't like the breakdown in religious and monastic discipline,
and the failure of the Carmelites to maintain their original ideals.

Tere read that this infuriated the leaders of the church (at this she
felt another strong kinship with the saint, as Tere had a reputation for
stirring up trouble in her department).
     "Carmelites…Carmelites…" She got out her phone and did a
search online, a resource she hadn't had as a student in the eighties. She knew it was an order of the Catholic Church, but that was
it. (Her aunt would be horrified.) "Okay, they have their origins in
the Mount Carmel region of Palestine, the word 'karmel' means
'garden.'" Tere stopped and looked out the sliding glass door at the
sun setting over the maple tree, painting the backyard in golden light.
"Garden, huh?" She shivered but kept reading. "A brotherhood committed to live in the footsteps of Jesus Christ." *Brotherhood, priests,
yadda, yadda, yadda.* How did a nun figure into all this patriarchy?
She skimmed through a bit.

In the 15th century there were relaxations of discipline in various communities, and St. Teresa of Ávila initiated the most famous reform, splitting the order into the calced, or shoe wearing, and the discalced, the barefoot order, who were committed to returning to a dedicated life of poverty and prayer as the order was originally intended. It is also referred to as the Teresian order.

Tere stared straight ahead, her mouth open. "Holy shit." She couldn't imagine having an adjective made of your name.

She was often sick and obsessed with mortification of the flesh.

Tere saw that she'd had to look that term up and define it in her notes:

Ascetic Mortification:
In Christianity, mortification has been an element in a more general practice of the ascetic life. Among its most extreme forms are self-flagellation and the wearing of a hair shirt. Flagellation is intended to reproduce the scourging of Christ, while the hair shirt—made of coarse animal hair that was intentionally painful, an ancient penitential symbol—functioned as a kind of continuous flagellation.

"Good God," she said out loud. "You'd think being a smart, strong woman in the Catholic Church during the Spanish Inquisition would be flagellation enough!"

Santa Teresa of Ávila was the first woman to be named a doctor of the church on September 27, 1970.

"Whoa." Another thing they had in common; Tere had been granted her doctorate just twenty years after her saintly relative. She was beginning to realize this woman's story was way more interesting than she had found it in her youth.

She sipped her tea, then went into the kitchen to grab a yogurt, since with all the "excitement" that day, she hadn't had time for lunch, and her stomach was growling. As she walked back to the living room, she realized she was looking forward to a long night of research. Just the idea of it felt like putting on an old warm sweater, one so familiar, it held your shape even when you weren't wearing it. She would snuggle down and shove the memory of the day beneath it.

"Self-knowledge is so important that, even if you were raised up to the heavens, I should like you to never relax your cultivation of it... Begin by entering the room where humility is acquired rather than flying to the other rooms. For that is the way to make progress, and, if we have a safe and level road to walk along, why should we desire wings to fly?"

—Santa Teresa de Ávila,
Interior Castle

CHAPTER FIVE

Tere woke up the next morning drooling on the couch like a freshman, a *Scientific American* article about using sound to levitate objects glowing on her laptop's screen. She brewed some coffee, ate a hard-boiled egg that was on the border of going bad, and watered the other half of the garden without incident. Midday found her sitting at the design table in her friend's tattoo studio, looking at a beautiful drawing of a spray of stargazer lilies, their ombré white-to-pink freckled petals spreading out like rays, their orange stamens dusty with pollen.

"It's beautiful," Tere said, then fell silent.

Esmé watched her for a bit. "You hate it. That's okay! We can—"

Tere put a hand on her friend's arm. "No! No, it really is lovely."

"Are you sad because they make you think of Carl? These were your wedding flowers, weren't they?" Esmé asked in a gentle voice.

"They were. It's not that, really. It's just…" Tere looked at her arm and examined the work they'd done over the years. A vintage Goya acoustic guitar for her late mother. A rowboat in honor of her long-deceased father. A stylized camera for her cousin Carlos, who'd died unexpectedly a few years back. Tere was started to feel like a walking, talking tombstone. She turned to Esmé. "Would it be a huge pain in the ass to do something else today instead?" She put her hand on the flower drawing. "This is so beautiful, but…maybe a different flower?"

"Of course! What are you thinking?"

"Peonies. Giant pink ones." She smiled big as soon as she named them. The wedding flowers were from when they'd been kids fumbling through life. They were the past. "There's something about peonies that feels more appropriate to this stage of my life, while still honoring Carl." She hadn't even known this part of her reasoning until she said it, but it just felt…right.

A huge smile spread across her friend's face. "I love this idea." Esmé typed away, then turned her iPad around. "Like this?"

Tere smiled at the colorful image; she could almost smell their scent, see Carl watering them in the early-morning light. "Yes! Perfect."

Tere was not a last-minute-change kind of person, and Esmé knew it. As she worked on the new design, she would occasionally look over at her with a question in her eyes.

Esmé showed her the finished drawing. "Something like this?"

"Yes!" Tere clapped as if she were five and had just been asked if she wanted ice cream. Whenever she got tattooed, it felt that way. Carl had called her addicted to the body art, and he wasn't wrong.

Twenty minutes later, Esmé's tattoo machine was buzzing like a swarm of bees, the tiny needles a constant burn against Tere's arm. She welcomed this particular pain. It was localized, mild, containable—and focusing on her body instead of her mind seemed right after the past twenty-four hours.

"So, why are peonies meaningful at this stage of your life?" Esmé asked, her face inches away from Tere's skin and brightly lit by the lamp.

Tere paused, unsure how to answer. "Carl planted them for me in the garden. I like the way they've flourished, even after he..." She didn't finish the sentence, just looked over at the flowers blooming on her arm, the deep purply pink of the petals bright against her paleness. She loved the magic of tattoos, the way her skin slowly filled with deep, new, forever color. The needles reached the crook of her arm, and she flinched.

"Sorry, sensitive area. You want me to stop?" Esmé ran her gloved fingers over the spot with a soothing gesture.

"No, let's get this done today."

As she went back to work, Esmé tilted her head of long blond locs in that way she did when she was thinking deeply. Tere thought her academic colleagues could learn a lot from the artist. With her head still down, Esmé said over the whir of the machine, "I'm sensing a restless vibe from you today. Unusual for you, Tere Sánchez."

Damn. How does she do that? Tere used to think Esmé's "burning palo santo and asking the body's permission to tattoo it" was all Vermont crunchiness. But she was beginning to wonder if there was much more to it. "Hmm. Can't imagine why. I never go anywhere these days." They were both silent for a bit, the sound of a dance class starting up from the floor below providing a rhythm section to their thoughts. "Esmé, you're into mysticism, right?"

The machine buzz stopped, and Esmé looked up with her huge blue eyes. "Yes."

Tere worked to keep her voice casual. "Like, levitation and such? Do you believe in it?"

"In levitation? Of course, I do!" Another look over her black-gloved hands. "Why do you ask?"

Tere shrugged, the raw skin where they'd been working twinged with pain. "No reason. It's just...yesterday I remembered my family is descended from Saint Teresa of Ávila, and I've been reading a lot about her."

Esmé put the machine down on the plastic-covered worktable. "What? Why have you never told me this?"

"You know about her?"

"Are you kidding? She's one of the two great Spanish mystics! Her and Saint John of the Cross."

"Wow. I mean, I studied her books in an Iberian lit class in my undergrad, but I guess I never gave her a thought after that, until… recently."

Esmé tilted her head again, never taking her eyes off Tere. She knew something else was up, but she was too respectful to press. "In all your years in college, you never studied mysticism?"

"No."

The artist stood up and walked to the bookshelves on the other side of the studio. She ran her fingers over the spines before pulling out several books. As she walked back, she said, "You're clearly entering a transformative part of your life, and the field is calling to you." Esmé handed her the pile.

Tere didn't know who or what was calling to her, but she was always open to reading books. She looked at the covers: *Quantum Realities*, *History of Mystic Experiences*, and *Sacred Places*. She glanced up at the tattoo artist.

Esmé folded her arms across her chest. "Oh, don't you give me that judgy academic attitude."

"What? No, I—"

"I chose these specifically because they're about the *science* of mysticism, knowing you're a hardened academic."

Tere was about to explain that she might not be an academic for long, but she didn't.

Esmé just tapped the top book. "Just read them, Dr. Sánchez. I think you'll be surprised."

She smiled. She was twenty years older than her friend, but often in the ten years they'd known each other, Tere had thought the younger woman was the wiser. She smiled and pulled the books to her chest. "I'll read all of them. Thank you."

Esmé smiled back, then straddled her stool once more. "Good. Now let's get this tattoo done before you go a-wandering."

But I'm not going anywhere, Tere thought.

Am I?

———————————

That evening Tere took a long hot bath, careful to keep her new tattoo out of the water. She had taken the protective bandage off before dinner, and the colors were incredibly vibrant in the way they only are when brand-new, the skin slightly raised as if done in the puffy paints she'd used on her jeans in middle school. She loved all her tattoos, but this one was particularly exciting, as the subject had been so unexpected, mirroring the past few days.

When she got out and dried off, she put on her pajamas and nestled into the corner of the sectional in the living room. It was only seven thirty, but that year she had been sleeping on and off around the clock, not even noticing what time of day it was. She ran her hand over the couch's soft chili pepper–red chenille upholstery. She had fought with Carl about this purchase. She could still see him standing in the middle of the furniture store's showroom floor, his straight hair windblown after the walk from the parking garage, his hands on his hips in what she called his Superman pose.

"Tere, it will be perfect!"

"Carl, I don't know. The cushions on the back are attached. You know I hate that—harder to clean. And a custom-made sectional? It'll cost a fortune!"

He smiled at her, that smile that went all the way up, crinkling at either side of his deep-brown eyes in a way that made her knees week. "Oh, c'mon, honey. We no longer have to worry about Rowan drawing with Magic Markers on it or using it for a trampoline. Why are we working our asses off if not to be comfortable as we grow old together?"

"I thought we were already doing that?" She folded her arms, fighting off a grin. "I mean, *you're* already old anyway."

"Exactly! An elderly man such as myself has earned a comfortable couch!" He was flailing his arms in the dramatic way he only did when he was excited about something. Rowan did the same thing; it was like their own dialect of emotional semaphore. "Just picture it…" He stepped closer and pulled her into him, one hand gesturing to the floor sample sitting there, taunting her to spend two thousand dollars. Every other piece of furniture they'd had over the years was somebody's hand-me-down: items from Carl's rich clients who spontaneously decided to redecorate, her mother's dusty velvet chesterfield they used until it started bleeding straw stuffing all over the carpet. "We'll both be able to stretch out at the same time. We can read, talk, watch movies—" He leaned closer and whispered in her ear, "Do all sorts of things together on it."

The touch of his breath on her ear and his suggestive words sent a woosh of heat through her body that melted any remaining resistance. The man knew exactly how to get through to her. They ordered it that day. It took months to come and was a bear to wrestle into their tiny Vermont farmhouse, but she had grown to love it.

Tere glanced over at Carl's empty side of the sectional. She still never sat there. She ran her hand over the slight indentation of his body that the deep cushions still held like an upholstery ghost. She pulled her hand back and lay down all the way. A text buzzed in, rattling the phone across the glass coffee table. It was from Nivea.

After we spoke I checked with Georgina
and it seems our cousin in Ávila is
indeed alive. At least for now.

What do you mean "for now?"

She has heart trouble. But she's my
age, so, only to be expected.

Do you have a phone number for her?

Ha! No way. She lives in a convent, they
pride themselves on being removed
from modern technologies.

Hmm. Interesting, Tere thought. Then she put the phone back down and cracked open *The History of Mystic Experience.* She was excited about the pile of books that awaited her on the coffee table. It was a subject she wouldn't have touched a year ago, but by the third page, she was pulled in, lost in the introduction. She wasn't sure how this would help her discern why she had started levitating or how to stop it, but she couldn't go back to teaching without solving this "issue," and if she didn't go back, they would rip the academic rug out from under her. And it wasn't as if she could go to her primary care doctor and say, *Doc, so, I've started levitating.* That would earn her a shot of Haldol and a trip to the psych ward. Besides, if Esmé thought this book was important information on the subject, Tere would read it cover to cover.

Turned out it didn't take that long.

In fact, what she needed was on the last page of the introduction. The paragraph was headed "The Spanish Mystics," and there, right in the first sentence, was Santa Teresa de Ávila.

Tere sat bolt upright.

She might be a "hardened academic" as Esmé had called her, but she also knew a sign when it whacked her in the face. She looked for the chapter, flipping through the pages until she found it. There was that classic beatific painting of the saint, her hands clasped, her other-worldly eyes looking toward heaven. Tere skimmed the pages... The saint had visions...was pierced by a golden arrow with fire at its tip...

Levitated.

On more than one occasion.

Nuns who'd attested to the miracle, who'd said they had to hold her down during mass. There might be notes on this in her under-grad notebook as well, but the book dove right in, focusing on the mystical acts.

The author talked about the church and convent of Santa Teresa in Ávila, Spain, built on the property on which she was born, relics of her remarkable life there for visitors to see. Tere *felt* something as she read about the city—a spark of connection. Ávila had already been in her thoughts from the conversation with her aunt the day before, and learn-ing that the cousin there lived (at least for now) only fanned the flame, bringing with it the scent of predestination. After reading through the chapter twice, Tere closed the book and held it to her chest. She imag-ined walking the same medieval streets as her long-dead relative, visiting the holy places that had been important to her life. There were answers to be found within those medieval walls; she felt it in her bones.

"I'm going to Ávila."

It was as if someone else had said it, and she swung her legs around, put them flat on the floor, and said it again. Louder this time. "I'm going to Ávila."

She liked the sound of her own voice stating this fact to the empty house. It lent a sort of gravity to it.

Because she was who she was, she ticked off the list of practical considerations: she still had six weeks until summer session started, had no small children or husband to keep her close to home, and had a damn compelling reason to go. Cousin Isabella would not live forever, and she was the only family member who really knew the city, who had a connection to the Spanish branch of their family, and who, just maybe, could help Tere figure out why this was happening to her and even how to control it. Yes, it was a long-ass shot, but where else did she have to turn? She could literally float around the house for the next few weeks, or she could take one fucking wild and crazy shot.

She texted Esmé.

> Seems I'm going to Spain.

The response came through immediately.

Of course, you are! See? A-wandering!
We were meant to talk about that today!

> I think we were.

I know we were. Send me details
about your trip when you have them.
I'm so fucking stoked for you!

First, she'd have to plan an actual trip. But that would come later. Before she lost her nerve, Tere called her son. More than buying tickets, this would be a true confirmation she was going.

"Hey, Ma. Did you make it to the class in time yesterday?"

"Yes! Did you really doubt me?"

A warm laugh, like a Labrador's contented rumbling before a fire. "Until yesterday? Never. But after that convo? Yeah, I was wondering. How did it go?"

Well, other than having to hook myself to Richard's desk by my feet… "Actually, it was fun." And it had been. Mostly.

"Excellent! A nice chance to get back in the saddle before you have to do it full-time again."

She didn't miss that he "happened" to use the same expression Richard had yesterday. "Yeah, about that…"

"You are going back, aren't you?"

Why did it feel as if their roles had reversed? "Yeah, sure. I just feel like I could use some brushup study on my Iberian literature. I have some friends at the University of Madrid…" Was there even a University of Madrid? She didn't know. Tere was making this up as she went along. It was kind of thrilling. "And I want to spend a few weeks…immersed." She hated lying to him, but circumstances being as they were…

A pause. "You're going to Spain? Now?"

"Well, not *now* this instant, but later this week, yes." She was winging that too; hopefully she could find a flight. Perhaps she should have done that first after all.

"Ma, do you think that's the best idea? I mean, it's been a difficult year…"

She bristled a bit at his questioning. She didn't need his permission, didn't need anyone's, but she pushed that aside for the moment. "Exactly why I should go! It will be a nice bridge to jumping back in."

"I guess." She could imagine his face flushing as it did when he was caught off guard.

A cacophony rose on his end: the slap of bare feet on hardwood, little voices yelling and blaming each other.

"Oh, I just love the sound of those two. I also love that I don't have to hear it all the time." She laughed.

"Lord, Mom. It's constantly wild. I remember things being calm at our house after school, but these two just set each other off."

That was an experience she'd never had as a mother. She and Carl had tried to have a second child, but Tere had miscarried at twenty-one weeks. Why was it that a woman "miscarried," like it was an action *she* took, a mistake *she* made—like it wasn't the last thing she wanted? In this case Tere thought they should use passive language, a miscarriage "happened." It was a miscarriage, like a miscarriage of justice. Yes, she preferred that.

"Mom?"

"Hmm?"

"You just seemed to go somewhere else."

"I was thinking about your brother. Even after all these years, thinking about him still has the power to make me sad."

"I know. Me too." He let out a long breath. "Okay, maybe the trip isn't the worst idea you've had."

"Oh, I'm so glad you approve." She couldn't keep the sarcasm out of her voice. It was an old dynamic, but even though he was an adult, they sometimes fell back into it.

"That's not what I meant. Don't put words in my mouth! God, I always hate when you do that."

There it was, the back-and-forth they had gotten so good at. They were too alike and used to bash their thickheaded skulls together and push until someone gave. This time, instead of snapping back as she usually did, she closed her eyes and let the old responses tumble by her like waves on a ship's hull, lifting her above the well-worn ruts that she and her son had formed beneath their relationship.

She could hear him breathing on the other end, waiting for her to fire back with equal anger, as was their usual dance. But she kept her eyes closed, smiled into the phone, and said, "I know, honey, and I'm sorry."

He stammered a bit, as surprised as she was.

She continued. "I'll send you my travel information later. Give Angela and the kids kisses from me. Love you, Son." Tere pulled the phone away from her ear, hearing his faraway voice saying he loved her too, the sound of something crashing, yelling, the call disconnecting, then silence. The phone in her hand faded, the room faded, and she felt connected to Rowan across the country, as if she were watching him herding the kids, bringing them into their kitchen to be placated with snacks. It was as if she were anywhere and everywhere. When she opened her eyes, she found she was hovering, her slippers dangling several feet above the rug.

The room looked so different from that vantage point, the small living room feeding to the small dining room, which led to the narrow kitchen. It was like the Habitrail she'd had for her gerbils when she was eight—plastic "rooms" connected by tubes, designed to give the illusion of freedom of movement while containing its inhabitants. No wonder those gerbils had eaten each other.

It was then that she noticed the breeze coming from above and getting stronger. She looked up and saw the industrial-grade ceiling fan spinning a foot above her head.

This was bad.

Really bad.

Tere felt the panic rise from deep in her belly, roaring like a campfire that had just caught, hot and orange and feverish. "No!" The sharp edges of her scream echoed off the Sheetrock walls. She looked down at the couch and reached out for it, upending her body as she floated in midair at an angle now. Her heart was galloping, as if its rapid beat alone were powering her flight, additionally marked by the *click/woosh* sound of the fan blades measuring out the remaining minutes of her life. She stretched her arms out, the tips of her fingers reaching for the pillows on Carl's side of the couch, reaching, reaching, until she tipped a bit more, and her fingertips brushed the fabric. She was able to grab the trim on the cushions, then the pillows themselves, slowly pulling herself closer, down toward the couch. With a guttural bellow, she finally wrapped her arms around the cushions, pulled them to her chest, and hung, desperately attached to the back pillow of the couch. In her head she apologized to Carl for complaining about them being sewn on, but since the damn industrial fan had been his idea, she figured they were even. Slowly, so slowly, her body lowered, until it finally sank down into the couch, and gravity returned.

She lay there, breathing heavily, her arms still grasping the cushion tightly, her teeth biting into the dusty chenille. After a few minutes, when she truly thought it was over, she let go and rolled onto her back on the couch. She looked up at the ceiling and thought about how close she had come to having her head in between those quickly rotating blades. She knew it wouldn't have killed her, but it would have injured her pretty severely. But the thing that frightened her most of all? How high would she go if there were no ceiling to stop her?

That thought rekindled the rush of anxiety, and she started counting her breaths. *In through the nose, out through the mouth.* After that first experience in the garden, she had felt the unreality that set in when you were being told something terrible you didn't want to believe, like, *You're fired,* or *The baby has no heartbeat,* or *I'm afraid your husband has had a stroke.* In those moments, you teetered on the precipice of your life as it had been before, and what it was going to be now that everything had changed. It felt unreal, dreamlike. When it had happened at the university, she'd been worried about being exposed, fired, humiliated. But this time? In truth, Tere was petrified, unmoored (literally and figuratively), and knew she *had* to go to Ávila, *had* to do something, anything, before it killed her.

Once her heart stopped racing, she texted Richard. They'd left it at a weird place, but she didn't have the spoons to smooth it over then. She had a trip to book.

> Hi. Can you water the garden for a few weeks?

A few weeks? Why? You going
to Cali to see Rowan?

> Nope. Going to Spain for a bit, immerse
> myself before the summer course.

What? Tere, I'm sure that's not necessary.
You could teach that class in your sleep!

> You know where the key is hidden. If you could
> come every few days, that would be great.

Her phone immediately started to ring. Richard, of course. Why did these guys feel they had some kind of say over what she did and where she went? She switched it to Do Not Disturb, and typed, Thanks!

Okay, so to be fair, it was an impetuous trip, which was massively unlike her, but they didn't even know the half of how crazy this all was. No, without a doubt, it was a leap of faith, something Tere didn't think she'd ever taken before. She'd had jobs since she was fourteen, always had health insurance, had her car's oil changed on time, and flossed her teeth daily. Nothing left to chance, all boxes checked. No wonder they were wigged out.

As she looked up the weather this time of year in that region of Spain, she thought about the Spanish translation of "leap of faith" as "salto de fe," a literal translation. But another one bobbed to the surface of her memory, one she might have heard in childhood. "Saltovacio," or "empty jump." But that didn't sound right. Her Spanish was growing rusty from living in Vermont for so long, so she googled it and found it was actually "salto al vacío."

Jump into emptiness.

The void.

But the first one resonated with her more, the single-word version, incorrect though it was. She didn't know if it was a Puerto Rican saying or if she had misremembered it, but she decided to keep it that way.

Saltovacio. Empty jump, like she was screaming it on the way down after leaping off a cliff.

Jump into the void.

While reading her notebook the night before, she had learned that Santa Teresa did many such leaps: going against the wishes of her father to join a convent, against the leadership of the church to establish her monasteries, and against the powers that be by talking about her ecstasies. Now Tere was leaping too, taking off to a city she'd never been to, hoping to track down an old nun cousin who *might* still be alive when she got there, in order to figure out her connection with a relative from five hundred years ago, with no solid plan of action for how to solve the mystery of why she was levitating before she lost her multi-decade career or floated into the engine of a Miami-bound 747.

Saltovacio indeed.

"It has wings now: How can it be content to crawl along slowly when it is able to fly?"

—Santa Teresa de Ávila,
Interior Castle

CHAPTER SIX

Tere was petrified of flying. Every time she stepped on a plane, she was certain she was going to die. She knew her life was more at risk driving around Vermont in the winter, but there was no logic to her fear. She had flown constantly as a child, back and forth from New York to Puerto Rico to see family, and it had never bothered her; she used to fall asleep before the huge 747 had left the runway.

The fear began about a year after Rowan was born. She was heading to a conference in Miami, and it was the first time she'd been apart from him for more than a day. Tere looked out at the shadow of the plane silhouetted on the tarmac as it lifted, and she thought, *How the fuck does this big thing get off the ground? Or stay in the air?* Then she thought of her young son, her gentle husband, and all she had to lose, and the panic attack followed. Her therapist had tried to help her. They had done exposure therapy, EMDR, even hypnosis, but nothing worked. So, from then on, she had to be sedated to fly. It had been easier when she flew with Carl. Knowing he was right beside her with his reassuring manner, she had felt somewhat better. She had never let her fear stop her, but she also didn't go out of her way to hop on a plane. Life was hard enough without Tere intentionally scaring the shit out of herself.

The flight from Vermont to New York City was quick, a puddle jumper, but the flight to Spain was a different story. She had the chemical assistance of some Ativan, and as she clicked the seat belt buckle, she felt better knowing that if she levitated during the flight, the belt would keep her in place. After the bland and tasteless chicken dinner with broccoli and rice pilaf that tasted like elevated hospital food, Tere dug into the section of her notebook about Teresian art. She wondered what the saint would think about having an adjective based on her name. She'd probably hate it, given how modest and self-effacing she had been. The image that adorned several of the more popular books was the oil painting by eighteenth-century French artist François Gérard. It depicted a younger Teresa, her hands clasped, oval pale face surrounded by a wimple, and huge brown eyes staring almost coyly at the viewer. Her robes were painted in red, black, and white, while the Carmelites' clothes were hewn of rough brown wool in keeping with their commitment to humility and detachment from material wants (not to mention their commitment to self-flagellation). It is a beautiful yet incorrect and idealized portrait done via the male gaze.

But the most famous depiction of Santa Teresa was the Bernini sculpture, *The Ecstasy of Saint Teresa*. The Italian baroque artist had created a marble portrayal of the transverberation of the saint, the vision she'd had where her heart was pierced by the golden flaming arrow of a seraph, an angelic being. Tere hadn't seen an image of the piece for forty years, but her dog-eared copy of the saint's autobiography, which she'd brought along, featured it on its cover.

After finishing her third bottle of water, Tere realized she couldn't put off a bathroom trip any longer. She hated those closet-like stainless steel rooms that smelled of chemical deodorizer and urine. She slid the lock closed behind her, peeled down her jeans, and sat, almost missing the seat thanks to the wooziness that accompanied the Ativan. As she peed, she put her face in her hands and let out a long breath. Questions buzzed loudly in her head, as if coming from the speakers above the paper towels: *What are you doing? Flying across the Atlantic to do what, exactly? What do you think you'll accomplish there?* It was as if she were being interrogated by a part of her own psyche, and that part was a relentless bitch. So, though she missed her comfy reading chair in her bedroom and the warm smell of coffee and toasting bread in her kitchen, she began to answer: *I don't know. I'll know when I get there. At least I'm taking some kind of action.*

Then the top of her head hit something. Her eyes snapped open to see the toilet below her. She looked over at the metallic mirror to see she was squatting in the air, her jeans down around her ankles, the final drops of urine falling to the floor.

"No!" she yelled, shocked by the loudness of her voice in the tiny room.

The knocking started almost immediately. "Señora? Señora, are you all right?"

More knocking.

She grabbed on to the opening of the towel dispenser, trying to pull herself down. "I'm fine! I'll be right out," she yelled in a quavery voice. But the truth was she was now hanging upside down, her hair dangling alarmingly close to the blue chemical toilet water, her feet brushing against the metal ceiling. She almost laughed from the comic absurdity of it all…well, that and the meds, but the truth was, the flight attendants could force the door open at any moment, and she couldn't let them find her this way.

Knocking. "Are you sure you're all right?" Knock, knock. "Señora?"

"You're not making this any easier," Tere mumbled as she grabbed on to the faucet, then the almond-scented hand soap dispenser that was secured to the edge of the sink, spurting it all over. Slowly, she managed to force her legs down, her feet mere inches from the industrial-gray floor. "Coming!" Gravity was returning in this metal tube propelling her and five hundred other strangers through space. Finally, her boots thumped to the floor. It was over. She looked at herself in the mirror, patted her wild hair down, pulled up her underwear and pants, then opened the door. The dark-haired flight attendant was staring at her.

"Are you certain everything is okay, señora?" the woman asked, looking at Tere with wary eyes, probably wondering if she was going to be a bigger problem.

Tere put her hand on the young woman's arm. "Yes, dear. I'm sorry, sometimes I have a bit of a digestion problem," she whispered, giving the attendant her best dotty-little-old-lady smile that faded as soon as she turned around to walk back to her seat. Hovering against the ceiling of an airplane bathroom had not been on her "Tere's life-changing year" bingo card.

Not fun, not fun at all, she thought as she buckled herself in once more. She swore off drinking water for the rest of the flight, unwilling to risk another bathroom trip.

Tere made it safely to Madrid, stumbled through customs, and, still in a haze, boarded a train to Ávila. The minute she sat in the half-empty car, she dropped her suitcase to the floor, put her head against the glass, and promptly fell asleep.

As the train rumbled west, Tere had the same dream she'd been having for months. She was traveling for work, in a city that she had once known well but no longer recognized, looking for her car. In her belly burned a paralyzing fear that her vehicle had been stolen or towed, and she'd have no way to get home to her family. In the dream, she kept pulling out her phone and trying to dial Carl, but the call wouldn't go through, or an irritating game would be running that she couldn't turn off. She wandered up and down the increasingly seedy streets as darkness fell, and with it came the certainty that she'd never make it home, that she was stuck there forever.

When next she opened her eyes, it was to the sight of miles and miles of dusty earth and brushy dark green trees hugging rolling hills. Tere'd had no idea Ávila was surrounded by so much country-side. It was a welcome discovery, as she was always comforted by nature. She was starting to nod off again when she saw movement among the trees. As they came into focus, she saw dozens and dozens of deer placidly grazing near the trees, their heads rising simulta-neously to stare at the train whizzing by. Tere was comforted by a setting so reminiscent of Vermont. In many ways the trip already felt like a coming home. Perhaps her aunt was right that this was her motherland.

Her aunt. *Shit!* She had texted Nivea from the airport and told her she was going to Spain, but Nivea had asked her to let her know when she had arrived safely. Tere texted her to say she had made it and was on the train, then asked if Nivea could track down some contact information for their nun cousin.

Along the way, the train would occasionally stop at small towns, each station surrounded by medieval stone buildings, with fewer and fewer people disembarking. By the time they pulled into Ávila, the car was almost empty, and Tere was bleary-eyed. The train sta-tion was in the lower part of the city, and according to Google Maps, her rented apartment was an eight-minute walk uphill. Eight minutes was a long time, given she hadn't slept much in thirty-six hours and was still slightly sedated. Her suitcase suddenly seemed massive and unnecessarily heavy. She'd used it on many trips before; why hadn't it felt heavy then? But as she struggled to haul it over the cobblestoned parts of the streets, she realized that Carl had always handled it, in addition to his own. The thought left her mouth feeling cottony, so once she had hauled it up onto the sidewalk, she took a big gulp from her bottle of water and reminded herself that she had birthed a child and earned a doctoral degree, she could damn well handle an eight-minute walk with her behemothic luggage. She worried that people would look at her with her gray hair and think she needed help, that she was an old lady. Not yet, she wasn't. Not yet.

The central part of the city reminded her of Old San Juan, with its low stone buildings packed in tight, store fronts topped by apartments, and people moving languidly through their days. Was it a weekday? She didn't even know. Not that long ago, Tere's life had been divided into Rowan's school and sports schedules, the university's semesters and course blocks, and all three of their doctors' appointments. Each hour of every day was neatly scheduled both in her planner and the magnetic calendar on the refrigerator, so everyone knew where to be and when. As she slowly made her way up and farther into the heart of the city, she realized how freeing it was to live outside that prescriptive calendar, to no longer have each minute dedicated to someone else's needs.

She was sweating bullets and out of breath when she found the building with the little park in front of it, as the Airbnb host had described, one of Ávila's many churches keeping watch ahead in all its stone and stately glory. She was early, so she sat on a bench, let out a breath, and looked up into the trees that encircled the park. The light was filtering through them in patterns, and the sky was the blue that kids drew, crayon layered on thick until the wax had its own shimmer. There were so many birds singing in the branches above, their song became a single avian chorus, and she closed her eyes to listen…

———————————

"Señora!"

Tere jolted her head up and looked around wildly. *Shit!* She'd fallen asleep.

"Are you Señora Sánchez, or are you not?"

She looked up to see an old man—hunched over, but still very tall—scowling down at her, clutching a leash that led to a tiny wiry dog that was looking at her with an equally derisive stare. Tere realized she must have looked like a vagabond sleeping in the park. "Yes, that's me, I—"

"You were early," he rebuked.

She stood abruptly, knocking her suitcase to the ground in the process. "I'm sorry, I managed to catch an earlier train." Lord only knew how her Spanish sounded to him. Born and raised in New York City, she spoke Nuyorican Spanish, and even that was terribly rusty after thirty years in Vermont. She held out her hand to him. "I'm Tere. You must be Señor Cruz?"

"I most certainly am not! I am Arturo Avellaneda González Diaz," he chastened, peering at her proffered hand as if it were diseased.

"Oh…" She dropped her hand and looked down at the dog. "And what's your name, cutie—"

The minute her fingers got close, the dog growled, bared its teeth, and snapped at her. She yanked her hand back like it had been burned.

"That's Sancho. He doesn't like women much."

"I can see that." She didn't think Señor Diaz did either. "So…
you're the owner of the Airbnb?"

"Of course not!"

Tere was so confused. Was it the sedative?

"I'll take it from here, Don," someone said from behind him.

A woman's hand with fashionable long stiletto nails appeared on
his shoulder. The hand's owner stepped to the side a bit, and Tere saw
an elegant, tall woman with pale skin and cascades of burgundy hair.

The old man turned around, started to hobble away, and huffed.
"Just damn absurd that the condo board allows you to rent out your
apartments to these strangers." The dog turned around and glared
at the two women. "I think this one's even an American." He shuddered, took out his key, and disappeared inside the glass door of the
building.

The woman turned to Tere. "Sorry about that."

"I thought he was the owner."

"Well, he acts like he is half the time. That's why I call him *Don*."
She held out her hand. "Yolanda Cruz. We spoke on the Airbnb app?"

Tere smiled and shook the woman's hand warmly. "Of course! So
nice to meet you. Tere Sánchez."

"Welcome to Ávila! Can I help you with your bag?"

"No, no. I've got it, thanks."

"Well, let's check out the apartment, shall we?" Yolanda gestured
toward the red building behind them and began to walk toward it,
her heels clicking on the cobblestones.

Tere was glad Yolanda wasn't looking when she stumbled (even
with her flat-heeled boots). The woman opened the glass door and
held it so Tere could get her suitcase through. While they waited for
the elevator, a nearby door opened, and they could see a human and
dog staring out at them.

"Just ignore them," Yolanda stage-whispered, and Tere snorted before she could stop herself. Then they both fought off laughter until they got in and the elevator doors closed.

"So, what brings you to our city?"

"Well, I've never been, and my family is originally from here."

"Wonderful! So, in a way, you're coming home, yes?"

Tere laughed, having had that exact thought not that long before. "Yes, I guess I am." Close up she could see the woman was older than she'd first appeared, probably only a few years younger than Tere but miraculously preserved, and her bold hair color added an edgy look. Yolanda was dressed in a black trench coat with high-heeled boots, giving her a *Matrix* vibe Tere coveted. She liked Yolanda. Women their age were always portrayed in soft hues, wearing white on the beach, a straw hat tilted on their heads. They were children of the sixties, the most radical of decades, and most of them were *not* coastal grandmas.

The Airbnb was on the third floor, the hallway close and dark, and Tere began to worry it would be depressing. But when Yolanda opened the apartment door, sunlight spilled out. The living room was filled with golden light. There were arch-topped louvered wooden doors and a glassed-in balcony with windows that opened. The wood floor gleamed, and the furniture was simple but neat. It was a lovely nest of a place, a perfect home base for Tere's…quest. Though that word made it seem so much nobler than it felt. To Tere it was more about survival.

"It's so lovely," Tere said with an awed voice. She remembered the owner had several nice apartments; she'd had trouble picking one. "You're the owner?"

Yolanda nodded, then added, "With my siblings. We own five apartments between the three of us."

"That's amazing. I don't share anything with my brothers and sister except neurosis and angst."

A wave of manicured fingers. "Oh, honey, we have plenty of that too. Don't worry!"

She went on to show Tere the nuts and bolts: where the washing machine was, how to use the coffee machine, where to put the garbage, etc. Then they stood at the front door, and Tere looked back into the living room. "It's perfect, thank you."

The host smiled and handed her a card. "If you need anything, just text." As Tere took it, the other woman seemed to notice the tip of the guitar tattoo that reached onto Tere's hand. Then Yolanda went to walk away, but she seemed to change her mind and turned. "Or if you want to grab a coffee or cocktail some afternoon." Yolanda looked at Tere for a bit. "I like you." And with that, the host was gone before Tere could respond. She liked Yolanda too, but after a year sequestered in her house, she seemed to have lost some of the finer points of social interaction.

She threw herself into the task of settling in: placing her haphazardly packed toiletries on the glass shelf in the bathroom, tucking jeans and underwear into the dresser, and hanging up her shirts. Before she closed the closet door, she glanced in and realized she'd automatically left space for Carl's clothes. She gave a sad chuckle, then spread the things out on the rod until they were evenly dispersed from one wall to the other. When she was completely unpacked, she dropped into the tan-striped upholstered armchair in the living room with a groan. Tere was so very tired. More tired, she thought, than she'd ever been before in her life, but she was also proud of herself. She'd done it. She was in Ávila, a place she'd heard about since she was six years old. Why had it taken her until sixty to get there? Well, other than the debilitating fear of flying and the twelve hours of travel. She could still hear the birds singing in the trees, even through the glass, and smell citrus oil that had been used on the woodwork, likely just hours before. Tere closed her eyes and drifted off into a blissfully dreamless sleep.

She awoke to the tolling of bells. So many bells. The sound was pure and joyous, and she jumped to her feet, stepped onto the balcony, and unlatched the windows. The ringing was coming from everywhere, bouncing off the surrounding buildings, filling the little square in front of the apartment. The last clang echoed as if it were going off into the distance, and she stayed perched in the balcony window. She watched the people go to and fro, walking dogs and pushing children in carriages. And there were couples. So many couples arm in arm as they walked, in no rush to get where they were going. *Must be a very romantic city*, she thought. Once again, she wished she had not waited so long, that she had come with Carl when he had been...well, when he *had been*.

Tere dropped into the armchair and closed her eyes again.

It hit her then, dropping on her shoulders like a yoke: She was alone. Really alone.

It's not like she was unused to being alone after the past year, but to not know a single person in the entire country was a completely different level of solitude. It reminded her of the time when she had been five and she and her mother were Christmas shopping at Gimbels. Tere saw a bright pink teddy bear on a perfume display, and she let go of her mom's hand to go run her fingers through its deep fur. When she looked up, the sea of people had swallowed her mother, and the terror that racked her small body was unlike any she'd ever felt.

A wave of anxiety enveloped Tere as she sat with her eyes closed. Her heart started to race, and it felt as if she were tumbling upside down, completely pulled off her moorings. She opened her eyes and gasped for breath. *I have to get outside*, she thought. She grabbed her purse and the keys, then tore out of the apartment, down the stairs, and out onto the street.

When she heard the building door close behind her, she put her hands on her knees and gulped air. It was the same feeling she'd had in the café with Richard earlier that week: being inside felt like being restrained, imprisoned. But this time, in this unfamiliar place, Tere knew she needed people around her, familiar or otherwise. She needed confirmation that there were indeed other humans in the world, that life continued beyond the confines of her brain.

She continued taking deep breaths as she rounded the corner and joined the afternoon flow of foot traffic. People moved around her like waves, and she started to feel better, buoyed by humanity. As she passed the church, she found herself in the middle of a large pedestrian plaza. On either side there were strips of restaurants, bakeries, and cafés. The plaza was made of squares of concrete arranged so that they led the eye to the center.

In the middle of the plaza stood a tall stone statue. With its base, it was nearly two stories high, elevating a woman who perched on a column that then perched on a platform. The statue was white stone, and the drapes of fabric the figure wore flowed like cascades of water. A wimple covered her head, and she looked off into the distance. In one hand she cradled a book. Tere walked up, shadowed her eyes from the sun, and read the name that circled the frieze beneath the hem of the woman's gown: "Santa Teresa de Ávila." The demeanor of the saint was one of stewardship, looking down over the square with attentive concern, as if worried the tiny humans below might dart in front of a car. They had that in common, these two women of the same blood separated by over four hundred years, accustomed to

taking care of everyone other than themselves. Tere walked right up
to the base of the statue, put her fingers to the cool stone, and whispered, "Nice to meet you, Santa Titi."

Perhaps calling her "auntie saint" would be considered blasphe-
mous in some circles, but it was just between them, Teresa to Teresa.
The last of the panic bled from her body then. It was going to be
okay. Even if she didn't find her mysterious cousin, she knew somebody there.

"It is a great advantage for us to be able to consult someone who knows us, so that we may learn to know ourselves. And it is a great encouragement to see that things which we thought impossible are possible to others, and how easily these others do them. It makes us feel that we may emulate their flights and venture to fly ourselves, as the young birds do when their parents teach them; they are not yet ready for great flights, but they gradually learn to imitate their parents. This is a great advantage, as I know."

—Santa Teresa de Ávila,
Interior Castle

CHAPTER SEVEN

The famous walls of Ávila were straight ahead, already familiar from hundreds of photographs Tere had perused online, and she was drawn to them as if they were made of magnets and she of metal. She was familiar with stone fortifications, having visited the bookended forts in Old San Juan more times than she could count, but these...these were older and more imposing but at the same time simple, like what children drew when they imagined a medieval city filled with knights and turrets and dramatic archways. Just the idea of fully enclosing a city in a protective stone embrace was fascinating to her; hadn't her Vermont house served the same purpose for her over the past difficult year? She was so focused on the walls that she almost proved the Santa Teresa statue right and stepped in front of a car.

There was a huge arched gateway directly across from the Teresa statue, and Tere wandered under it like a child at Disneyland, gaping at the vaulting overhead as it surrounded her. When she exited on the other side and looked back, the sun shone on the walls, and from that angle, they had the cinnamon-sugar coloring of the sand in Luquillo Beach, where they used to go when she was a child—bleached seashell pale with hints of coquina red.

Having officially entered the old city, she continued walking, admiring the cross-shaped burbling fountain, looking into the small food shops with whole hams hanging in a row and the bakeries displaying different sugary pastries as if they were jewels. And she saw restaurants, so many restaurants, the scents of searing steak, garlic, and baking bread spilling out into the street. The smell made her realize just how hungry she was. It was early afternoon, no longer lunch and not quite dinnertime, but there was no one else's body clock to consider, only her own waxing and waning of blood sugar and exhaustion.

There were so many choices of places to eat, Tere was overwhelmed, and she felt the beginning notes of panic rise again. Whenever Carl had asked where she wanted to eat, she was the one who didn't care, who could eat anywhere. He had been the picky eater. But he was not there. She decided to choose randomly. On a side street, she ducked into a small restaurant filled with older men talking, eating, and jingling the change in their pockets. It was like stepping back in time with its traditional masculinity; she could almost see her father with his cuff links and smell of Briggs pipe tobacco. There were display cases with tapas along the counter, and though she didn't know the names of anything, she pointed to three and asked for water with gas. She grabbed her spoils and settled at a nearby table.

Food had never tasted so good. There was a meat patty, a small plate of chorizo, and what she thought were mashed sweet potatoes (she would later learn they're called patatas revolconas, mashed regular potatoes with smoked paprika, fragrant garlic, Spanish olive oil, and pork), all served with freshly baked bread. When she had emptied the three small plates, she sat back and sighed. She felt better. So much better. As she was digesting, she moved the plates to the empty spot across from her and pulled out a small notebook she'd bought at the airport. Pen in hand, she stared at the fresh page with the intention of coming up with a plan of attack, a series of actionable items to embark on and give structure to this ridiculous and impetuous trip. After a long fifteen minutes of staring alternately at the blank page and at the choreographed movement of the restaurant staff, she accepted she could start fresh in the morning. Besides, her mind was still fuzzy from the sedatives.

Yes, tomorrow was another day.

She put her pad and pen away, paid the ridiculously low tab, and stumbled out the door.

Tere headed back toward the apartment, her belly and brain full. She had seen and felt more in the previous forty-eight hours than she had in…well, a year—good and bad—and she felt alive. When she got to the apartment, she dropped onto the bed, fully clothed. In the instant she let out a long breath of relief, her phone buzzed with a text. She groaned and dug her cell out of her jeans pocket. It was her aunt.

> At mass I told Cousin Ileana all about your pilgrimage and asked if she knew where Isabella lived. She said no, but that we better hurry, since our nun cousin does ministry work at an orphanage in Quito, Ecuador every spring. I will keep looking. Besos!

Great. Yet another ticking clock. No pressure. Tere threw the phone across the bed. She was too tired and full to be excessively frustrated. She rolled over and was asleep in minutes.

Tere slept for fourteen hours, awoke, and threw wide the wooden louvered doors to the balcony. The sun shone in, spreading across the white bedspread like liquid gold. As she leaned on the balcony railing and breathed deep of the clear, bright morning, she remembered Nivea's text about the time pressure on finding Isabella and groaned. But the lovely day almost made up for it. Almost.

She didn't even bother with the individual-pod coffee maker. Carl hadn't been able to get dressed for the day before his first cup of coffee, so while traveling together, they'd had to make any coffee available immediately upon rising, regardless of the quality. But she was alone and in Spain, where coffee was rich and strong, so she was not willing to settle for less. Tere threw on some clothes, put on minimal makeup, and at the last minute, shoved the worn paperback copy of the saint's autobiography in her backpack, then headed out the door.

She stopped into the Santa Teresa Café and got an excellent café con leche and an almond pastry to eat while she walked. She wandered a bit and saw an entrance to walk on top of the walls. Tere loved the idea of seeing her ancestral city from above. She paid her entry fee and took a cursory glance at the gift shop wares. She was relieved they were not as commercial as she had expected. No Saint Teresa bobbleheads or Funkos, to which she gave a sigh of relief. Though she was sure she had no right to it, she felt defensive of her saintly relative. For Tere there was an aura of the sacred around the woman, and it seemed perhaps the city felt that way too. She made her way up the winding staircase.

When she finally breached the top, the sun shone onto the stone and lit the walls, almost as if from within. Looking off to one side, she could see the tips of the city's buildings—some new, most old, all beautiful. And on the other? Miles and miles of countryside. The city still spilled beyond the walls, but not far, and then it was just earth and trees with an occasional road cutting through them.

She was aware of other people walking the walls—there were tourists of all backgrounds, most her age or older—but it was less crowded than she had anticipated. However, it was early in the season. Midsummer it was probably flooded with tourists of all ages from all over the world. She took photographs of the vistas from different viewpoints so she could remember them and lost herself in the act of putting one foot in front of the other as she reflected on Santa Teresa, on how she must have lived her life in this very city four hundred years earlier. As she walked, she pulled out the autobiography from her bag and read the saint's first line:

"If I had not been so wicked, the possession of devout and God-fearing parents, together with the favour of God's grace, would have been enough to make me good."

Tere remembered finding it amusing that the saint referred to herself as wicked throughout the work, but especially when recounting her childhood. She'd tried to attain martyrdom at seven years old. Tere? Well, according to Nivea, she had been a feral child with skinned knees and no shame.

She continued to read about how when Santa Teresa had been in her forties, she was "commanded" to write the autobiography by her "confessors," men who had positions of leadership in the church, so as to prove her ecstasies were not of the devil but of God. She had written this book and others to literally save her life and avoid execution by the Inquisition for heresy. Tere stopped short, leaving a pair of Japanese tourists no choice but to bash into her from behind. "Sorry! ¡Perdón!" She'd called after them in the only two languages she knew. After they passed, she stood with her back against the ancient wall, breathing hard and staring at the words on the page until the individual letters seemed to lift and shift as her eyes blurred with tears. No wonder Tere hadn't wanted to tell anyone about her levitation: she was descended from people who'd had to worry about being executed for the exact same experience. Tere must have known this at one time, but because it was so far from anything that she thought would affect her life, the knowledge had fallen away. But in that moment, the knowing sat in her belly like one of the bricks that comprised the wall.

With the book in hand, Tere climbed up into one of the turrets that afforded an even wider view of the city and the surrounding countryside. She leaned her arms on the wall and pressed the book against her chest, feeling as if there were tendrils growing between them, connecting her to her namesake's words, to her story. Tere took a deep breath in and looked around, really seeing the city and its surroundings for the first time. It was impossible not to be awed by God while standing on top of the ancient and magnificent city, for the love of Him was soaked into the very soil and stone, was built into the foundations of its many churches and monasteries. She closed her eyes and felt the wind whip through her hair, the smell of freshly mown grass and narcissi reaching from the garden that hugged the wall behind her. She felt light, joyous, like spring itself. Tere opened her eyes and looked at her feet.

They were planted firmly on the stones beneath her.

Interesting.

She continued on her way. The farther she got from the main gates, the more the press of tourists thinned, the youngest and oldest unwilling or unable to go that far. When she got to the end of the open and walkable section, she stopped and looked off the parapets, wondering what everything had looked like back in Teresa's time. She spent a while lost in thought, and when her phone beeped, she jolted. A FaceTime call from Nivea. When Tere saw her aunt's image on the screen, she felt a wave of warmth as if she were on the island too, the Caribbean sun having come out from behind a cloud.

"Titi! You'll never guess where I am!" She held the phone out and gave her aunt the 360-degree view.

"Oh my. It is just as beautiful as I remember it." Nivea's voice was soft with longing and memory. "Oh, I so envy you, m'ija. I had hoped to go back there one day."

Tere turned the phone toward her face once more. "Let's go next year! Together." Titi was in her eighties. They both knew the odds of such a trip were getting slimmer with each passing year, but it comforted Tere to imagine they would.

Nivea laughed, the sound as warm as the sun-soaked stones. "Sure, and after we'll climb Everest."

Tere shrugged and grinned into the camera. "I'm game if you are."

Her aunt waved her hand impatiently. "Enough of such ridiculousness. I called to tell you that I found out where our cousin the nun is."

Tere's heart thrummed. "Wonderful! But wait, are we going to continue calling her 'our cousin the nun' and not her actual name?"

"Fine. I don't know if she ever took her vows, but her full name is Isabella Lope Sánchez."

"So, when I meet her, I should call her 'Sister Sánchez' or 'Sister Isabella,' something like that, right? I don't know the protocol in such situations." She was getting excited. Maybe this trip wasn't as far-fetched as she had imagined.

"That's thanks to your heathen upbringing. I blame your parents."

Tere rolled her eyes at the phone.

"Either will be fine, I'm sure. Listen, I'm told she's at Sacred Heart Convent. I don't know where that is, but you should be able to goggle that, right?"

Tere snorted. "Google it, yes, I can do that."

"Cousin Ignacio says that's the most recent information he has for her."

Tere tried to picture Cousin Ignacio. She had a vague image of a tall baldpate man with an old-school mustache at a wedding of some other relative she couldn't remember. "Okay, I've walked as far as I can here. I'll goggle it and go there as soon as we're done."

Nivea nodded. "Bueno. So, is the city everything you imagined it to be?"

"It's amazing. Beautiful, like history is soaked into every stone. But it's kind of weird being in a city where I don't know anyone. It isn't like when I traveled for work without Carl. I knew academic contacts or conference coordinators, someone. This? I don't know a single human being in the entire country." She thought of Yolanda, but she'd only spoken to her for ten minutes, so she didn't think that counted.

"Well, you are going to fix that soon, yes?"

Tere smiled. "Yes." It was so comforting to see the environs of her aunt's comfy home on the small screen, Tere was hesitant to sign off.

"Keep me posted, okay?"

"Of course." The sound of Puerto Rican Spanish was soothing, the familiar music of it sweet and earthy like fresh-picked mangoes.

Her aunt blew a virtual kiss, and when the picture winked out, rather than feeling happy and connected to her, Tere felt exposed.

Vulnerable.

Alone.

"Any unrest and any strife can be borne, as I have already said, if we find peace where we live; but if we would have rest from the thousand trials which afflict us in the world and the Lord is pleased to prepare such rest for us, and yet the cause of the trouble is in ourselves, the result cannot but be very painful, indeed almost unbearable."

—Santa Teresa de Ávila,
Interior Castle

CHAPTER EIGHT

Leaving the walls behind, Tere headed across the Plaza de Santa Teresa and started down the hill to the address she'd found for Sacred Heart, though it took a lot more digging than she'd expected for a convent. A couple of blocks down from the apartment, she saw she had left the touristy area and entered a more working-class neighborhood. The stores' offerings were more practical—hardware, kitchen goods, eyeglasses—and there were fewer meandering sightseers. Most of the buildings were newer, mid-century housing of glass and cement, but there were medieval buildings tucked here and there among them like sentries from the past. Since meeting Carl, Tere had found she loved the mixture of tradition and practicality that blue-collar areas offered. He had been a carpenter, raised poor in rural Vermont, and built his own business from the ground up. Tere remembered when she'd suggested they buy a house in Shelburne, a bougie area outside Burlington. They drove around for an hour. Over coffee in a neighborhood café, she asked him what he thought.

"I don't know, Tere. I mean, where do these people buy the things they actually need for life?" He was gesturing dramatically with his free hand. "What if you need a mop or toilet plunger? You have to drive to Williston." He took a distracted sip of his coffee, then stopped, holding the cup out to her. "Look at this coffee. It cost five dollars, and I prefer the taste of the ninety nine cent cup at the gas station." He paused and then looked into her eyes in that intense way he had where she believed he could see into every corner of her being. "I'm just not comfortable here, honey."

In the end, they'd bought a house in the Old North End, ethnically diverse and the last bastion of working-class neighborhoods, and she found that she too was more content in less pretentious company.

She started to think that when she next came to Ávila, they would stay in this neighborhood, Carl would like it…until she remembered. Sometimes she would forget he was really gone. Then it was like waking up to a slap.

It took the GPS a couple of tries to identify the correct street, but finally Tere stood in front of a medieval building, bookended by a tile store and a tattoo parlor, the ancient wall pockmarked and graffitied in spots. There were two large arched doors, the wood thick and cracked, generations of brown paint gathered in the crevices, with huge metal hinges. In front of the one on the left, a young man with a tumble of thick black hair stood, holding a silver tin.

She approached him with a smile. "Excuse me?"

The boy turned and looked at Tere, and she froze. He was a handsome young man, with full lips and a strong Roman nose, but it was his eyes that drew her attention. They were deep brown, dark but also bright, as if there were twin candle flames right behind them. She had once seen a baby in a restaurant in Stowe, and when she looked into its eyes, she'd felt a pull, like there was a much older, evolved soul in there looking out. This boy's eyes gave her that same feeling. She realized she was staring, so she gave him an embarrassed smile and continued. "Do you know if this is Sacred Heart Convent?"

"Si, señora. It is."

"Any idea where the entrance is?"

He pointed to the other large door. "I think there's a bell on that one."

She dug into her pocket and placed a two-euro coin onto his plate. "Thank you." She waved and walked off, still a bit stunned by the young man. When she arrived at the other door, she saw there was no sign identifying what the building was and no bell or knocker evident. She was confused, and the building was completely uninviting. She had started to walk back to talk to the boy again, when the door behind her opened quickly, disgorging a priest. She turned around again, hoping to catch it before it closed, but she was too late.

Tere called out to him. "Father! Father, excuse me? How do I get in? This is Sacred Heart Convent, yes?"

He paused, looking flustered, and reluctantly bustled back toward her. "Yes, señora, it is. I'm afraid I don't have a key. You have to ring the bell."

Her gaze skimmed the entirety of the door. "What bell?"

"Here." He pressed somewhere on the wood—she didn't catch where—and a buzzer sounded within. The priest scurried off before she could thank him, as if he couldn't wait to put distance between himself and the convent.

She waited for some time but didn't hear any movement within. *What kind of place was this anyway?*

Tere was trying to find the hidden bell to ring it again, but when her face was closest to the door, it suddenly swung inward, almost pulling her off her feet with the vacuuming air.

A grimacing nun, who looked to be about Tere's age but with dyed-black hair harshly pulled back from her face, stuck her head out, a lit cigarette dangling from her mouth. She looked left, then right.

Then she glared at Tere through eyes narrowed from the smoke. "Did you ring the bell?"

"N-no." It was the truth, but she had to admit the woman frightened her. The nun was still regarding her, and Tere felt sweat begin to gather on her upper lip despite the cool day.

The woman looked around as if wishing someone more interesting had rung. Then she eyed Tere up and down and sighed. "Well? What do you want?"

"I'm—I'm looking for someone. This is Sacred Heart Convent, isn't it?" She coughed and waved her hand in front of her face, trying to push the gray smoke away.

The woman examined Tere for a long second more, then stood to the side and shooed her through. As the nun closed and locked the door behind them, Tere stepped into a courtyard, very old indeed, with green grass shooting up from between the ancient stones, reaching for the blue sky as if looking for escape, kind of like the priest. There was a lovely calico cat sitting on a step to an interior door, lifting its paw as it groomed itself calmly. Where were the people, though? There was another courtyard off to one side with a large stone sculpture in the middle, and two floors of rooms lined the square. It still appeared ill cared for, but she had to admit the inside was more welcoming than the outside.

"Well? Who are you looking for?" the woman barked next to her.

At least the *setting* was welcoming. "Isabella Lope Sánchez."

The nun pulled back with exaggerated raised eyebrows, then appeared to chew on the name as if it were something she was unsure was edible. "She's been gone a couple of years now."

Tere's shoulders dropped with disappointment and sadness. "She passed then."

The woman screwed up her face and swiped the thought away

with her entire arm. "No! Did I say that? What kind of Spanish do you speak anyway?" She growled. "I didn't say she was dead. She just left the convent."

Tere was relieved to hear about Isabella, but damn, the nun was beyond rude. "Okay…" Tere dragged the word out, patience waning. "Then can you tell me where she is now?"

The woman took a long drag on her cigarette, then gave Tere the squinty-eyed regard again, the lines on her face thick, as if a heavy-handed cartoonist had drawn them. "Who wants to know?"

"I'm her cousin. I'm a Sánchez," Tere added, certain that the name at least held some regard.

The nun cackled. "Oh, honey, aren't we all? I don't have the name, but I am too. Half the damn city is." Then she picked up a nearby broom and threw it at the cat, screaming at it in her gravelly voice as it shot off through the other courtyard.

Tere began to suspect she had entered the fifth circle of hell.

Then the woman was staring at her again with her smoky judge-and-jury eyes that made Tere feel as though her skin were flayed off and she stood there all shiny red muscles and stretched tendons like the anatomy dummy in the university's science lab. "Why do you want to find her so badly? It sure isn't for her personality." The nun cackled, actually slapping her thigh.

Tere was surprised this horrible woman seemed to have some sense of her need for answers. Perhaps it was that surprise that made her answer honestly. "I'm looking into levitation, why Teresa levitated, and given that Isabella is a Sánchez, I thought—"

"Why? I can tell you why. She was a saint, end of story. It's not the place of ordinary people like you and me to understand the divine."

"But wasn't Teresa an ordinary person once? She came from a

family just like you and I did, she had chores and read books just like we do—"

The nun was already shaking her head. "No. She was always blessed. She needed that life so she could understand the rest of us mortals, have empathy for us. The levitation was part of her ascension."

The thing was, Tere had thought about all these things—they were basically the tenets of the Catholic Church—but that didn't change the fact that she too was levitating. She knew in her heart and soul she was no saint, not to mention that she was already sixty years old. No. There was something missing from this pat theory. You couldn't excuse miracles as being inaccessible to all but a precious few. Miracles. Did Tere think of her experience that way? She was starting to think miracles came in different sizes and weren't always welcome.

Tere looked at the woman to find her cutting her fingernails with a clipper that was attached to her key fob, the thin strips of dirty nails flying left and right.

Tere had to get out of there. "So, do you know where Isabella went or not?"

The woman looked up from her makeshift manicure and shook her head slowly, a mean smile lifting one side of her mouth.

Many choice words ran through Tere's head like subtitles, but she had been taught to be polite to nuns, though some clearly deserved it less than others. "Okay, well…I'll just be on my way then." She started inching back toward the door.

The woman was shooing her out with waves of her hand. "Yes, go, go." When the nun got to the door, she stood with one hand on the lock and with the other pointed to a donation box mounted on the wall. She looked at Tere with raised eyebrows and narrowed eyes.

Oh, hell no. Tere folded her arms across her chest, daring the woman to outright ask for a donation. She probably used the money from the box to fund her smoking habit.

They stood there for a moment of high noon standoff. Then the nun scoffed and opened the door for Tere. After she'd stepped out, the nun yelled at her back, "And when you find her, tell her Sister Inés wants the twenty bucks she still owes me from poker!"

And then the door slammed, followed by the metal clanging of locks being thrown.

Tere couldn't help but wonder why her cousin Isabella had left such a lovely place. But she had, and now Tere was frustrated by her lack of progress. Dropping on a nearby bench in the small square in front of the convent, Tere dug out her copy of Teresa's book and stared at the cover, as if she could find answers there, as if the photograph of the saint's marble effigy might speak and tell her where to find her cousin, maybe even what was going on and why the hell it was happening to her. She closed her eyes and tried to slow the galloping of her mind and heart. An unhealthy cocktail of rage, fear, and frustration flooded through her veins.

She heard a tearing sound and felt the bench shift. Tere looked down and saw that her jacket had caught on one of the boards of the seat, the black fabric ripping as her body worked to rise.

"Oh, for Christ's sake! Now?" If you'd have asked her to guess what caused one to levitate just a week earlier, she would never, in a million years, have thought an episode could be triggered by a cranky-ass nun and an overwhelming feeling of impotence. With heat rising behind her face, she quickly grabbed her coat's belt and tied herself to the metal frame of the bench. Tears stung her eyes as she realized she was destined to be an unemployed, desperate old hermit, aimlessly floating around the ceiling of her house, all alone. Once she was as secured as possible given the haphazard mooring job, she put her head in her hands and held back sobs. She could feel her body struggling to pull away from the bench, desperately trying to launch her neurotic ass into the cosmos. She felt so powerless that for one desperate moment, she wondered if she should just let it.

"Señora? Are you okay?"

Startled out of her reverie, Tere looked up and saw the young man with the astonishing eyes standing over her, his face shadowed in the afternoon sun. She looked around, worried that her current state was obvious, but she'd already started to descend, and she could feel the pull lessening. Tere coughed, wiped her face, then arranged her mouth into a facsimile of a smile. "Yes, thank you, joven. I'm just…tired."

He pointed to the convent. "You didn't find the answers you sought there?"

Her heart skipped a beat. A common expression, but Tere swore she actually felt her heart skitter. "How do you know I went there with questions?"

He shrugged his shoulders. "You looked like a seeker."

As she looked at him, she thought, *It takes one to know one.* Instead of voicing it, she smiled sadly and said, "Well, you're very perceptive." She put out her hand. "I'm Tere, Tere Sánchez."

He looked at her hand for a moment, surprised, then shook it. "Teresa, like the saint?"

She nodded, again struck by this boy's extraordinary…aura? Vibe? All the words that came to mind were trite.

"I'm Juan."

"Nice to meet you, Juan." She pointed to the empty half of the bench next to her and wished it filled, just while the exhaustion from the "episode" wore off. "Won't you join me for a bit?"

He smiled, then sat down. Juan glanced over at the book on her lap. "You're reading Santa Teresa's book?"

She had forgotten about it and looked down. "Oh yes. I read it back when I was your age, but I've been reexploring it."

"There is so much wisdom in that book. The Spanish edition has a different image on the cover, though."

Tere looked down at it. It featured a close-up of the famous marble sculpture. "Yeah, I'm not a fan of the Bernini interpretation of her. It has too much of a creepy rapey feel for me." She glanced over at Juan. "Sorry! I—"

"Oh, don't apologize. That is definitely true. Particularly when you see the entire tableau."

"Wait, 'entire tableau'?"

"Oh, there are a series of sculptures on either side of the room. Have you not seen them?"

She pulled out her phone and searched for images under "Ecstasy of Santa Teresa," the title of the piece.

Juan slid closer on the bench. "Try adding 'full tableau.'"

She gazed over the results, the orgasmic face of the saint duplicated over and over on the screen, the disturbing leer of the angel holding the arrow over her.

"There." Juan pointed to an image. "That's one side."

Tere clicked, and when it enlarged, her mouth fell open. She focused in on four bearded men in a balcony on either side of the alcove, watching, discussing, one of them consulting a book. "You have got to be kidding me?"

"No, Bernini created a balcony on either side, filled with members of the wealthy family that commissioned it. Most of them were Cardinals or high members of the church or the government."

She looked over at him. "Watching? Balconies of men, watching her 'ecstasy.'"

"Yes."

"This takes the problem of the male gaze to an entirely different level. Why are these never shown in the images of the piece?"

"Perhaps for the same reason you and I are so horrified. But probably just because they are hard to photograph all together."

One of the captions actually said, *Members of the church assisting in Saint Teresa's ecstasy. Assisting.* They'd almost had her executed! Tere kept scrolling through images, hoping there was some mistake, but no.

Juan stood up. "Well, if you'll excuse me, I have a shift at the soup kitchen on the other side of town."

Tere started to get to her feet, forgetting she was tied to the bench causing the book to slip and fall to the ground. She awkwardly jerked back down, her thighs slamming on the wood. She adjusted her hair as if that could set right her bizarre behavior. "Oh! Of course." Remaining seated this time, she reached her hand out to him. "Thank you, Juan."

He gave her a small smile. "For further ruining a piece of art for you?"

"No!" She laughed. "Well, yes, but I believe it is always important to learn as much as you can about a subject."

"Are you a teacher?"

She looked at Juan again. "Yes, I am. Well, was." She smiled. "Am."

"May God bless you, profesora," he said, bending in a small bow before walking away.

A homeless boy wishing that God should bless *her*. Now that was more Teresian than the nun inside the convent who'd actually taken vows. As Tere watched him walk away, his begging pan tucked under his arm, she couldn't shake the feeling that the young man was something very special.

The encounter with Juan served as a balm to her frustration over having had yet another episode. She was still a scholar, so she would put the awful visit to the convent of Sacred Heart behind her and do what she did best. As she untied herself from the bench, she thought about the options of where to begin her research. Her undergraduate days of wandering into a library and announcing to a librarian that she wanted to know more about X were long over. She would do some preliminary exploration, then approach things the next morning with a specific strategy in place.

Yes, she felt better already.

As she stepped away from the bench, she tripped over something and looked down to see the book with the odious cover. She picked it up and tucked it back into her backpack. She would keep it but would never look at the sculpture the same way again.

Before bed, she called Nivea and filled her in on the experience at the convent—a challenge, since her aunt kept laughing so hard, Tere often had to pause for her to catch her breath.

"Any true ecstasy is a sign you are going in the right direction... Don't let any prude tell you otherwise."

—Santa Teresa de Ávila

CHAPTER NINE

Tere woke up the next morning with a burst of energy and a plan to find her cousin Isabella. The night before, she had looked up the city's Catholic archdiocese. It was the most concrete place to begin with the highest probability of finding answers. They'd have to have a record of her. Rather than call, she decided she'd get farther in person, and according to the map, it was on the other side of the old city, a mile walk. Her stomach was growling, and they didn't open for a couple of hours, so Tere took herself out for breakfast. She ended up at a table in Santa Teresa Café with a traditional Spanish breakfast of a thick piece of freshly baked bread topped with thin slices of cured Ibérico ham drizzled with fresh olive oil and sea salt, a glass of fresh squeezed orange juice, and a café con leche spread out on the table in front of her.

As she took a bite of the delightfully crunchy toast, she realized she was downright giddy. She knew it was because that morning she had a plan, albeit a simplistic one, for the first time since she'd arrived in Ávila. She loved itineraries, to-do lists, even the work involved with creating the university's strategic plans. So much of her life she had been guided by her intellect, led around by her brain. With intellectual parents, over twenty years of school, and straight into academia, she had lived in the realm of thought, not feeling.

Until she met Carl.

That man led with his gigantic heart. From the first afternoon of their honeymoon trip to the island of Virgen Gorda, when he convinced her to pick up two young boys who were hitchhiking, something the New Yorker in her would never have done. Those lovely kids not only gave them the inside scoop on the best hiking trails, but also led them to a locals' shack that served caught-that-morning grilled mahi-mahi smothered in fresh mangoes, the thought of which still made her salivate. They'd spent the night dancing on the beach to drums and drinking rum with a group of men and their families who worked in construction and bonded with Carl. Those families still sent Christmas cards each year, the photos of the light-strung palm trees bringing a whiff of ocean breeze to snowy Vermont. She didn't write back to the one sent this last Christmas, as her message would have been too sad for a holiday card.

Though it had been as slow as a sea change, she had been influenced by Carl during their long years together. In fact, from the moment she decided to start this quest, Tere knew she would have to tap the energy he had brought into her life. So, other than during this visit to try and find out where Isabella was, she made a pact that she would not wile away hours in libraries and dusty archives, conversing only with pages of text. That was why she'd traveled halfway across the world on a whim, after all, which was, now that she thought about it, the most Carl-like thing she'd ever done.

After her food and caffeine sustenance, the walk went quickly. It was another beautiful day, and she breathed deep of the blooming spring flowers spilling from planters everywhere, listening to the myriad of languages spoken by people as she made her way through the streets. This trip skirted the increasingly familiar old part of the city, and she enjoyed discovering new neighborhoods.

She arrived at an open black iron gate and a paved road that led directly to the Roman Catholic Diocese of Ávila, a stately stone building with a slate roof and a courtyard at its center. As she walked down the sidewalk, she noticed there were no cars going up and down the road. The whole complex seemed as if it were sleeping.

It had been forty-two years since she'd set foot in a Catholic administrative building. Her high school, Saint Michael Academy in New York City, had a similar imposing vibe, and whenever she'd entered, it had always made her feel as if she were in trouble for something (of course, the ten-foot statue of Saint Michael, sword held high, his foot on the writhing head of Satan right at the entrance hadn't helped).

There were three arches at the building's front, and she felt small as she walked through the center one and into the cool marble interior. There was a tiny chapel to the side, the altar draped with a white cloth that had an embroidered image of Santa Teresa in the center, rows and rows of battery-powered candles glowing on top and in front of the altar, and behind, a life-size statue of the saint looked upon the tableau with resolute patience. Tere made her way to the main desk opposite the entrance and stepped up, feeling tiny before the tall marble slab. She stood on her toes and addressed the man typing away on an ancient PC.

"Good afternoon."

He looked up through his thick glasses, then back down at his screen. "Can I help you." It wasn't really posed as a question, more as a statement.

"Yes, I'm trying to locate some information on where to find a relative of mine, a nun here in Ávila."

He looked over at her again, then back at the screen. "You'd have to check with the records office."

"And that is where?"

Without saying anything or taking his eyes from the screen, he pointed to the left hallway.

"Thank you." She started walking, her heart beating a bit faster, feeling like someone should be saying, *Warmer, you're getting warmer,* like that game she used to play as a kid.

But before she got more than a few yards away, he called out, "But you need to make an appointment."

She stopped, her boots squeaking loudly on the tile floor. She turned around. "Really?"

He nodded as he typed. "And they're closed on Mondays."

She put her hands out in frustration. "You couldn't have told me that when I first asked?"

He just shrugged and held out a business card with the phone number of the records office. "You can call them tomorrow."

Tere walked back, snatched the proffered card, and resisted the urge to give him the finger. Even she was not that irreverent, but she was frustrated. One step forward, two back. *Colder, you're getting colder—ice-cold!* The taunting childhood voice spoke in a singsong in her head. Before she exited, she stepped over into the chapel and looked up at the statue of Teresa over the altar.

Tere gazed up at the beatific ceramic face and whispered, "Hey, Titi. Maybe you could give me a little help here? I'd really appreciate it." After waiting for a beat, as if expecting an answer, Tere sighed, then headed out into the sunny morning. For a moment, she felt angry at the beautiful clear day because it did not at all reflect her mood. It was two days nearer to her expected return to teaching, and she was no closer to finding answers. As she made her way, she stared at the ground, feeling so weighed down, she was surprised she could walk, let alone float as she had the day before.

She decided to take a longer route back that led through the old city. At least she could walk on the same streets Teresa had frequented. *Maybe I can get some information by osmosis.* She snorted at the thought, and a woman walking by glanced at her warily. When Tere reached the top, nearing one of the gates in the wall, she looked up and realized that ahead was the Ávila Cathedral, the biggest church in the city. She had seen it from above when she walked the walls but could not properly comprehend its size and grandeur until she was standing in front of it. The building itself was incorporated into a section of the wall, ensuring the safety of its congregation during dangerous times. It had been built over a span of four centuries, so it represented a mishmash of architectural periods. The result had a Frankensteinian vibe, but as she looked up at the front, Tere had to admit it was impressive and quite stately.

"What the hell," she mumbled. Thanks to the records office's lack of Monday hours, she had nothing else to do at that moment, so she joined the flow of the crowd feeding through the entrance.

She was surprised they charged a five-euro entry fee—to a church (she wondered if there weren't laws against such things). Later she learned that it was a "suggested donation," but nothing she'd seen indicated it was a choice. To add insult to injury, once she paid, she had to follow a U-shaped path that led through the gift shop, with its beaded rosary bracelets, key chains bearing Santa Teresa's image, and religious-themed coloring books, before even setting foot in the cathedral proper. Though she usually hated audio tours, Tere needed distracting, so she downloaded the tour and set it to play in her earbuds as she walked into the main entryway. When the audio began, she put her phone away, looked up and into the cathedral, and gasped. She had seen Saint Patrick's Cathedral and the Cathedral of Saint John the Divine in New York, Saint Peter's Basilica at the Vatican in Rome, and the Duomo in Florence, but this? This was beyond magnificent, the huge building filled with art and drama from marble floor to vaulted ceiling.

She walked along with the audio tour, looking into each of the endless side chapels, admiring the paintings done in rich dark colors as the man's cultured voice talked in her ears. She entered an area that had crypts built directly into the walls, then stopped at one in particular when she noticed "Sánchez" engraved on the plaque. Was this a relative? *At least I found* one *family member.* She scoffed. Her gaze passed over the pocked and worn stone that made up the effigy of the long-dead Sánchez, his hands calmly folded across his chest, his nose half chipped off, his eyes closed for his endless sleep. It was so weird to think that his body, or what remained of it, lay right there, in the stone box for all who paid five euros to gawk at. Before Carl, Tere had only seen one dead body.

Her father died of ALS when she was eight. She'd watched the disease eat his body over five years, shrinking him from 280 linebacker pounds to 140 and in a wheelchair. She was devastated when he died; in her mind he was still her wide-shouldered, unbelievably strong father who lifted her up on his shoulders as they walked. Her mother refused the mortician's request for an open casket, as neither of Tere's parents believed in embalming. The undertaker argued so vehemently over the phone that her mother intentionally dressed Tere's father in his favorite around-the-house outfit of a white undershirt and torn khakis. Tere remembered her mother and the man with the bad toupee having one last argument in a small side room in Saint Paul's Chapel on the Columbia University campus.

"But he looks so handsome, just like he did in life! You have to admit, it is incredible work."

"Whose suit is that, even? I dressed him how he wanted to be buried, and I expect him to be re-dressed before the service. Plus, I made it abundantly clear there was to be no embalming," her mother said through her clenched jaw, waving a pointed finger. While they fought in hushed voices and the church filled with hundreds of her father's academic colleagues, Tere tiptoed over to the shiny box in the corner. It was reddish wood with carved curlicues like apostrophes around the edges. She made sure the adults were not paying attention to her and very gently pried open the lid. There was no creak to call attention to her transgression, just a smooth lift, a flash of white satin, and there he was. Her father's face was filled out like it had been before he got sick, his white hair neatly brushed back, his bright-blue eyes shrouded beneath powdered lids. His skin looked perfect, too perfect, like the plastic skin of her Ken doll. She was just reaching out to touch his cheek when a hand fell on her shoulder. She looked up and saw her mother, the lower part of her face shadowed by the coffin lid, but her hazel eyes were lit golden by the afternoon light coming through the room's stained glass window.

"Come on, honey. It's time to say goodbye to him."

Tere looked at her mother with disbelief. That was it? What kind of a goodbye was that for a man who had been half the foundation of her life? Could her mother just walk away and leave him?

The mortician appeared beside them and moved toward the casket with the discarded clothes to re-dress the body with a disappointed shake of his head. He gave Tere a tight smile as if they were bonded in their dissatisfaction with her mother's decision, but she didn't like his strong scent of lilies that did little to mask the chemical odor beneath. Her mother took her by the hand, stood tall, and led her away, toward the front of the church, where her older siblings were already seated.

Tere had twisted around and strained to see the coffin, hoping to catch one last glimpse of her father.

Seeing Carl's body hadn't been anything like that.

He had passed in the time Tere took to eat in the cafeteria, the final stroke shorting out his brain as she sat choking down tasteless pork roast and gravy two floors below. They were just unplugging his machines when she arrived, and when she realized what was going on, a low moan escaped her lips. She could feel her heart contract with pain and a dizzy spell coming on.

She sat on the side of his bed and held his hand, ignoring the staff's suggestion that they take him away, their whispered questions about who they could call for her or if they could get her a priest. In that harsh industrially lit room, she watched the blood slowly settling to the bottom of his body, leaving his tanned Native American skin with a ghostly pallor. She didn't know how long she sat there when a familiar voice reached her.

"Tere. I'm so very sorry."

She looked up and saw Richard standing in the doorway, his face drawn, his hair wild as if he had just gotten up.

Tere was relieved to see him but, at the same time, upset at being disturbed. "Wait, how did you know? You're not on Carl's emergency-contact list."

He stepped into the room. "No, but I'm on yours." He stood next to her and put a warm hand on her shoulder. "The hospital staff was worried about you." He looked down at Carl's still form. "You're going to have to let them take him."

She took a swallow of breath and was about to yell, *No!* But she knew he was right. Instead, a sob escaped her mouth, and she leaned into Richard and broke down. He held her, crying himself at points, and she felt a flurry of emotions leave her in a whoosh.

"C'mon, let's get you home. Rowan's flight gets in at eleven tonight. I'll stay with you till he gets there."

She turned back around, leaned over her husband of more than thirty years, and pressed her lips one last time to his newly cold ones. She could not watch rigor mortis stiffen those limbs that had been so strong and nimble just the week before. The huge rough-skinned hands that had so gently held their son for the first time and then loaded his furniture into a truck for a cross-country move twenty years later. Like her mother before her, Tere would have to put the physical remnants of her husband in her rearview mirror.

———————

As Tere stood in that stately cathedral in Spain, pulling herself back from two deep layers of memory, she realized she had been raised by a widow for most of her childhood and then had become one herself. One would think she would have been better at it, with all that experience, but instead she had ground her life to a stop for a full year while her mother had had no choice but to go on since she'd still had three children left at home. Tere felt like a failure as a widow.

She took a huge gulp of air, like she'd just breached the surface of the water after too long beneath. Then she held herself up straight, turned much as she had a year earlier, and put the Sánchez man's crypt—and the thought of his dusty bones—behind her.

"I wanted to live, but saw clearly that I was not living—but rather wrestling with the shadow of death. There was no one to give me life, and I was not able to take it."

—Santa Teresa de Ávila

CHAPTER TEN

Still somewhat distracted by the flood of memories and the tour narrative running in the background, Tere pretty much stumbled into the main chapel. She looked up and around like waking from a dream, then gasped at the towering arches lit by electric lamps, the sun beaming through tall colorful stained glass windows. It was spectacular.

As she walked around the central nave, she was appalled by the egregious show of wealth with all the gold accents, priceless art, and precious carved woods; but on the other hand, she had to admit that all together, it was awe-inspiring. Literally. This realization was a perfect metaphor for her relationship with the Catholic Church: it enraged her with its hypocrisy of saying we were all one under the Lord, then in the next breath adding, *Oh, well, we didn't mean gay people. And all those other religions that have been around for centuries? Heresy. Oh, and only men can be priests and popes.* Meanwhile sexual abuse was rampant among their clergy. But there were things she loved about the church: the rituals, the teachings of Christ, the community, and the symbolism. The Ávila Cathedral seemed a testament to both the good and the bad.

The last leg of the tour was around the central courtyard, a square of columns with glass in between, protecting a well-kept garden. Why on earth did they wall off the garden as if it were an exhibit? She would have welcomed sitting for a spell on a bench near the perfect green grass, the blue sky above offering a bit of brightness after the dark majesty of the cathedral.

As she walked out and back onto the ancient streets, Tere realized just how drained she was. She had started the morning energized and determined, but the dead end of the diocese and the memories in the cathedral had taken a toll on her.

She had twenty-four hours until the records office opened, but she refused to do nothing. She decided that, in the interim, she would do some old-school digging. The public library was literally across the street, after all. The moment she stepped through the archway and into the open gated courtyard, she released what felt like a breath long held.

At the circulation desk, she requested a variety of materials about Santa Teresa and Spanish mysticism, then gleefully settled at a table in the corner, neatly piling her resources around her like the city's walls.

By the time she lifted her head again, two hours had flown by. She had gone down a rabbit hole reading about the friendship between Teresa and Saint John of the Cross (who, it seemed, had also been known to levitate). It was fascinating, but Tere felt no closer to finding answers than when she had awoken that morning. She pushed away from the table, the chair's metal legs scraping loudly against the light wooden floors, and started piling the books and bound articles once more, angry at herself.

She had learned nothing that would be useful in solving her levitation problem, yet she was hours closer to losing her tenure.

Though libraries were Tere's safe space, comfortable and familiar, something told her that since nothing about this entire situation was comfortable nor familiar, her answers lay elsewhere. She strode over to the desk and placed the materials on the return cart with a huff, then abruptly turned to walk out and slammed directly into a young man who also appeared in a hurry to get out of the library. The thunk of their skulls hitting still rang in her head as she bent to help him retrieve his manila folder, which had disgorged its contents all over the floor.

"Señora, I'm so sorry! I—"

She looked up and met the electric eyes of the boy who had enlightened her about Bernini's sculpture. "Juan?"

"Oh! Señora—"

"'Tere,' please." She smiled as she rubbed her head and stood, handing him a few of the papers.

"Tere." He gave her a shy smile as he rubbed his own. There was a round red mark on his forehead as he stood as well. "I'm so very sorry—"

"Is the library on fire?"

He looked around, alarmed. "What?"

She chuckled. "I just meant you seemed in quite a hurry to get out of here." The two of them fell into step next to each other as they resumed their walk toward the exit.

He ran his hand through his tumble of hair. "I come here every day to use the computers, and I'm afraid I got a little...frustrated today."

"Don't they have someone who can help you?" she asked, though she had a feeling it was about more than tech support.

His face flushed. "I'm trying to apply to college, but they make it so complicated, and"—he waved the folder back and forth—"I'm not even sure what documents they're asking for. I don't have an address—"

She stopped short.

He realized she wasn't beside him and looked back at her sheepishly. "I'm sorry. You don't want to hear all this, señ—I mean, Tere."

"Yes, I do. And Juan? We ran into each other today for a reason." Finally, she felt as if her day would not be a complete loss. She might not have made progress in her search, but she could help this boy. She took his hand in hers. "Come with me." She gently pulled him back toward the building.

"Where are we going?"

"Literally the only place I've ever worked in my adult life has been in higher education. And I started in admissions all those years ago. I'm going to help you with this, and we're going to get that application in."

"I can't ask you to—"

"You're not asking. I'm insisting! C'mon." Yes, this was just what her battered heart needed, and it was something much closer to what Santa Teresa stood for.

They settled in at the bank of computers, going over the materials he had in the file, talking about what admissions teams were looking for. She was thrilled to be back in a territory she knew so well, to have a purpose amid the wildest time of her life. When he pulled up the college's website, Tere was somehow not surprised that the local institution was Saint Teresa of Jesus Catholic University. While he pulled up the application form and entered his information, Tere printed out and read his personal essay, thinking she could help with a suggestion or ten, but she was delighted to find it didn't need much feedback at all. "Juan, this is excellent."

"Really?" His eyes lit up even more than usual.

"I'm serious, this is outstanding. The sensory descriptions of your life now are so powerful, the connections with your childhood insightful. And that you used reverse chronology? Brilliant! I just indicated a few typos and grammatical issues here and here." She sat back in her chair and looked at him. "Seriously, this is better than some of the graduate essays I've read. Have you ever thought of studying creative writing?"

He looked flushed, but she could tell he was proud of his work. "Yes, though my high school guidance counselor said I couldn't make a living at it."

"Psh! I heard the same thing from every guidance counselor I ever had. That I was not working up—"

"—to my full potential." They said it together and laughed.

"You too, huh? Guess they give them the same script in every language. Well, screw them. It's your life, not theirs." She gestured toward the computer. "Keep going so you can prove them wrong."

Tere got an inspiration, so she fired up the computer next to him, and they typed away side by side for about twenty minutes, until Tere pressed Send and turned to him. "Okay, check your email."

He toggled away from the current application, checked his Gmail, then opened the attachment from her, his eyes glancing over the lines on the screen. "But…what's this?"

"A letter of recommendation. In my experience a letter from a college professor weighs—"

He lurched over and pulled her into a hug.

She was surprised and frozen for a moment, then hugged him back warmly. She felt his body shake a bit and the soak of tears on her shoulder, so she ran her hand over his hair like she used to do with Rowan when he was upset. Tere found herself missing her son and the intimacy they'd shared, so warm and full of trust. Then she was crying too.

Eventually he pulled away, careful to wipe his eyes before he fully sat back. "I cannot thank you enough, Tere."

She put her hand on his arm. "It is absolutely my pleasure, Juan. To tell you the truth, this is what I needed today too. Now let me enter my credit card for the application fee, and we'll get this submitted."

He put his hand out. "No, Tere, I cannot let you do that. I've saved—"

She pushed her rolling chair out of the way, stood over the keyboard, typed in her information, then pressed Enter. "Well, you don't have any choice now, do you?" She smiled at him. "Now, finish this up and submit it!"

Ten minutes later, a grateful and flustered Juan ran off for a volunteer shift at church, so she logged them out of the computers and just sat there for a moment. Tere felt good, better than she had in some time. Working with Juan had reminded her of the best parts of her academic career. Not the politics or the power grabs among faculty. It was the students. Young people who were hungry to learn. Helping them seemed to feed her in ways nothing else did.

When she put the credit card back in her wallet, Yolanda's card fell out and onto the table.

Yolanda…

Her outgoing and vivacious landlord was definitely someone who was connected in the city…

And her family was from Ávila.

"Yes!" Tere pumped her hand into the air as two young girls at a nearby table stared at her. She mouthed "sorry" and dialed the number.

"Yolanda? It's Tere Sánchez. I'm the one—"

"Tere! How lovely to hear from you!" Yolanda's voice was so genuine and warm, Tere's eyes filled again. "Everything okay with the apartment?"

"Oh! Yes, perfect! I'm calling to ask for your help with something. I know that's weird, since we just met, but—"

"Of course! I'm at an open house, but it's dead as a crypt this afternoon. Here's the address." Tere's phone dinged with a text. "Come by and we'll chat."

"Great! Thank you." When Tere pressed End, she smiled to herself. *Not warm, but not cold either,* her childhood voice said as she headed out of the library and onto the afternoon streets.

"It is certain that a man who has no need of anyone has many friends: in my own experience I have found this to be very true."
—Santa Teresa de Ávila,
The Way of Perfection

CHAPTER ELEVEN

To reach the address Yolanda had sent her, Tere exited the walls through the nearest gate, one that was new to her. The day was warming up, but it was still cooler than the day before. Once the sun hit the walls, however, it was as if they were stone radiators encircling the city, spreading their warmth until the sun set beyond the hills.

Following the GPS, she turned down a side street tucked between restaurants all touting their steaks, with photos of bleeding meat posed with glasses of rustic red wine. Tere was afraid to go into one, order a steak the way she liked it—medium well. They would probably throw her out of the city on her ass for desecrating a quality cut of beef. She just couldn't eat it any other way; it used to make Carl insane. He would throw his hands up in frustration when she asked him to put hers back on the grill. "It doesn't even taste like meat anymore when it's cooked that much!" If she had come to Ávila with him, they would have had many a late-night flesh-eating dinner, and she would have relished seeing his eyes close with pleasure when he bit into his disgustingly bloody meat like some sort of feral creature.

Halfway down the block, next to a small jewelry store, she saw the sign advertising the apartment's open house. Tere stopped and gazed up at the three-story building, with its two levels of balconies framed in black wrought iron, ivy trailing down in cascades, bringing to mind once again the beautiful streets of Old San Juan. In addition to talking with Yolanda, Tere wanted to see what an apartment would look like this close to the walls, tucked right up against history.

The building was unlocked, so she climbed to the second floor. Her knees snapped and cracked loudly in the quiet stairwell. Tere rarely thought about her age, mainly because she didn't feel sixty at heart, but then something like creaking joints reminded her with a sharp poke. The apartment door was propped open, and she jumped when excited squealing erupted from inside.

"Yay!" Yolanda rushed over, enveloping Tere in a warm hug that brought with it the delicate scent of gardenias. "I'm so glad you called me! Come on in."

When they separated, Tere glanced around. "I'm surprised there isn't a line of people here. This apartment is beautiful."

"Oh, young people don't want to live in Ávila anymore. The city is tiny, in the middle of nowhere, and there really isn't much to do beyond go to mass and eat."

Tere smiled. "I see your point."

Yolanda leaned back against the kitchen counter, folding one lean leg over the other. "My kids couldn't get out of here fast enough! One's in Madrid and the other London, last I heard anyway. She makes it a point not to keep me updated. Thinks it makes her more independent or something."

"My son felt that way about Vermont. Too rural and too damn cold in the winter."

"I saw that on your profile. Where on earth is Vermont?"

Tere wasn't surprised; no one seemed to know where Vermont is outside the United States. "In New England." Yolanda was still staring. "A few hours north of Boston."

"Ah! Okay."

That always worked.

"So, on the phone you said needed help with something?"

"Yes. Though it's a little weird."

Yolanda clapped. "Oh good! I love weird. Let's have a glass of wine and sit in the living room."

Tere let out a sigh of relief. "I'd love that." She followed her new friend, Yolanda's stride punctuated by the tap of her high-heeled pumps, a bright cherry red like her dress. Bold and edgy.

They settled into the furniture with their glasses of red wine and talked for a bit about general things: life, children, and husbands. It was not meaningless small talk, but rather filling-in-the-blanks-of-life talk. When was the last time Tere had sat and shot the shit with another woman? She honestly couldn't remember.

Yolanda raised her wineglass and smiled. "I like you, Tere Sánchez."

Tere did the same. "And I like you, Yolanda." After taking a sip, she put the glass on the table and leaned forward. "Okay, I'm trying to locate a relative of mine, a cousin who may or may not be a nun. Her name is Isabella Lope Sánchez, and last we knew she was at the Sacred Heart Convent, but I went there yesterday, and it was a whole... thing." How else would one describe that experience? "Anyway, she wasn't there anymore. Do you think you might know some way to help me find her? I wouldn't ask, but there's a time crunch, as she does volunteer work in South America, and I'm afraid to miss her."

Yolanda tapped her long fingernail on her lips. "I can try someone I know in the city office. Or a friend who works for the local dioceses."

"Oh, I went there this morning. Their office was closed, and the guy at the desk wasn't overly helpful."

Yolanda snorted. "Not surprised with the stories she's told me. But I can text her directly. She owes me a favor since I looked after her ill-behaved children for a weekend. Let me make a few calls."

Tere smiled, grateful. "Thank you."

Yolanda took a sip of her wine, then asked, "So, finding your cousin is not the entire reason you came to Ávila, is it?" She peeked at Tere over the rim of her glass, the merlot matching her hair perfectly.

Tere jolted a bit but recovered quickly. "What makes you think I'm not here to track down Isabella and maybe sightsee?"

Yolanda waved that away with her elegant hands. "Oh, c'mon! I've only known you for forty-eight hours, and I know you're not here to kneel in every church in town like the religious tourists. They're the only ones who come for more than a day tour, and you sure as shit don't fit the pious mold."

Tere snorted into her wine, spraying it all over her face, and they both laughed. "That obvious, huh?" She wiped her face with a cocktail napkin, grateful the furniture was leather and not white linen, then fell back into the cushioned chair. "My husband died a year ago."

Yolanda leaned forward and took Tere's hand in hers. "I'm so sorry."

"It's okay," Tere said automatically, patting Yolanda's hand as if comforting her. Then she stopped herself. Something about this woman and her straightforward manner made Tere realize something. Why was that her default answer? "Actually, you know what? No, it's not." She looked at Yolanda. "It's not okay. Nothing about losing him was okay. So much so that I haven't gone back to work after my bereavement leave."

"No, that kind of loss is never easy. What do you do for work?"

"I teach at a university, but everything that seemed so important before Carl's death seems trivial now." They sat in respectful silence for a few minutes. Tere was surprised to be talking so openly with someone she'd just met, but she was also relieved. Then Tere sighed and said, "As to your original question of why I'm really here, I guess I'm trying to figure out what the next stage of my life is." *And why I'm floating in the air at seemingly random and sometimes dangerous times,* but she kept that part to herself.

"But, honey, you've been through so much, no? Raised a son, had an important career. You're not interested in slowing down?"

"Hell no! I'll slow down enough when I'm dead."

Just then, they heard the building door open, and footsteps and voices made their way up the stairs.

Yolanda sat up, put her glass on the table, slipped on her high heels once more, and stood to her full and rather impressive height. "Well, this has been such a wonderful visit. But I'm afraid duty calls."

As Tere stood, she picked up both glasses to put in the sink. "Thank you so much, Yolanda. I appreciate your taking the time to hang with me and help me with my search."

Yolanda grabbed the glasses back. "Give me those. That's my job." Then she reached over and pulled Tere into a one-armed hug. "And it is a pleasure."

The smell of gardenia was soothing, almost as much as Ativan, and Tere's heart slowed deliciously. As they separated, she said, "It really was wonderful to see you again."

"I'll get in touch with you the minute I find something about your cousin, and trust me, I will. It might not surprise you to learn that I'm a tenacious bitch when I want to be."

Tere chuckled. "Another thing we have in common."

"And maybe we can sneak in a coffee date?"

"I'd love that." After twelve months of avoiding human contact, Tere realized she meant it.

A young couple stepped through the door, and Yolanda greeted them and began asking them questions about themselves, about what they were looking for in a home. Tere was not surprised at just how good Yolanda was at her job; everything sounded fresh and not at all like something she said over and over. As Tere was walking out, she saw the info sheet on the apartment on the counter and took a copy before folding it away into her backpack and waving goodbye to her new friend.

She was lost in thought as she started down the stairs, excited to have a new possible source for locating Isabella. As her hand slid on the ornate wrought iron handrails, she took the next step on the marble stairs, and it didn't land, as if the stair had been pulled out from beneath her. Tere looked down and saw her foot was floating, her back foot beginning to follow.

"What? Not now!" She hissed.

Tere reached over and gripped the railing with both hands as her lower body rose behind her.

Shit!

Voices rose from the open door of the apartment above, but they couldn't see her. Yet. She had to do something. She pulled with all her might and slowly guided her legs down and toward the railing. Awkwardly she managed to push one shoe between two of the twisted posts. Then, with a loud grunt, she got the other one through. She joined her hands on the other side of the railing and wrapped her legs around each other, securing her entire body to the banister, her chin leaning on the handrail. Just then the building door downstairs opened, and she watched an older man unlock his mailbox, pull envelopes out, and examine them as if he had all the time in the world, while Tere desperately tried to at least put her butt on a stair so it wouldn't be obvious she was still floating.

He started up the stairs, and when he got to the landing and turned the corner, he saw her and stopped short.

Tere gave an awkward smile and went to wave to him but realized she couldn't let go. She nodded at him instead. "Buenas tardes."

He was just standing there in all his trench-coat-and-business-suit-put-togetherness. He coughed, then asked, "Are you all right, señora?"

She tossed her head, like she clung to stair rails every day. "Oh yes. Just needed to take a bit of a rest. These stairs are steep!" Then she cackled in what she hoped was not a maniacal manner. "But thank you."

He paused for a second, nodded, then picked up speed, giving her a wide berth as he passed. She listened to him walk to the third floor, then heard a door being unlocked. When it finally closed, she let out a long breath. She rested her head against the handrail, the smell of metal, cleaning fluid, and sweaty hands somehow comforting, and felt her body slowly lower, her limbs relieved and aching to let go.

The whole thing was getting terribly complicated.

"What proud humility did the devil plant in me, when I gave up my hold on that pillar and staff whose support I needed to save me from making a great fall."

—Santa Teresa de Ávila,
Interior Castle

CHAPTER TWELVE

As Tere walked across the plaza, still shaken from the experience in the stairwell, the bells from a nearby convent began to ring, and with the timing, it felt as though they were for her. She stopped, stood, and listened. There was something magical about being in Spain and hearing medieval church bells echo off the buildings. But she was most comforted by the ordinariness of the kids and dogs running back and forth across the open square, old men in suit coats gathered at the outside tables with glasses of amber beer before them. Those exact things had been happening there for hundreds of years, with generations of dogs and children and old men. She found that changelessness comforting, particularly given all that seemed to be changing within her.

As she walked through the square, Tere stopped at the statue of Santa Teresa. "Hi, Santa Titi," she whispered up, running her fingers along the edge. Though she hadn't planned to, she sat on the marble base and waited for the family walking by to pass out of earshot. Then she looked up at the statue, the sunlight a corona around the saint's head, and began to whisper. It was a conversation she felt needed to be out loud, since she couldn't speak about this with anyone else.

"It happened again, and it's getting harder and harder to hide.

How am I to live my life if I have no control? Not to mention that I have no one to ask for guidance. But I know *you* understand, if no one else can. I'm scared and totally lost, Titi. I get why you levitated—your strong connection with God and all—but why me? I am no saint and have no desire to be. I'm just trying to live my life, to understand how to move forward after losing so much." Tere lifted her hands in a kind of surrender. "Look, I'm not even going to ask you how to make it stop, since this experience is clearly happening for some reason, but I need—no, I'm *hoping* for answers. I guess what I'm asking is if you can help me discover why."

The sun shifted, and she could see the contours in the statue's face, the texture of the stone. She began to feel silly talking to a carved rock, and her eyes filled. Then she felt someone take her hand. She looked up and saw a nun in a brown habit standing in front of her. She was a tiny woman with brown skin and large, bright brown eyes bookended by deep wrinkles like quotation marks. Behind her, a group of other nuns waited and watched with kind smiles. Without a word, the woman opened Tere's palm and placed a small wood rosary in it. In the center where the beads met, there was a picture of Santa Teresa. Tere looked up at the woman and asked, "Thank you. But why are you giving this to me, Sister?"

But she just closed Tere's fingers over it and patted her hand. One of the other nuns came forward and put an arm around the shoulder of the smaller woman. "Sister Luisa is visiting from a convent in Trinidad, and she has taken a vow of silence. She signed to us that you were praying, and she needed to give something to you. She was quite insistent."

Tere looked at the woman, put the fingertips of her flat hand to her lips, and then moved them down toward the sister—the ASL sign for "thank you." The nun responded with her hand sideways, doing the sign of the cross for "God bless you," bowed slightly, then shuffled off arm-in-arm with the other women.

Stunned, Tere sat there staring at the small rosary in her hand. There was more to that encounter than a simple gift of prayer beads. She glanced up at the statue and whispered, "Is this your answer?" But she didn't understand what it meant. When she looked back at the women, they were already making their way up a side street. Tere stared, wondering if she should run and catch them, but she didn't even know what she would say if she did. Then they were out of sight. She couldn't shake the feeling that the other Caribbean woman knew about what Tere was struggling with, that just perhaps, Luisa levitated too.

But that made no sense.

Still, she carefully tucked the rosary into her coat pocket.

Tere started walking home, but it was as if her body were moving of its own accord, her mind still trying to understand the experiences of the previous hour. She was almost home when a FaceTime call came in. Richard. No matter how they'd left off in their last conversation, she was happy to see his face on her screen. She stopped walking and settled down on the low wall that surrounded the neighboring church so she could sit in the sun to take the call. "Richard! How's my garden?"

He laughed. "Wild and out of control, as it seems you are too, of late."

"You have no idea."

He leaned into the screen, glancing around, and smiled. "Hold on, that doesn't look like Madrid. Are you in Ávila?"

How the fuck did he know that? Well, there was no denying it. "Yes."

Richard's eyes narrowed. "I didn't know there's a University of Madrid in Ávila."

"There isn't."

"So, what kind of research are you doing there?"

"Did I ever tell you we're descended from the family of Santa Teresa of Ávila?"

He pulled back. "Um, no? Are you serious?"

"Yeah. I never thought about it much before...well, before. But I've never been here, and I felt the need to connect with her, with the city."

"Hell yes, you do! That's astonishing, Tere!" He was excited; she could tell from the way he was gesturing wildly. "And talk about Iberian literature! I mean, her work predates Cervantes's by fifty years!"

"True."

"You going to add that to the summer class's curriculum?"

Ugh. That was the last thing she wanted to talk about. "I'm thinking about it." Vague enough and practically true.

"Have you gone to the Four Posts yet?"

"The what now?"

"The Four Posts. It's outside the walls, just west of the city. It's by far the best view of Ávila."

"So, you've been here?"

"Sure, in 2005, Denise and I did a tour of Toledo, Ávila, and Salamanca. She's a good Catholic, wanted to see all the sacred places in that neck of the woods. But she only adheres to the parts of the religion that serve her, though. She wasn't so devout that she couldn't divorce my ass." He gave a chuckle.

Tere knew he wasn't really angry about it; it was just a script some men his age followed, like the "ball and chain" trope. "Oh, c'mon, some people just grow apart. And you stayed close friends. Honestly, those are harder to come by these days."

"Yeah, I actually like her better now than when we were married."

"Besides, ecclesiastical prohibitions are grossly outdated, and you know it."

"True, true." He nodded his head absently. Then: "So, Tere, I had lunch with Mike Sampson last week, and I didn't give him a name, or anything"—he held his hand out to the camera to ward off her response—"but I asked him about that issue you had while we were hiking last month—"

Tere could feel anger stoke in her belly. Sampson was a cardiologist who taught at the university. "You did what?"

"Dizziness, passing out—"

"I did not pass out during that hike!"

He leveled his gaze at her. "Tere, you weren't conscious to see it, but you did, just for a few seconds. Scared the shit out of me."

"Yes, Rowan told me." These guys were really starting to piss her off.

"And given the history of heart trouble with your mother, he said those could absolutely be symptoms of a heart problem, and that you—or the person who is experiencing such symptoms—should get a series of tests right away—"

Tere put her hand up, closed her eyes, and took a deep, calming breath. She spoke slowly and clearly. "Richard, my dear friend, though I appreciate your concern for my well-being, I am a grown woman and more than capable of taking care of myself."

His shoulders slumped a bit. "I know, I know. We're just worried about you." His eyes softened. "Look, it's not just the hike. Not coming back to work, this last-minute trip… You're just not acting like yourself lately."

It was all true, but there was no way she could talk about it, particularly not with Richard.

He gave her his best grin, "Besides, you must know that Santa Teresa was the patron saint of heart disease and had her own issues, so it goes *all* the way back in your family."

She chuckled and her own heart softened a bit. "Again, I appreciate it, but I'm okay. Really." She even rustled up a smile to prove it.

A swell of muffled voices rose on his end, indicating a break between classes. She could picture the youthful energy bouncing from wall to wall like atoms. The sound was so familiar but also far away, like the memory of a place you hadn't been to in many years. "All right, Dr. Sánchez. If you say you're okay, then you're okay." His voice sounded sad. "Office hours are about to start, so I better let you go."

"Thanks for caring, Richard."

"And I always will." A wink, and then he was gone.

She shook her head a bit. Tere knew he had good intentions, but still. She stood and walked around the corner to her building.

Just after she'd closed the door behind her, Señor Avellaneda González Diaz popped out of his apartment on the first floor, Sancho barking feverishly by his leg. "Señora Sánchez, Señora Cruz came by on her way home. Seems her cell phone died, so she asked me to give you this." He handed her a half folded piece of paper.

"Oh, great. Thank you." She took the note and turned back toward the stairs.

"I guess she thinks I'm a messaging service now." He harrumphed.

Tere glanced over at him, amused to see him standing with crossed arms and a deep scowl, like a toddler about to throw a tantrum. "Well, I appreciate it," she responded, trying to read the note as she walked up the stairs.

"Why are you interested in a convent?" he called after her.

Tere stopped halfway up the flight and looked down at him. "Now, señor, I know you didn't read my private correspondence."

He waved his arms. "What do you expect? It wasn't in an enve-
lope, and it's not like it's state secrets, for God's sake!" He was still
ranting as he closed the door to his apartment and then yelled at
Sancho to shut up.

Convent of Saint Michael

She stood in the dark hallway searching the name and found a
listing on Calle Don Lopes de Segovia. She looked at the map—it
would be a walk—then at her watch. Damn. It was too late to go that
day; showing up at five would not ingratiate her to her elderly cousin,
but she was pleased she once again had a plan for the next day. She
just hoped the nuns at this convent would be friendlier than the last.

Tere tried to relax, but she was just too restless with all the day's
events. She headed out into the late afternoon in order to investi-
gate a new part of the city.

There were countless cobblestoned side streets that seemed to
always lead to yet another plaza, the city's layout as intricate and beautiful as a snowflake. She let her feet lead and headed down the big hill.
The storefronts were mostly closed, and there weren't many pedestri-
ans, so there wasn't much to check out. She was about to turn around
and head back, when she saw half a dozen bikes parked outside a store
just ahead. "A bike shop!" she exclaimed out loud.

Tere excitedly made her way toward the entrance. Riding bikes
was something familiar, an activity she had done in Vermont often
before Carl's death. She always smiled while riding a bike because it
reminded her of childhood, of the kind of freedom you only have
when you're young. The last time she and Carl had ridden together,
she had one of those dizzy spells Richard was going on about, and

Carl ended up having to ride back alone, get the car, and pick her up. He had fussed over her all evening, worrying. Ironic since he was the one who had died a month later.

Tere glanced at the models outside—mostly mountain bikes and cruisers with wide tires, which made sense. She didn't imagine road bikes would be possible with all the cobblestones. She went in. The bell over the door was cheery, and she looked around at the brightly lit shop with its rainbow of bicycles and immediately felt comfortable there. It had a good, welcoming atmosphere. The only customers were a man and a boy standing at the register, so she looked around at the different options until the clerk was free.

She was admiring an elegant bright green mountain bike when the man and boy passed by her, calling thanks back toward the counter, the boy wheeling his brand-new bright-blue bike with a huge grin on his face. She smiled as she watched them.

"There's nothing like the excitement of a new bike when you're that age, huh?"

"Isn't that the truth? I—" She sputtered a bit when she turned around and saw the man who had just spoken. He was striking, slightly taller than her, younger—she guessed midforties—with a full head of wavy silver hair. His skin was tan and weathered, much like Carl's had been from years of working outside. She continued talking, though she was slightly flustered. "I remember getting my first non-hand-me-down bike for my seventh birthday, and for a whole week at school, I would remember it was in the garage at home, waiting for me, and I felt this current of joy just at the thought."

He smiled and nodded. "Banana seat with sparkles?"

She grinned, surprised at the accurate description. She could see it so clearly in her mind. "Yep, and rainbow streamers that flew from the handle grips as I rode."

"Mine was metallic blue with chopper handlebars."

They kept smiling at each other, enjoying their shared memories. But then Tere looked at him through squinted eyes. "Wait a minute, you're too young to know about banana seats. Those were in the seventies."

He answered as he shifted the bikes a bit, filling the hole the boy's bike had just vacated. "Oh, style-wise we're always ten years behind here. Besides, my older sister had one just like it, with groovy flower stickers all over the seat." He gave her the peace sign.

"Yeah, mine had them too."

"I was partial to playing cards in the spokes, myself." He put his hands on his work-aproned hips and smiled at Tere. "So, can I help you with something?"

"Oh! Yes. Do you rent? Bikes, I mean?" She worried she sounded like an idiot. Her social skills really had suffered over the past year.

But the man simply grinned at her. It was disarming. "We do. Do you ride?"

"Yes. I used to all the time back in Vermont."

His face lit up. "Oh, I love Vermont! The bike trails in the mountains are unlike any other."

This warmed her heart. "You've been? Most people just stare at me blankly when I say where I'm from."

"I have a friend in Burlington who is a very serious mountain biker."

"That's where we live!" She caught herself. "We." She was so used to saying it. "I mean, where *I* live." Tere swallowed hard.

The man was looking at her like he saw what was behind her eyes, like he could see the pain hiding there, buried behind the cornea and iris, clouding her vision, keeping her from looking forward. "It's interesting."

Could he see inside her head? Nothing would have surprised her at that point. "What is?"

He folded his arms across his chest, and she noticed the profusion of tattoos that reached down onto his hands. From what she could see, they were a collection of tribal images and Eastern spiritual symbols on his forearms, plus a stylistic compass on one hand and a death moth on the other. Tere approved. "You don't speak Spanish like you're from Vermont."

"That's because I'm originally from New York City." He was still looking at her. "And I'm Puerto Rican."

He put his index finger up between them. "Aha! I knew it!"

Tere laughed.

"So, when are you planning to go for a ride, Señora Boricua from Vermont?"

"I don't know." Truthfully, she hadn't thought that far ahead. This was all a whim, like the whole goddamn trip. "I guess, soonish?"

"So, are you here with your…husband?"

Tere felt a familiar weight thud in her belly, settling within her pelvis as if it had just been returned to the cradle that was made for it. "No." Suddenly the overhead lights seemed too blue and bright, reminding her of the university hallway or…the hospital. Her breathing began to speed up.

He put his hand on her arm, the one with the compass tattoo. "Hey, are you okay? You look a little—" He didn't get to finish. The bells over the door clanged, and a crowd of younger people flooded in, all energy and rapid-fire Castilian Spanish.

Tere stepped back, overwhelmed by the rush of activity, the noise, and the echo of grief she could still feel in her chest. One of them seemed to know the man, as she immediately pulled him into a hug and started introducing her friends. Grateful for the diversion, Tere slipped out while the man was distracted with all the names and questions being thrown at him. She heard him call out for her to wait, just before the door shut behind her. She took off, walking fast, back toward the apartment, an empty feeling spreading in her chest, like a black hole that was absorbing everything around it. There had been many times in the past year when she'd missed Carl more than she could bear, but what she'd felt with that guy—what was it, an attraction?—made her grief feel sharper, its edges pointed and painful like shards of glass.

When she closed the apartment door behind her, she took a deep gulp of air, and the sobbing began. She strode to the bedroom and threw her body on the bed, covering her head with the pillow. Tere could hear the shuffle of everyday life on the street, the birds singing outside her window, and she couldn't imagine how life could just go on as always. That was when she felt the now-familiar stirrings, her body slowly pulling away from the mattress. She jolted up to sitting, hurled the pillow across the room, and screamed, "Fuck you!"

Then she carefully crawled under the tightly made overlarge bed, which held her down like a cocoon, curled into a ball in the center, and sobbed herself to sleep.

"Let us now, with the help of the Holy Spirit, come to speak of the sixth Mansion, in which the soul has been wounded with love for the Spouse and seeks more opportunity of being alone, trying, so far as is possible to one in its state, to renounce everything which can disturb it in this solitude."

—Santa Teresa de Ávila,
Interior Castle

CHAPTER THIRTEEN

Tere awoke the next morning with swollen eyes and a dry mouth. It felt as if she were rising out of layers of sand. Part of her wanted to crawl deeper beneath the covers, but the rest of her, the majority of her, was determined not to spend more time indulging her grief; there had been enough of that in the previous year. It was time to find the elusive nun cousin and hopefully get some answers.

She half-heartedly applied some makeup in an attempt to make her eyes appear less swollen and headed out. Tere didn't bother with breakfast; she wanted to make sure to get to Saint Michael's early, and when she was nervous, it was hard to eat anyway. According to Google Maps, the convent was on the other side of the old city, about a two-kilometer walk, so she bought a bottle of water, put on her sunglasses, and started following the route that ran along the walls on the outside. Away from the bustle of the tourist area, the path was empty, and even as tense as she was, she was still able to enjoy the sun on her face. Below the walls and the path, there was much traffic, a main thoroughfare that was buzzing with cars, motorcycles, and trucks.

The walls were imposing from that vantage point—four stories of solid beige rock that rose like a continuous monolith around the city. She almost preferred seeing them from the outside. The impossibly green grass that surrounded them contrasted with the sterility of the stone, and she loved how the walls hugged the city in their protective embrace with an eternal promise to never let go. The path went on for some time, heading downward, and the street she needed was just beyond the halfway point, the farthest from the Plaza de Santa Teresa. The turn was up ahead, and as she looked to the hill above, she saw the silhouette of four Doric columns against the sky.

Those must be the Four Posts Richard mentioned, she thought. Tere decided she would stop there afterward as a reward, which she might need to inspire her if the experience bordered on traumatic like her last visit to a convent.

She crossed the road when there was a lull in traffic and made her way to the walkway that traversed the river. She could hear a cacophony of voices and looked over to see a crowd of uniformed teenagers outside an institutional-looking building, laughing, and running, and kicking out their long limbs like spring calves in their first foray from the barn. Watching them and their untamped kinetic energy made Tere think of her son. Had he ever been that young? At that age Rowan was a study in contrasts. He would make her drop him a block from the school so no one would see him being driven by his mom, but he always kissed her and told her he loved her before he got out. When they weren't arguing, they swapped iPods and shared new music, talked about horror movies for hours, and laughed until they couldn't breathe. His twenties? Those belonged to Carl. Something changed after high school, and the two men bonded over their love of cooking and sports, but Tere enjoyed seeing them connect. That's why he'd taken Carl's death so hard. In the future she and Rowan would have to find their way as a family without Carl, perhaps connecting in the manner they had in the past. She would try when she got home.

As she walked, she thought about what had happened at the bike shop that had sent her firmly on a grief spiral. The silver fox seemed very nice, but it was not as if his face were hovering in her mind like she was a lovestruck youth. Rather, his attractiveness had only made her miss Carl more, bringing up memories of how he'd smiled at her in that way that reached all the way to his eyes. It was the kind of smile that touched off an electric feeling across her skin. She was surprised that even after a year, the wound was still so fresh, but she was beginning to realize that was part of the reason she'd come to Ávila. It was time for her to find a path forward, *without* flying off into the cosmos, and hopefully her cousin could help.

After she crossed the river, she came to a traffic circle. She always found the floating arrow on the GPS hard to discern when walking, waggling around as it did, but it appeared her path led in the opposite direction of the posts and to the west. Tere took a long draw from her water bottle and started off. It was clear from the way the sidewalks were cracked and the storefronts dingy that she was far from the touristy areas of Ávila. But it did not feel dangerous, like the New York City of her childhood. No, this was merely real life, and after her years with Carl, she was most comfortable around real life. That was why academia had come to frustrate her. In the last years before she went on leave, she had started to see it differently. The academy was filled with so many people theorizing and analyzing all the aspects of human existence, while the rest of the world was busy living it. She had the least use for what she referred to as "armchair academics," people like her white male anthropology colleague who taught and spoke five African tribal languages but had never set foot on the continent.

It was getting hot in the sun with no trees lining the streets, and she was nearing the dregs of her bottle of water. She stopped to take a breath. When she looked behind her, she couldn't believe how far she was from the city. Her legs were warm and limber, and her breath was coming in harder, but it felt good. She took the next left turn up a side street that appeared abandoned, like the town had forgotten it existed so the street didn't get swept, nor were the branches that overhung the road trimmed. But to her gratitude, there was no lack of shade. The map proclaimed her destination was on the right, so Tere looked up at a formerly grand, but now quite ramshackle, building. There were large chunks missing from the stone facade, and all that remained of the fallen pieces were piles of dust in the bramble.

This can't be it, she thought. *Who would allow nuns to live in such a place?* Then she recalled the monasteries Teresa had founded throughout her life. The saint preferred the buildings that no one wanted, tumbledown and inexpensive. She would buy them before the leadership of her order knew, and then she and her nuns would travel under the cover of night, sweep and clean the buildings as best they could, and hold the first mass there the next day. With the mass the monastery was founded. She had been a "better to ask for forgiveness than permission" kind of woman, and Tere respected that. So, really, the building in front of which she stood was more in keeping with Teresa's teachings than the gold-strewn buildings the Catholic Church was so fond of.

There was a pathway bisecting the ridiculously overgrown lawn that led to the establishment's main entrance—only a path in the theoretical sense—so Tere picked her way through. Off to one side she could see the edge of a large garden that was beautifully tended, which gave her hope. When she arrived at the tall wooden door with its heavy iron hinges, she saw it was warped from the years and weather. She curled her hand into a fist and knocked, but the door was so big, the wood so thick, she barely made a sound. She pounded then, but even that made little noise. Other than the garden, there really was no other sign of life, and Tere wondered if Yolanda's contact had given her the wrong convent name or if the internet had the address listed incorrectly. The door didn't even look like it *could* open.

A voice called from the garden side. "Hello, dear. Can I help you?"

Tere looked over and saw a nun in a brown habit, her arms filled with bright vegetables, clearly fresh from the garden. "Oh!" She started to pick her way back down the path. "Yes, thank you. Is this the Convent of Saint Michael?"

"Yes, it is."

Tere let out a breath of relief. "Great! I'm looking for Isabella Lope Sánchez. I was told she might be here?"

"Sister Isabella, of course." The nun gestured with her head for Tere to follow as she disappeared around the building's corner.

Tere's body sagged with relief. Finally, some progress—or the possibility of it anyway. She jogged through the overgrown lawn, turned the corner, and stopped short. There were acres of vegetables and fruits and flowers, all arranged in neat rows, every color imaginable pushing forth from the ground. She could smell the loamy, rich soil, the spicy green scent of fresh basil, and the sharp tang of berries. There were rusted wire benches scattered around the outside of the garden, and several women bent down among the rows, their brown habits blending into the earth, making the rainbow of colors that surrounded them all the brighter. As Tere walked by, her mouth hanging open, they would each rise and wave at her, then return to their work.

"You look surprised." The nun was waiting for her at the entrance to a patio with an amused look on her face.

"You'd never know this was here from the condition of the front of the house." Then Tere realized how blunt that sounded. "Sorry, it's just—"

"Don't worry, dear, we know." The nun placed the bounty into a basket that sat on a nearby table. "Let me get you some water. You must be parched." She walked over to where a frosty pitcher of water sat with slices of cucumbers and lemon floating on the top, probably picked right from the garden.

Tere looked around as the woman poured. The back patio of the house was full of wire tables with mismatched chairs, each with an individual vase of freshly cut flowers at its center. The only sounds were the clean clipping of garden shears and birds flitting above from tree to tree.

The nun walked over and handed her the glass, the sweet green and citrus smell wafting up from the water in a cool wave. Tere smiled gratefully and took a long sip.

"We like that the convent looks that way to the outside world. Our order prefers to keep to itself."

Tere couldn't help it; she looked down at the nun's feet. Teresa's order was called the Discalced, the shoeless. But this nun had practical leather sandals on her soil-spattered feet.

The sister noticed her looking and smiled. "We have worn shoes for hundreds of years. Even Santa Teresa wore sandals with all her traveling."

Tere felt heat flush behind her face. "Right, right. I read that." She looked around at the compound of gardens and buildings as she drained the last of the water. "So, this *is* part of the Discalced Order of the Carmelites."

"Yes. May I ask why you're looking for Sister Isabella?"

Okay, they were protective of each other too; Tere respected that. She put her glass down. "Well, it seems we're related, and I'm doing some research about the family, and my aunt in Puerto Rico thought it important that I meet her."

The nun didn't say anything for a bit, just stared at Tere. She guessed the woman was weighing whether she was telling the truth. Ultimately, she seemed to believe her, as she turned around and headed toward the house.

"Bueno. I will be right back. I will go tell her you're here, though it is up to her whether she comes out or not." She stopped at the door and looked back at Tere. "We tend to discourage visitors here."

Yeah, no shit. Anyone who saw the building would know that. Still. "I'm sorry, I didn't know—"

"Of course, you didn't, dear." And then the nun walked away with a swish of robes and the soft patter of rubber-soled sandals. Tere wondered if perhaps Sister Isabella was very ill. She should have offered to go in to see her rather than have her come out, but she knew she would have been turned down.

Tere stood there for what to her seemed like hours but was actually twelve minutes, just watching the gardening nuns. They didn't speak to one another, rather communicated with gestures as they did their work. Was there a vow of silence in this convent? Tere thought of her experience in the square with Sister Luisa and absently fingered the rosary in her pocket. It was then she smelled something familiar. When she looked down at the table in front of her, she noticed the flowers in this particular vase were dark pink peonies, just like in the garden at home, like the ones inked on her arm. Her skin tingled.

The sound of shuffling came from the house. It didn't sound like the nun from earlier, so was this Tere's elusive relative? Would she finally get to meet her?

"Well, don't just stand there—help an old woman!" said a craggy voice from the shadow of the entryway.

"Oh, of course!" Tere ran over and took the woman's arm, helping her down the high step from the house and onto the stones of the patio. She could see silver hair neatly tucked beneath her wimple, her nose sharper than Tere's, but her hazel eyes were all Sánchez. The woman pointed toward a table and chairs, so Tere led her—no, that's not right—the nun led *her* there; Tere was merely holding on to her arm. From the way Isabella moved, Tere got the distinct feeling the fragile-old-woman thing was primarily an act. She saw no sign of a heart problem or infirmity.

"Well then," the nun said as she settled into her chair. "Who are you?"

Tere gave a nervous laugh. It seemed these nuns were not the restrained and overly pious breed she had known in Catholic school. "Sorry, I'm—"

"What are you apologizing for?"

Oh, they were related, of that Tere had no doubt. "Okay." She sat down. "My aunt is Nivea Sánchez, and she gave me your name."

"Oh, Nivea! Haven't heard from her in years. How is she? I hope she finally got rid of that venereal disease she got from that guy at the senior center." The nun slapped her thigh as she said it.

Tere choked. Literally choked on her saliva and shock.

Sister Isabella cackled, rocking back and forth in her chair with mirth. When she stopped, she looked at Tere. "What?"

"It's just...you're not like—"

The woman did a "get on with it" gesture with her hand. "Like any other nun you've ever met. Yes, I know. I get that a lot. But in truth, I've never taken the vows. Never felt the need."

"So, you're a novitiate?" Tere was pleased to have remembered the term; so many words were buried forever under the years.

Isabella smirked. "Look at me. I'm eighty-four years old. Do I look like a novice to you?"

"I—well—I'm not—"

"Just screwing with you, dear. What's your name anyway?"

"Um…Tere?" Her voice went up at the end as if she were asking if that was indeed her name, for at that moment she was so confused, she couldn't be certain of anything.

The nun looked at her as if she could see through her skin. "Ah, you're Elena's girl, God rest her soul." She did a quick sign of the cross. "Elena was the only one with the cojones to name a daughter after our saintly relative. How old are you now? Sixty-five? Seventy?"

Tere scoffed. "I just turned sixty!"

"Ah, well. Must be all that cold air. If I remember correctly, and I always do, you live in Canada or something, yes?"

"Vermont."

Isabella waved that away. "Same thing."

Tere wasn't sure what to say next, so she made small talk. "I'm glad to have caught you before your trip."

"Trip? What trip?"

"Oh, well, I was told you go to Quito, Ecuador, each spring to do missionary work."

Isabella waved her hand dismissively again. "Psh, I haven't done work like that in thirty years. I just tell Cousin Ileana that so she won't show up at my doorstep expecting me to play religious tour guide. She's the kind of woman who thinks she's so pious but bad-mouths everyone the minute they're out of earshot."

Tere just nodded. Talking with this woman left her feeling even more destabilized than she had been already.

Isabella leaned back in her chair and folded her hands over her belly. "So, Tere daughter of Elena, what do you want from an old woman?"

Okay, this is it. She had to be careful what she said if she wanted to learn anything from the elderly relative, didn't want to freak her out with talk of levitation. Tere cleared her throat. "Well, I'm here researching Santa Teresa, and—"

Isabella stood up. "Okay, I had a feeling."

What? "No, I—"

The nun brushed her hands over the fabric of her crisp habit as if it needed ironing. "We get hundreds of women a year wanting to 'commune' with Teresa, but they're only interested in the storybook version of her work, not in enacting real change in their lives. Instagram sainthood, I call it. Bah! Total bullshit." She turned around and started heading back to the building.

Oh my God. Tere had come around the globe to get answers, and her own relative wouldn't speak to her? What could she say that wouldn't sound superficial? *But I'm different?* They probably all claimed that. Her heart started thumping against the inside of her ribs, a fast-running river of disappointment and anger rushing through her veins.

Isabella called over her shoulder as she shuffled, "Let me guess, you're having marital problems or something."

"Actually, he was the love of my life, and he's dead."

The older woman stopped for a second, her back still to Tere. After a pause she said in a more serious voice, "I am sorry to hear that," yet she started walking away again. "But I don't have time to indulge—"

"I've started levitating!" Tere stood and blurted as Isabella went to take a step into the house. She had not planned it, had not intended to tell her until she got to know her cousin, but it seemed she didn't have that luxury.

The nun froze for an instant, then put her foot back down and just stood there.

Tere looked around, suddenly aware of the quiet and saw that all the nuns in the garden were looking at her, their heads popped up like groundhogs. Even the birds seemed to have gone silent.

Sister Isabella turned around and slowly headed back to the table.

Oh, thank God. Tere felt like crying with relief but feared that would only make her look weak and bring derision from her nun cousin.

Isabella sat back down into the chair she had just vacated with a sigh. "When did it start happening?"

Tere sat down too, but at the edge of the metal seat, afraid the woman would storm off again. "Just a few days ago, but it's happened many times since."

"Do you know why it's happening?" Isabella was firing questions in rapid succession, as if interrogating her.

Tere didn't mind; she was just grateful to finally be talking about it. "I mean, no. That's why I came to Ávila."

The nun said nothing.

Tere stammered, "B-but I'm thinking it must be because it runs in the family—"

Isabella dismissed that with a wave. "Look, just because something is genetic doesn't mean everyone inherits it." Then the nun looked at Tere, her face serious again. "The propensity is there, yes, but for those who experience it, there is usually a very profound and personal reason. For Santa Teresa it was her deep love of Jesus and commitment to her faith."

"I don't think I—"

"Yes, I figured that from the half-dyed hair, huge hoop earrings, and tattoos."

Ouch…

"My point is, every person who inherits this gift has their own particular impetus for why it begins."

"You mean there have been others?"

"Of course, there have been others. Did you think you were the family's special unicorn?"

"Um, no, but I'd like to talk to them, if at all possible."

Isabella cackled again. "Not unless you can talk to the dead too!" She looked at Tere and seemed to realize she was upset, and the smile disappeared. "Look, the only one who can answer why this is happening to you, and why now, is you."

"Well, that's not helpful." Tere said before she could stop herself, but Isabella just cackled.

"Life's a bitch, ain't it?" she asked in English, then put her hands on her knees and started to stand. "Well, I best go supervise in the kitchen. Sister Catalina is cooking, and she could burn an ice cube in Alaska." When she stood, Tere could see the nun's hips pained her, and the woman's advanced age became more apparent.

"Wait, that's it?" Tere held her hands out and looked around as if asking the empty courtyard if it believed this.

The nun shrugged. "Some answers, we have to find for ourselves."

Tere stood. "What kind of answer is that? I traveled halfway around the world to come talk to you—"

"Well, that's hardly halfway! What did they teach you in geography class?"

Tere gave a strangled moan, dropped to the chair, and grabbed her head with her hands. "I can't deal with this. I can't live like this, knowing I could start floating at any moment, anywhere." She looked up at her cousin. "I really think I'm going insane."

Isabella's face softened. "You're not going insane. The world is insane for not accepting what we're truly capable of. Look, when she spoke of her raptures, Teresa said that for those who experience them, the state that their souls have been living in is 'neither more nor less than a prison.'"

Tere threw up her hands. "Yeah, that about captures it. But how do I break out of that prison and shed this family curse?"

"Curse? I think you misunderstand. For many, I would say Teresa included, the experience of levitation comes at times of great change. The best kind of change. The evolution of self, which is never easy. Eventually, it will stop."

"Do you know anyone who also does this? Who"—she looked around as if it were still a secret and she hadn't publicly announced a few minutes earlier—"levitates?"

"It's not something one advertises. There are no social clubs."

"Well…can't you ask? You know, around the church?"

A long sigh. "Amor, at my age you ask something like that, and it earns you a diagnosis of dementia and a one-way trip to an assisted-care facility with doors that lock from the outside." Then she points at Tere with a scolding finger, eerily reminiscent of Nivea. "And I advise you to be careful who you speak to about it too. This world has never been kind to those who are different."

Tere's eyes filled as she looked up at the nun. "A period of great change? Lots of people go through great change, lots of women lose their husbands, so why aren't they all floating off the damn earth?"

"Only the Lord knows. Perhaps they are not thinking deeply enough about their change."

Tere felt hope rushing out of her like a blown tire. "It's just—" Her voice caught, and the next words came out as a sob. "I'm not sure how much more change I can handle."

Isabella didn't come closer to comfort her, but she smiled kindly. "M'ija, at the end of the day, we can endure much more than we think we can."

Tere sniffled. "Did Teresa say that too?"

"No, Frida Kahlo." Isabella stepped over to another table nearby, where someone had been making garden posts with a Sharpie and small white signs on sticks. She proceeded to scribble a series of numbers onto a sign, then thrust it at Tere, the sharp solvent smell of the pen reaching her first.

Tere took it.

"Just keep on with what you're doing, and if you need me, call."

"If?"

But the nun was already almost to the door.

"Sister Isabella?"

She turned around and looked at Tere with an impatient expression.

"Sister Inés said to tell you that you still owe her twenty dollars from poker."

Isabella waved it off with her hand. "Bah! Like hell I do! That woman cheats." As she held on to the doorframe and hoisted herself up, she yelled inside the house, "Catalina, don't you start those potatoes without me!" And she disappeared inside the building.

Tere was left standing there, grasping a garden marker, for a good five minutes.

What the hell just happened?

She looked at the marker in her hand, baffled. When she spun it around, she saw it said "garlic" on the other side in Spanish. She snorted, stuck it in the pocket with the rosary, and headed back to the front of the house, the gardening nuns giving her a group wave without lifting their wimpled heads from their work.

Tere left with more questions than answers, but that just proved one thing: Isabella was indeed a Sánchez.

"At times it gives me great pain to have to deal with others...as all my longing is to be alone... Solitude consoles me. Conversation, especially with relatives, seems burdensome."

—Santa Teresa de Ávila,
Spiritual Testimonies #1:6

CHAPTER FOURTEEN

The walk down the hill from the convent went by in a blur. Tere stumbled along, trying to figure out the puzzle pieces she had gotten from Isabella, but they weren't snapping into place neatly. When she got to the traffic circle, she stepped off the curb without looking, and a car buzzed by so closely, she felt it brush her shirt. Clearly this was not the kind of thinking she should be doing while walking.

She crossed the busy intersection, looking both ways this time, and arrived at the sidewalk that ran around the walls. This time she went right instead of left, choosing the opposite direction from where she had come less than two hours earlier. Had it only been that long? It seemed as if time moved differently in the Convent of Saint Michael, like Isabella and her sisterhood lived outside traditional time. Tere had always hated *Alice in Wonderland* as a child; it was weird and confusing, and honestly, it had scared her. But, in that moment, she really felt as if she had just crawled out of the rabbit hole herself, her own cousin evoking both the Cheshire cat and Mad Hatter.

Where the wall curved, there was a small arch that led back in— one of the nine gates that allowed entry to the old city. As she walked through, she imagined the armored guards who used to be posted there, deciding who to permit and who to deny. Given her heritage, she imagined her people had always passed through. They were pale-skinned and "noble," the very founders of the city. But Tere was haunted by thoughts of those who had been expelled during Teresa's time—primarily Jews and Muslims—simply for having different beliefs. She found it disappointing that humans hadn't yet evolved beyond such conflict as a species.

Looking up, she found herself in a small and familiar plaza. She had seen pictures of it and realized where she was when she saw the dark bronze sculpture of Santa Teresa sitting in front of a church, the saint's eyes looking to the sky in religious ecstasy. There were tourists taking photos with their phones perched on selfie sticks and tripods, a tour taking a group shot next to the sculpture. Up ahead, in all its stately glory, was the church erected in Saint Teresa's honor.

Where better to sit and process all the thoughts and feelings she was struggling with than the place where she might feel Teresa's presence the strongest? It was built on the family's property, so it must've held some echo of holiness, some predestiny mortared between the stones of its foundation, and boy, how Tere needed that right then. As she walked in, she saw a sign advertising a lecture on the saint. She found the church cool, shadowed, and hushed, the naves lit with golden light, the small stained glass windows featuring images of Santa Teresa glowing from the sun that beamed through. Somewhere in the recesses of Tere's brain—the Catholic guilt that had been there since she was ten and didn't confess to Father Ignatius that she had shoplifted candy on a dare—she worried that she might spontaneously combust upon entering a church due to her transgressions. But in sixty years it had yet to happen, and besides, any religion that made children worry about being incinerated just by entering a building had issues.

There was a priest in the pulpit, speaking to about ten rows of people, so she quietly took a seat in the back. He was talking about Santa Teresa's childhood, about her teenage years of vanity. When he got to her raptures, he spoke of her vision of Jesus and the devil, then the deepened commitment to the Lord that resulted, but he made no mention of levitation. He seemed to rush through that section, as if it embarrassed him. Or was Tere merely reading too much into it? She tuned him out and just sat staring at the large statue of Teresa in the front, worrying Isabella's words like the beads of a rosary.

The experience of levitation comes at times of great change.

The past year had been like a bad dream. According to her cousin, Santa Teresa had spoken of life before her raptures as being a sort of prison. Tere was not naive; she knew she had incarcerated herself, that she was judge, jury, and jailor, but Carl's death had not been of her making. It came out of nowhere, like a stray bullet. He was healthy and fit, and they'd had another twenty years of life planned together. Richard and Rowan had implied it was time for her to move on. But how did one do that? There was no on-off switch to grief; she wished to God there were. People acted as if it were something you just decided to do, you simply got over it. Well, she hadn't a clue how to do that, so did that mean she would have to worry about levitating for the rest of her life?

Tere was aware of movement and realized the lecture had finished, and everyone was heading toward the front. When the couple in front of her got up, she tapped the woman's arm. "Excuse me, but where is everyone going?"

"The priest is giving us a tour of the Chapel of Santa Teresa and the re-creation of the room where she was born."

Tere thanked her, got up, and followed, curious. The group funneled into a small room on the left side, and Tere managed to slip in along the wall. While the priest talked about the history of the chapel, she looked around. On the far end, there was a massive tableau almost entirely in gold, with ornate columns on either side that featured disturbing painted angel heads, some of them vomiting red ribbons. A bust of Santa Teresa was at its center, her face, hands, and wimple painted in "natural" colors, while all the rest was gleaming gold. She was depicted gripping her obligatory quill and book, looking up in what Tere imagined was intended as a beatific gaze but just seemed scared and exhausted. It was a spectacular display of opulence and idolatry.

Well-coiffed women pushed by her to take selfies with the gleaming and exhausted saint, their lips plumped with filler and faces arranged in artificially worshipful expressions. *She would hate this*, Tere thought; she was by no means an expert on the saint, but she knew that much. In fact, Santa Teresa had been much hated by other clergy for her insistence of the poverty of the order that she claimed God had demanded. *So, they honor her with this mountain of gold?*

"Any questions?" the priest asked. As often was the case in lectures, no one raised their hand. After a beat, Tere raised hers. "Yes, señora?"

"I'm curious about Teresa's experiences of levitation. Why are those powerful and deeply mystical events never depicted or discussed in lectures and informational brochures about her life?"

She could see the priest work to keep his expression neutral, his long gray brows hanging over his eyes like awnings. "Santa Teresa de Jesus had many ecstatic experiences, visions, transverberation—"

"And levitation," Tere added.

"And levitation, yes. All are symbols of her deepening commitment to God and the church."

"Yes, but levitation was the one experience that was witnessed by others, a physical manifestation rather than a symbol. It is the one aspect of her ecstasy that could be proven. I find it surprising that it's so readily ignored when it clearly has historical importance." The crowd didn't seem annoyed by her question; in fact, they were looking from her to the priest as if watching a tennis match.

He made that harrumph sound she'd only heard from men of her parents' generation. She could tell he didn't like being challenged, probably made worse by the fact she was a woman. "Well, there's only so much that can be covered about her long and fruitful life. If this is truly of import to you, we can always discuss it afterward," he said with a patronizing smile.

From his tone it was clear he did not want to talk with her at all, and everyone in the room knew it. Many biting responses came to mind; she had verbally eviscerated much smarter men in her academic career and had met many priests like him in her youth—self-important, elitist. But no, it would be a total waste of her time. "No need, Father. Please continue." She gestured for him to go on, as if it were her leading the event, not him.

He harrumphed again, then gruffly hustled them into the next room, where the tiny cell where they had reproduced Teresa's bedroom, replete with austere furnishings and rustic bedding, was tucked behind a glass door. After a few words about the reproduction, the priest led the group back into the church. Tere didn't follow. She waited until they had all filtered out. When she stepped back out of the side chapel, she noticed the wall ahead was actually a large glass window. She stepped closer, and a story below lay a carpet of green bathed in sunlight: a small garden surrounded by ivy-covered stone walls. With a gasp, she realized it was Teresa's garden, the one true piece of the original property that remained. A tingle ran across her skin, and for the first time since arriving, she felt she was witnessing a truly sacred place.

At the far end, near the back wall, were two statues: Teresa and her brother Rodrigo as children. The boy was kneeling on the ground before a small toy castle, and Teresa was standing with an open book to her chest, as if preaching. Perhaps it was meant to depict the moment when she'd suggested they run away and become martyrs, but either way, her reading at all was a subversive act, as women had not been permitted to read in her time. Tere was overjoyed to see this representation of her, particularly depicted in granite and surrounded in grass and ivy and stone rather than gold.

Tere stayed gazing at the garden for a long while, smiling and happy, and if her ecstasy had been about joy, she wouldn't have been surprised if she had levitated right there in the church. But early on she had learned her impetuses were not that simple, and luckily her feet stayed firmly on the black-and-white marble tiles.

The church was almost empty when she finally walked through, and as they went to the exit, most people stopped to genuflect, make the sign of the cross, and put money in a box next to the door before leaving. Tere just walked by the box with the praying hands and slot for donations, then out the front door, feeling frustrated at the amount of money that was poured into the church already. She committed to finding someone on the way home who needed it more and giving them her donation instead.

That was what Teresa would have wanted.

When she stepped out into the midday sun, it took a bit for her eyes to adjust. When they did, she noticed a group of nuns walking down the steps of the church. She was about to look away, focused on getting some food, when she recognized one of the nuns from the square. Tere put her hand in her pocket and held the little rosary. She recalled that feeling she'd had when the Trinidadian woman had given it to her, like she understood. Isabella had driven home the lesson that she couldn't go around talking about levitation, but if Tere could speak to the woman directly, one-to-one…

Tere tapped the nun on the shoulder. "Excuse me, Sister?"

The woman turned around, her eyes soft and gray in the sunlight. "Yes, my child?"

"Sorry to bother you, but I was wondering where I might find Sister Luisa? The nun from Trinidad?" She looked at the group but didn't see the Caribbean woman among them. "I'd really love to talk with her."

"Oh, I'm sorry, but she flew back to the island this morning."

Tere's whole body sagged. "Oh."

The nun touched her arm. "May I help you with something, dear?"

All the nuns were looking at her now, their kind faces soft with concern.

She smiled. "No, that's all right. But thank you, Sister." She nodded at the group, put her hands in her pockets, and fingered the rosary as she walked, accepting that her hunch about the other Caribbean woman would remain unproven.

"Now let us see how this garden is to be watered, so that we may understand what we have to do, and what labor it will cost us, also whether the gain will outweigh the effort, or how long it will take…"

—Santa Teresa de Ávila,
The Life of Saint Teresa of Ávila by Herself

CHAPTER FIFTEEN

Tere felt better on the walk through the city, like seeing Teresa's garden had been a balm for the sting of disappointment after visiting the Convent of Saint Michael. But was it fair to have expected to show up at Isabella's home and have the woman answer all her questions, solve all her problems? No. In fact, she felt like her expectations had been a lot like those of the women her cousin had complained about, who came to commune with Teresa but didn't care to do any real work. Tere was not afraid of hard work.

She realized she was starving, but it was the time of the siesta, so most of the restaurants and stores were closed. She passed a supermarket on Calle Alemania, and though she could tell it was smaller and bougier than the bigger ones outside the walls, she was exhausted, and it was convenient. Plus, she had been craving a brown rice dish Carl used to make, though she didn't have the recipe and had very few culinary skills. She grabbed a rolling handbasket and ventured in. Supermarkets gave her a low-level feeling of anxiety, the surgically bright lights, the array of choices, the riot of colors and scents. Carl had always done the grocery shopping. In their relationship he had been the chef and she, the baker; they had balanced each other out perfectly. Now she was left with only her skills, and she had discovered they were markedly less useful. Over the past year, she had just ordered premade meals from a local Vermont farm online or skipped eating altogether because she just couldn't "deal," so she felt ill-equipped to navigate a supermarket, particularly given her state of mind of late. As she went down the aisles, she grabbed a premade sandwich to eat as soon as she got back, some brown rice, and some cans of chicken broth for the recipe. After adding a few yogurts to her basket, she decided to hit the produce section and be done with it.

The colors of the varied fruits and vegetables always soothed her, especially when she caught their green, earthy scent and breathed deep. She ran the tips of her fingers over a dozen kinds of oranges before grabbing a few that were labeled "Berna." The tag said they had a pear-like aftertaste, and she liked the sound of that.

"You don't have to touch them all, you know."

Tere turned around to see a small pinched-face woman in a store uniform with an apron over it. "Excuse me?"

"And you have to weigh them first before checking out. Over here and put the label on. You Americans never know that."

Tere stepped back a bit. "How do you know I'm American?"

The woman gestured at her with a jerk of her head. "Those earrings and black boots, like you're in the military or something."

Tere looked down at her outfit, surprised. She had dressed in her nicer clothes to go to the convent, and the Blundstone boots were comfortable for the walk.

"Only an American woman would wear those at your age." The woman rolled her eyes and began reorganizing the oranges with jerky movements, as if Tere had somehow destroyed the display.

She was taken aback, but just for a second. "Wow. Are you this kind to all the customers?"

"And your Spanish, what kind of accent is that anyway?"

Tere felt the New Yorker within whoosh through her body, and she put her hands on her hips. "Look, you bitter little—"

"Leave her alone, Sandra."

They both whipped around to see the silver fox from the bike shop standing behind them, dressed in running clothes with a basket over his arm.

He indicated Tere. "The poor woman's just trying to get some groceries."

Sandra sneered, but she visibly backed down and shuffled away, pretending to be very interested in a display of crackers.

Tere looked over at him. "I can handle myself, you know."

"Oh, I can tell. Trust me, I wouldn't have bet on Sandra in a fight. I could imagine you ripping her head off with your teeth."

"I thought about it, let me tell you." But she felt the flash of anger fade, and all it left behind was exhaustion. She used to feed off self-righteous altercations like those, with the priest and now this woman, but that day they just made her tired.

"You have to forgive her. She's miserable and likes to take it out on other people."

"I *don't* have to forgive her, actually." She sounded like a Karen. Did she sound like an American Karen? Tere went back to looking over the vegetables, determined to get scallions and get the hell out of there.

"When you came into my shop the other day, you left before I was able to introduce myself." He put his free hand out. "I'm Rodrigo."

"Tere." She shook his hand, gave him a tight smile, then made her way to the onion section. There were a dozen variations of scallions, all different sizes and shapes: large bulbs and dark green shoots; smaller, thinner ones with straight stalks; other bendy ones. Her hand hovered over the variations of greens, and a small spark of panic touched off in her chest. She looked around and saw Rodrigo busy rustling through the tomatoes and another woman nearby assessing the lettuce. She turned back and tried to remember what Carl had said about which scallions were best, but nothing came. In that moment, water started spraying from the rack above the produce, lightly misting the vegetables and her face, quickly steaming up her glasses.

As she stood there, blinded, exhausted, and reminded of lying in the grass in Carl's garden, she began to cry, her tears mixing with the water that ran down her cheeks. She put her face in her hands and sobbed.

"Tere, are you okay?"

His voice was so kind and gentle, she pulled her hands away and looked over. "No! I don't even know why I'm crying."

Rodrigo's brown eyes softened. "That's okay. Nothing wrong with crying."

"No, it's ridiculous. It's just that my husband always did the grocery shopping, and I can't even remember what I'm so supposed to look for in goddamn scallions, and I don't like feeling so fucking helpless—" She stopped in order to suck back the snot that was dangerously close to running down her face. Lord, she was losing it, and in public, no less. Plus, now Rodrigo would pity her, and she had definitely proven she was, indeed, helpless. That only fed the shame spiral.

"It's simple." Rodrigo reached over and grabbed the larger of the scallions. "You don't want these; they're mass-produced and imported, so God knows how old they really are. Besides, the thicker stalks aren't as flavorful. Now these, over here"—he reached across and grabbed one of the skinnier bunches—"they're grown locally, first of the season. Don't be misled by the skinny stalks; they're full of flavor, and this deep green color is a good sign. And see how the bulb is white at the top? Also good." He handed her the bunch with a smile. "Now you don't have to feel helpless around scallions. Though I know they can be intimidating in their scallioness."

That made her laugh.

"Nice to see you again, Tere." And he walked away with a kind smile.

She watched him stride toward the registers and greet the guy behind the counter by his first name, while she just stood there, holding the green onions. After a breath or two, she dropped them into the basket, wiped her face, and decided that after she tracked down some mineral water, she was out of there. She was going to hide in the apartment, read, and sleep. That was quite enough of the world for the day.

———————

Later, Tere was lying on the couch, eating an orange, and reading a different biography of Santa Teresa when her phone rang. The ringtone took her by surprise. *Who calls anymore?* She looked at the screen. *Ah, of course.* "Richard, is this going to be a daily occurrence?"

"Tere, you're not going to believe this." He was out of breath, whispering while walking.

"Why are you whispering?" she practically yelled into the phone just to irritate him. Richard could be so dramatic.

The sound of a door closing. "I just left the academic council meeting. Thought you'd want to know that Pearson, the brand-new chair of your department, just got fired."

She sat up straight. "What?"

"Yep. Seems he said some rather incendiary things in a diversity, equity, and inclusion meeting."

"Ha! What'd he say?" She was dying to know. Probably something spectacularly clueless and offensive. She glanced at her saintly ancestor's beatific face on the cover of the book she was reading and felt momentarily ashamed for taking joy in the man's blunder. But then she shrugged, turned the book over, and put her attention back on the academic gossip.

"I don't know. Look, what I needed to tell you is that afterward, Dean Hammerston asked me what your status was."

"Asked *you*?" Her eyebrows rose at that.

"Yeah, he knows we're friends. Look, Tere, that's not the point." She could hear the impatience in his voice. "Are you sitting down?"

This time, she gave a full eye roll. "Yes, in fact, I am."

"He says the chair position is yours if you want it."

Wow. Didn't see that one coming. Department chair had been her goal for so long. She put in nights at seminars, spent weekends traveling to conferences, published numerous articles, and took point on projects. Putting in extra hours to prove her worth when she could have spent them with Carl and Rowan. But the third time they'd passed her over for the promotion had taken the wind out of her sails.

"You're not saying anything. I thought you'd be pleased."

"Well, I mean, I'm flattered, I guess."

"Flattered? Tere, you worked toward this for years!"

"Yeah, but they passed me over for the position how many times?" Even she was surprised by the resentment in her voice. "Besides, they were about to take away my tenure if I didn't teach the summer class, remember?"

"Someone else can teach that, but you'd have to come home

immediately. Tere, this is the chair of the whole department! You'd finally have power."

Part of her loved the idea of being head of the English department, the first woman in the history of the university. It never ceased to amaze her how fucked up that was. But then she thought about levitating in a damn faculty meeting. A fate worse than death. No, she had things to figure out first. "I'm going to have to think about this, Richard."

"You've been thinking about this for twenty years! This is the dream. *Your* dream."

It had been for a long time. Her mind was spinning faster than it had all year, imagining what changes she would instigate, how she could decolonize the canon so students like Constanza could see themselves in what they read. But was it her dream now? "I don't know. So much is changing."

"Can't some of those changes be good? Tere, my dear friend. You're only sixty! You could have twenty more years in academia. Why would you want to give up on your life so young?"

"Academia is not my whole life, Richard."

A fraught pause. "I really don't understand what's going on with you lately, Tere. I mean, the extended leave, the last-minute Spain trip, the disinterest in the chair position…"

"To be totally honest, I don't know what's going on with me right now either. That's why I don't feel I can commit at this moment."

He let out a breath, but not a tension-relieving one; he was more like a bull blowing air out his nostrils. "Fine. When are you coming home?"

Another pause. "I'm not sure… I have to take care of some things here."

"Like what? Isn't your career more important than whatever you're doing there?"

Tere didn't say anything, another thing that was unlike her.

"Look, when you figure it out, just let the rest of us know, will you?"

And he was gone.

Tere dropped the phone to the coffee table and slapped her knees. "Well, this sure was a fun day!"

She got up and went to the kitchen to brew herself a cup of tea. As the water heated, she thought about how much she had loved teaching. Helping young minds learn interesting things about the world. Exposing them to art and literature for the first time and seeing who was moved by it. Like what she had seen in Juan's eyes when they talked about the Bernini sculpture or worked on his college application. But it wasn't teaching that Tere dreaded going back to. It was the politics, the exact kind of thing Richard had so excitedly called with and injected into her soul-searching trip. Not long ago, she had seen herself so clearly as the chair, adding spoken-word poetry to the course options, finally bringing the department into the twenty-first century; she had already compiled a list of exciting faculty to attempt to woo there. Besides, wouldn't taking this job be "moving on," as she was supposed to be doing? Then why didn't it feel like it was?

Damn it. She wished Richard hadn't called. It was like he had pulled half of her backward in time.

"For at times it happens that some trifle will cause as much suffering to one as a great trial will to another; little things can bring
much distress to persons who have sensitive natures. If you are
not like them, do not fail to be compassionate."

—Santa Teresa de Ávila,
The Way of Perfection

CHAPTER SIXTEEN

For a few hours, Tere tried to nap. She'd lie down, get comfortable, start to nod off…then her brain would be wide awake again. So many things—good and bad—had happened that day, the hamster wheel of her brain was spinning around and around, the metal against metal getting scratchier, shriller with each revolution.

She wandered into the kitchen and stared at the definitively incomplete ingredients to Carl's rice dish that she had laid out, but she was overwhelmed by the idea of cooking anything. Tere looked at her watch. It was only seven thirty, too early to go to bed, and she was hungry again. She hadn't yet gone out to dinner on this trip, mainly because traditional Spanish dinner was served late, and she'd lived in Vermont too damn long for that.

Screw it.

She put on her most presentable jeans, a lightweight sweater, and platform boots, then took herself out. The night was cool, and she was grateful she'd grabbed her leather jacket as an afterthought when she was leaving. The walls were lit from below, and the bottom of the evening sky was still bright from the setting sun, so the sky that touched the walls was glowing deep blue. She breathed in the crisp evening air, proud of herself for getting out and into the city. After all, she could lie around the house back in Vermont.

She followed the ambling crowd through the arch and into the old city. Sax music from a busker gave the street a jazz-club feel. She walked for a while, listening to the hum of conversation, admiring the sheen on the cobblestoned streets, a souvenir from a quick afternoon rain. *This city is magic*, she thought, feeling much better than she had after Richard's call.

Tere had no idea where to eat, so she just wandered. She walked across the Plaza Mercado as the bells from several churches rang at once, calling people into evening mass. When she arrived at the center of the square, she just stood and listened to them, the same metallic chorus that had been ringing for hundreds of years, the same Santa Teresa had heard, perhaps from that exact spot. When the last bell echoed off the buildings, she strolled off onto a side street named Calle de Caballeros and saw a restaurant that was buzzing. The front was glass almost from ground to ceiling, and it had an informal wood-and-stone ambiance that felt welcoming, so she entered. Right away a handsome dark-haired host inquired if she wanted a table and for how many.

"One, please." That number still felt so new to her, probably because she rarely—actually, never—went out to dinner alone. And as he pulled out a chair and she sat down, Tere remembered why. As she looked around at the tables of two or four, conversation tumbling fast like rain on a tin roof, it felt a little like those dreams where you were in a public place and realized you were naked. *Look at me! All alone! Aren't I sad?*

She scanned the QR code on the table and perused the menu. When the waiter came back, she ordered the pork like a good Puerto Rican and pulled out a book from her bag, the next on Esmé's literary tour of mysticism. She was lost in a chapter about quantum realities when the waiter returned and placed a caramel-colored drink in front of her, the ice sparkling like diamonds in the low light.

Tere looked up at him, confused. "Oh, I didn't order this."

The waiter pointed toward the crowded bar. "The gentleman over there sent this with his compliments."

She scanned the shifting sea of people that surrounded the bar and saw a distinct swath of silver hair and the kind of smile you couldn't help but return. She would be lying if she said her heart didn't jolt, just a bit, at seeing Rodrigo again.

Tere raised her glass in that direction with what she hoped was a smile but was probably closer to a grimace. To say she was out of her comfort zone was like saying the Empire State Building was kind of tall.

Rodrigo stood, put his hand on the waiter's shoulder, and made his way toward her table.

What the fuck am I supposed to do now?

And then he was standing there in all his faded jeans and soft sweater glory, smiling down at her. "Two times in one day. I feel very lucky."

"Me too. And thank you, by the way, for the drink and for your help this afternoon with my scallion crisis."

He grinned. "My pleasure. I mean, my specialty is root vegetable rescue, but I'm always willing to expand my services."

She giggled. When was the last time she giggled?

"Well, Tere, I didn't want to disturb you, but I hope you enjoy the Manhattan? You said you were originally from New York, so I thought you might welcome a taste of home." He raised his glass again.

She raised her drink in response, and he turned to go back to the bar.

The truth was, Tere hated eating out alone. *Fuck it.* She called out to him. "Would you like to join me?"

He turned. That smile, it was indeed infectious. "I'd be honored." He pulled the chair out and sat across from her.

Such a simple thing, sitting across a table from a man. How many times had she done it with colleagues, relatives in Puerto Rico, men other than Carl? But in that moment, it felt alarmingly intimate, like looking into someone's eyes while you slow danced. She felt a subtle shifting under her skin, so Tere did what she often did when she was uncomfortable: she asked questions. "So, Rodrigo, when I saw you earlier, you called it 'my shop.' So, is that your bike shop, or do you work there?"

"Oh, the shop doesn't make enough money to hire staff. No, it's mine, though lately it feels like more of a vanity project than anything." He shrugged. "I just love to ride and want to share that with other people."

"So, you can afford to own a shop that makes no profit?" The minute she said it, Tere gasped, horrified. She put both hands over her mouth to keep any more words from coming unbidden. When she caught her breath a bit, she said, "I'm so sorry! That was incredibly rude." Heat rose behind her face, and not for the first time, she cursed her paleness. "The truth is, I've never had much of a filter, but after I turned fifty, whatever remained of one vanished."

Rodrigo was just grinning at her, and then she started to laugh, which made him laugh, and her embarrassment dissipated.

"It's all right. I much prefer people who talk straight. I find it refreshing."

He looked like he actually meant it, so Tere let out a long breath of relief.

"As to your question, no, I can't really afford it. It's slowly eating away at the savings from my former corporate life, but it makes me happy." He took a sip of his drink and relaxed in his chair, draping one arm behind him over the back in a perfectly natural, expensive-catalog-model way.

"Now *that*, I find *that* priority refreshing."

"You sound like you're talking from experience."

"Yes, I guess so." She took the first sip of the Manhattan. The warmth of the bourbon spread throughout her body. It was comforting. "I took a leave from my job because of my husband."

"Yes, you mentioned him in the grocery store. So, is your husband back in Vermont?"

"No. He died a year ago."

Rodrigo leaned forward; his brown eyes softened. "Oh. I'm so sorry."

She took another sip and looked off in the distance. "Yeah, me too." It was so easy for her mind to spin off into thoughts of Carl, but she reeled it in and forced herself back into the moment. "Anyway, there I was, I was no longer a wife nor professor, and my son was grown and starting a family of his own across the country. The truth is, I don't know who I am anymore. I suppose that's part of the reason I came here." The other parts, she couldn't talk about. She hadn't said much of this out loud to anyone, and she had to admit it was a relief, like getting rid of clothes you hadn't worn in years.

"Well, I'm very glad you came here, but I wonder why Ávila and not Madrid or Barcelona?"

Oh, the question she didn't know how to answer truthfully without sounding unbalanced. She took a moment to think before answering, "Well, my family is from Puerto Rico but originally from here, and with this year of drastic changes, I guess I wanted to go back to where it all started." Not a lie, just a selective truth. She figured entire governments were run on those.

Rodrigo opened his hands in a welcoming gesture. "What better way to figure out who you are, yes?"

The waiter appeared and placed their food in front of them, and they dug in. The conversation flowed easily. Rodrigo was forty-five (she had called that one on the money), divorced, two kids in their twenties, one older sister. After his divorce and once his kids went off to college, he'd moved back to Ávila, where he was from.

They had filled each other in on the basic facts of their lives by the end of dessert, a delicate local yogurt with honey and lavender. Rodrigo dropped the spoon into his empty glass dish with a clatter, put his hands over his taut belly, and groaned. "Okay, I'm done. There's no room left after that."

Tere sat back, her spoon still in hand, the bliss of the meal spreading throughout her body. "That was amazing."

He was staring at her, making her shift in her seat a bit. Finally, he leaned forward and asked, "So, what's next for Tere Sánchez?"

"Oh, nothing, I assure you! I'm going to finish this yogurt, then go back to my Airbnb, and sink into a well-earned food coma."

"No, I mean, you've been away from your job for a year, so what's your plan for the future? Go back to the university, or try something new?"

Tere paused at that. People didn't often ask women her age about their plans for the future. It was as if they assumed they didn't need to plan since there was "less time ahead than behind." But as Richard had said, she could have twenty years left in her, maybe more. Moving on and all that. "You know, I don't know? I've always been the kind of person who planned everything out. I was all about the one-, two-, five-year plan. But my long-term life goal got shot to shit."

Rodrigo tilted his head a little.

"It was to retire at sixty-five, collect my pension, and spend time with my husband, Carl. We were going to get a condo in Puerto Rico and spend the winters hiking in the rainforest and the summers biking in the mountains of Vermont. Just spend time together like we did before we became parents."

"Yes, back when we had time and lots more energy."

"Exactly." Tere looked at her yogurt. "Well, clearly that can't happen now." She put down her spoon.

Rodrigo let the silence be for a bit. Then he said in a faraway voice, "It was always my dream to open a bike shop. I was clear with my wife from the time we were dating. That's what we were working toward the whole time we were living in Madrid, working hard, building a family. Or at least, that's what I thought."

"She changed her mind?"

"Yes. For years I stayed in the city, only seeing the kids half the week, working my soul-sucking investment banking job day in and day out. It was different when it was a means to an end, but when the kids were off to college and the day job became my whole life, I decided it was time to do what I wanted to do."

"What was that like?"

"You mean finally opening my shop?"

"Yes."

A slow smile spread over his face. "It doesn't feel like work, you know? My tío Esteban used to tell me that you never work a day in your life if you love what you do. I didn't know what that meant until that first day when I walked through the space where my store is now."

"That sounds lovely."

"Do you ever think about moving out of Vermont? Or are your roots dug in?"

She slowly shook her head. "Oh no, those were Carl's roots, not mine. Though I have come to love it there. No, I think mine were so tangled with his in Vermont and my family's in Puerto Rico that I have trouble seeing them as separate. Besides, the idea of being rooted anywhere *forever* panics me a bit. Too much like death."

He smiled. "Perhaps you're an air plant then?"

She cackled, thinking of the experiences that had brought her to Ávila and how close he was to the truth. "You know, I think you're right."

They paid their respective bills, he waved to the people he knew, and then they were standing out front, the night even brisker, the volume of the streets a few notches higher, the nightlife just beginning.

Tere took a deep breath of the crisp air and turned to Rodrigo. "Well, I have to say, that was the most enjoyable dinner I've had in some time."

He grinned. "Me too."

She was not used to talking about how she felt and suddenly found she didn't know what to do with her hands. She ended up digging them into her jacket pockets. "Well, I better get back."

"Which hotel are you staying at?"

"I've got an Airbnb, just behind La Iglesia de San Pedro."

Rodrigo slipped on his jacket. "Ah, well, that's great. I'm heading that way too. May I walk with you?"

Tere laughed. "Sure."

He tilted his head as he looked over at her. "Was something funny about that?"

"Oh, no! I was just pleasantly surprised you didn't say, 'Can I walk you?' You said, 'May I walk *with* you?' It's a very subtle difference in language, but a big difference in meaning."

"Oh, yes? How is that?"

She pulled up the collar of her jacket against the chilly breeze. "I don't know, men of my generation usually present it like they're your protector, like I couldn't get myself home safely without them. It's quite patriarchal."

"'Men of *your* generation?' But we are the same generation, no?"

"That's very sweet of you, Rodrigo, but we're from different generations. I turned sixty last year."

He stopped. "No! Seriously?"

She laughed and kept walking. "You're very good at that, but no need for flattery. I'm okay with my age." People were often surprised, telling her she looked ten, even fifteen years younger, but she was not vain in that way; she'd earned every one of those damn years.

He caught up. "It wasn't flattery—you have a very young spirit."

Surprised, she looked over at him, noticing his eyes sparkling in the light from the streetlamps. "Now *that's* a compliment that means something to me."

They walked by the church, seeing teenagers in jeans draped over the low wall and one another, running around, yelling, pouring music from small tinny speakers. "Wait, I recognize that song." She stopped. "Wow, that's really interesting."

"What?"

She pointed to the teenagers. "The music they're listening to, it's reggaeton."

"Yes, it's very popular here in Spain."

"But that's Bad Bunny, and the song before was Daddy Yankee. It's funny hearing Puerto Rican voices echoing in a plaza in Spain."

"Why is it funny?"

"I don't know—such a small island, so far away. Plus, does it mean the colonized have arrived to take over the colonizers? Well, their speakers anyway."

He laughed, a genuine belly laugh, and it pleased her.

They turned the corner of the church and saw a group of priests passing beneath a streetlamp on the far side of the little park, and she thought about the priest from earlier. She hadn't wanted to talk with him, but perhaps it would help to talk to someone more modern. "Hey, Rodrigo, do you know any priests? I mean, personally? I'm doing research, and I'd love to chat with someone."

"Yes, actually. I have a cousin who is one, Timoteo."

"I'm hoping for someone less entrenched in old-school church thinking, you know?"

"I think he's more progressive than most. But his parish is in Barcelona."

"Damn."

"He does come up this way from time to time, so I'll ask."

"That would be great, thank you."

"How long do you think you'll be in Ávila?" He rushed to add, "I mean, so I can tell Timoteo."

She let out a long breath. She was doing that a lot. "I haven't a clue, I'm afraid. But I have the Airbnb for another few weeks, so that long at least." They turned the corner, and she stopped in front of the door to the building. "Well, this is me."

"I'm so glad we ran into each other, Tere."

She smiled. "Me too. I like you, Rodrigo. You're good people."

"I like you too."

Cue awkward silence where normally a kiss might occur. She let it ride, pulling slightly back. "Look, Rodrigo, I—"

"May I see you again?"

Tere sighed. How was she going to express this gently? But he'd been so easy to talk with all night, her instinct told her she didn't need to worry about bruising his ego. "I would really like that; however, I have to say up front, it would have to be as a friend."

He nodded. "You're seeing someone back in the U.S."

"No, I'm not."

He looked confused, and she felt she owed him more of an explanation—no, not owed... She *wanted* to give him an explanation. But how would she do that when she didn't understand it herself?

She just started talking. "Since my husband died, that part of me, the part where romantic love comes from, has lost its pull over my life. Actually, it started happening when he was still alive. When you're married for that long, the relationship shifts, becomes more about companionship than sex." Lord, she was telling a man she'd just met the deep dark secrets of her heart in the middle of the street. But wasn't that how any meaningful friendship started? And he was listening. Really listening. Another quality she treasured. "You're a very attractive man, Rodrigo. I suspect if I were at a different time in my life, this evening would have ended very differently, but friendship is all I can offer anyone right now." Tere stopped talking and looked at him. She wanted to have this man as a friend, but if they were going to do that, she would not lead him on. She hoped he understood.

He smiled, put his hands on her shoulders, and gently kissed her on each cheek in the European style. "Friendship is the best gift anyone can give, amiga mia."

Her eyes filled instantly, and she felt a warm wave of gratitude flood her chest. "Thank you for understanding."

He pulled a business card from his pocket. "Here. That's my cell number. If you need anything, just call."

Tere smiled down at the small paper rectangle with his name beside the spokes of an old-fashioned bicycle. "Even if it's just a café and good conversation?"

"Especially if it's that. Or a vegetable emergency." He grinned, put his hands in his jean pockets, and walked off. She watched him until he rounded the corner.

Had she been tempted? Of course. Yet as she stood there, she knew getting involved with anyone would not be the "moving on" she needed to do. She closed her eyes and lifted her face, smelling the cool night air, the green scent of the leaves above. Perhaps she would figure out what moving on looked like for her by identifying what it wasn't and going from there.

Tere took one last deep breath, opened her eyes, and turned to put her key in the front lock to find it was a foot below where it should have been. She looked up and saw the stone cornice that ran over the door right in front of her face and felt the rapturous release of gravity's hold on her, her skin alive as if it were its own separate being. As she grabbed hold of the stone with her fingers, a sensation swelled in her belly, much like when a roller coaster dropped suddenly—safe but unimaginably thrilling. For a moment, she considered letting go, imagined letting her entire self go and becoming one with the eternity that blossomed at the edge of her known universe, but then a flame of fear built in her chest, that if she did, she would fly up into the cosmos and be lost forever. She gripped the stone with her hands and slowly pulled herself down until she could reach the door handle. She used it to get her feet closer to the ground, pried opened the building door, pulled herself in, and closed it behind her, letting out a relieved breath as the now-familiar feeling slowly dissipated, and she could take a step toward the stairs, hoping to get to the apartment before the exhaustion hit.

"I become very frightened if I feel the least stirring of attraction toward something. This is for you alone, because those who do not understand me will have to be guided according to their own spirit. And indeed, if there is anyone with whom I can allow this stirring, it is with the one to whom I am writing, but however small this may be, a free soul feels it very strongly, and perhaps God wants it to feel this to safeguard the part that is necessary for his service."

—Santa Teresa de Ávila,
"Letter to Madre Maria Bautista, June 1574"

CHAPTER SEVENTEEN

The next morning Tere marched out of the apartment building as if she were storming the beaches of Normandy. Though it was her life's work to teach and read books, there was one genre she'd always hated: mystery novels—the meted-out breadcrumbs of clues, the intentional misdirections, and the classic character tropes. She'd always preferred decisive action, and today's was to return to the saint's childhood home and scour every corner available to her. The museum below the church had been closed when she was there, so that was where she would start.

As she strode, she reflected on the night before. The dinner with Rodrigo, yes, but more importantly the latest experience of levitating. This time it had been more of a rush, the warmth of wine quickening through her blood—that is, before the fear flooded in. And it always flooded in. There had been times in her life when she thought she had moved beyond it, storing her anxiety under cedar blocks for eternal storage. She'd be going along, living her life, and something would jump out at her, setting her back once again. Carl's death had been the biggest jump scare of her life thus far. One she had yet to recover from.

The museum was in the level below the church, in the family crypt. Did all medieval houses have crypts in the basement? She would have to look that up. The basement of her Vermont house sure felt that way, the dirt walls wet and musty, spiderwebs hanging in every corner. Just the thought made her shudder. She refused to go down there, and when it came time to get the boxes of Christmas decorations each year, she'd made Carl do it. This past holiday she just didn't decorate rather than face it herself.

The museum still felt crypt-like, but Tere appreciated that it was laid out in a square of walkways, exhibitions running along the outside, all the way around. The design was intuitive, leading the visitor through the artfully lit exhibitions arranged by periods of the saint's life, starting with her birth and childhood. There were paintings of the holy people who'd influenced her and of her ecstasies, but once again, there was nothing about levitation. How was Tere to cure herself if everyone pretended it didn't exist?

The art was rich and beautiful, and the curation was excellent. When she got to the end of the first side, she saw a sun-illuminated patch of green straight ahead. Teresa's garden! She rushed up to it, only to find it glassed in there too. *What? Why?* What did they think would happen in there? That visitors would tear up the flowers or draw mustaches on Rodrigo's smooth face? Tere put her hand on the glass and wished she could step through it onto the grass. It was actual ground on which the saint had walked, read, and prayed. Part of Tere felt that if she could only get in there, she could connect with Teresa. She jumped when a man with gardening tools and a jangling set of keys materialized at her right and disappeared through a hidden door, reappearing a moment later on the other side. Would he notice if she followed? Would she get thrown out?

One of the docents who had been at the entrance came up behind her, making Tere jump again. "Are you enjoying the view of the garden?" she asked with a polite smile.

"Yes, though I envy the staff member who actually gets to go in and experience it." Tere pointed toward the man on the other side of the glass.

"Oh, he's a volunteer. There's a team of them that take turns tending to the garden, all church members or residents of the homeless shelter that the church runs."

She nodded. "I see, thank you." Though she was disappointed to not be able to go in herself, she looked differently at the older man pruning the ivy that ran along the walls; he did it for love, not money. He earned his time in her garden.

Tere made her way down the other rows. She looked in every case, admired every sample of Teresa's elegant handwriting, the deep colors of the oil paintings, and the cases of historical ephemera. When she finally left the museum, she headed back up toward the front of the church. She remembered there was just one more stop at this location: the reliquary. But first, she needed to rest. Though she hadn't levitated, she felt that bone-deep tiredness that followed an incident, and her head filled with fog. Maybe she would take Richard's suggestion and call Dr. Sampson when she got back to Vermont.

Tere sat next to the statue and looked into its bronze face, wanting to talk to this one as she had the marble version in the square. Perhaps even make a bargain. But it was impossible with the tourists shuffling about all around her, leaning over to take selfies with the saint, unaware of the desperation that grew in Tere Sánchez's chest.

Instead, Tere pulled out her dog-eared copy of the autobiography, and began to read the next chapter. She read the first few paragraphs and froze, all movement and people around the plaza becoming merely a blur. Santa Teresa was writing of how to make a garden of our faith for the Lord's pleasure:

"We have then, as good gardeners, with God's help to make these plants grow, and to water them carefully so that they do not die, but produce flowers, which give out a good smell, to delight this Lord of ours."

She went on to outline four methods of watering this metaphorical garden, but Tere could no longer read the words. Her mind kept returning to that first time, that first experience of levitation when she had been watering Carl's garden, the smell of the peonies, her sneakers floating above the mown grass. Where it had all begun. And there was a garden right behind her, tucked within stone and glass, an unreachable one that felt somehow sacrosanct. What did it mean, this connection of gardens? Then she remembered the garden stake Isabella had given her, still nestled in her pocket. She took it out and marveled at yet another garden symbol and thought that pretty much every aspect of the journey had felt if not predestined, then connected in some way, markers along some kind of trail, like the blue streaks on trees along a mountain path so hikers didn't go astray and end up lost in the woods. Tere had definitely spent the past year lost in the woods. She spun the garden marker once, then tucked it away, stood, and headed toward the reliquary.

At first Tere wasn't sure she had the right place; the low building, with its bricked-up arches and single gated entrance, felt more like a storage building than a shrine, but the sign on a leaning battered metal stand clearly stated "Reliquary." Tere stepped through the entrance and into a gift shop, where two cranky-looking old men stood behind the glass cases hawking overpriced medals and images of Teresa. Everything was faded and dusty, the atmosphere heavy and sepulchral (though it could be argued that the latter was appropriate, given the main feature of the reliquary). It was the most depressing store she'd ever been in, and she'd lived through the recession of the eighties. There was a wall of faced-out books to the left that she slowly perused. She considered buying one titled *Santa Teresa: Mystic & Subversive*, but she felt it was grossly overpriced at thirty euros for a thin paperback. She figured at that price, it had to be an academic text, and she was not in the mood for one of those.

She looked over at the men, wondering if there was an entrance fee, but one of them impatiently waved his hand for her to just go in. Slowly, she walked through to the little room in the back, expecting, well, if not guards and red velvet, at least some reverence.

She and Carl had once taken Rowan to a roadside "dinosaur site" in upper Massachusetts. It had mismatched cases filled with questionable rocks, and you paid four dollars to see the "fossils" out back. In fact, it was like somebody's uncared-for backyard, with bare dirt and a large flat rock that, supposedly, had "fossils" imprinted into it but just looked like random crevices. They'd left ten minutes later, their wallets twenty dollars lighter, Rowan clutching a made-in-China stegosaurus figure, all three of them massively depressed.

This was worse.

It was a room smaller than the gift shop, lit by flickering old-school fluorescent lights, with four glass cases around the exterior walls. Over each was a badly handwritten sign, dangling from yellowed tape, that forbade photographs and touching.

Wait, this can't be the *reliquary, can it?* she thought as she slowly walked around.

Tere glanced into the first few cases, but there were random things in them and faded fabric along the bottoms; everything inside and out was coated in dust.

No, this can't be it. She was about to give up, but as she glanced into the last case, she saw it, next to hair and bone from Saint John of the Cross.

The ring finger of Santa Teresa.

Tere had read that her body was said to be immutable and smell like roses.

For fuck's sake.

It was a skeletal finger, propped upward, with dried yellow skin over bone, a square emerald ring rattling around its base. Next to it was the impossibly small bottom of a sandal and pieces of hair, but her eyes kept going back to the finger, getting increasingly blurred as the tears gathered. A sob caught in Tere's throat, and every fiber of her being wanted to break the glass and free this body part that she shared DNA with. The saint had given so much during her life and beyond, and this was how they honored her? Didn't she deserve to rest and be at peace?

She rushed out, openly crying now, feeling the old men's eyes following her. What did she care about two more people questioning her sanity? They could just get in line.

Tere hurried up the block and onto a side street, her grief and anger dragging behind her like entrails still attached to her body, still bleeding. It was quiet there, no stores to attract tourists, only garages and blank walls. She slowed her gait and breathed deeply, wiping away the last of the tears. Turning the corner, she chose a direction at random. By the time she passed a middle-aged couple, Tere had somewhat pulled herself together.

She had gone to commune with her relative, to ask for help in learning, or better yet, to bargain for her freedom from this family curse. Instead, she ended up face-to-face with Teresa's withered digit on display like a circus sideshow. She couldn't help recalling her experience in the cathedral in front of the crypt, the memories of her father's body, the way her mother had put it behind her and moved on, and Carl's death, how Tere would have sat there until flesh turned to bone, then dust, if Richard hadn't taken her out. All the bones and bodies of the people she'd loved and lost danced around her in that moment, the memories jumbled and clawing.

The farther she got from the reliquary, the easier her breathing became. She needed to process the experience, to gauge whether her reaction was overblown or if that place was as horrific as she thought, and she didn't want to do it alone. She dialed her titi's number in Puerto Rico. Her aunt's recorded voice answered, and this was not something for a voicemail.

Tere remembered the garden marker. She pulled it from her pocket, sat on a nearby bench, and dialed the Convent of Saint Michael. A woman with a craggy voice answered.

"May I speak to Sister Isabella? I'm her niece."

Tere heard her put the phone down with a clatter, then the shuffle of feet.

Isabella was slightly breathless when she came to the phone, and once again Tere worried about the woman's health. She hadn't known the nun existed a week ago, but somehow, she had already elbowed her curmudgeonly way into Tere's heart.

"Teresa? What's wrong?" Isabella asked into the phone.

"I just came from the reliquary," she blurted out.

A pause. Then: "I see. And how did that go?"

"Well, actually? Kind of…horrifying."

"Yes, I can understand that." Isabella spoke slowly and precisely, the hint of her Puerto Rican accent nestled beneath the Castilian. "But it is a very old tradition representing a physical connection to a saint."

"How can one have a physical connection with a skeleton finger locked in a glass case? I don't understand Catholics, I—"

"You are Catholic too, my dear. I was there at your baptism."

"Wait, you were?" Titi had neglected to mention that. But that didn't matter. "It's just, I don't understand. It feels disrespectful to have it on display like that."

"I have always thought so too. Thanks be to God, we have gotten past the time when men of the church fought over the bodies of saints like a pack of hyenas."

"Yes!" It was such a relief that her cousin agreed with her. So often the older generation had felt Tere's attitudes were "radical," or she was being too "sensitive," and she'd been left feeling even more like an outsider than she already did.

"And there is no security. Any loco could take it."

Tere thought of the guy who'd attacked Michelangelo's *Pieta* with a hammer. A new thing to worry about.

"Well, m'ija, at least it sounds like you're connecting with her, yes? Santa Teresa?"

Tere let out a loud, dark-edge-of-sanity laugh. "I'm trying, I really am. It's just…though I know my feet are stepping where hers once did, that I'm standing in places that were important to her, I'm still not getting answers." She sighed. "The truth is, things are not as I expected."

"They never are, m'ija."

"At first it may cause a good deal of trouble, for the body insists on its rights, not understanding that if it refuses to admit defeat, it is, as it were, cutting off its own head."

—Santa Teresa de Ávila,
The Way of Perfection

CHAPTER EIGHTEEN

Tere tried to walk off the experience, but it wasn't working. She was worrying it, like a loose thread you couldn't help but fuss with, though you knew it was in your best interest to leave it alone. Before that day she had understood "reliquary" as a concept but not as a reality. Not when it was someone who shared her name, whose family blood ran through her veins.

She stopped into a café and ordered a coffee and a churro. She needed something after that experience, a reward, compensation, carbohydrate therapy. After settling down at a table, she did some searching regarding the reliquary; she wanted to find out where the rest of the poor woman's body was.

She learned that nine months after Teresa had died, nuns in the municipality of Alba de Tormes fought to keep her body there, where the saint had spent her last days, at one of the convents she herself had founded. In the end it was Teresa's own confessor, Jerome Gracián, who'd initiated the exhumation of her body. Supposedly, though the coffin and her clothes were molded and decayed, her body appeared as if it had been buried the day before and smelled of roses. In fact, many documents said that her body remained incorrupt.

"Yeah, no," Tere said out loud. She had just seen that finger, and it was a skeleton with dried yellow skin stretched over it. Okay, so she had to admit that after four hundred years, it probably should have turned to dust, but roses? No.

After exhumation it seemed Gracián had cut off her right hand to keep for himself but left an arm for the convent. Tere dropped her phone on the table. She was shaking with rage at the ghoulishness of the church. As she sat there, she imagined the priest cutting the saint's hand off himself, but she knew he would not have had the stomach for that. No, he would have made the coroner do it. After a few somewhat-calming breaths, she picked up the phone again; she needed to know the rest.

It seemed the remainder of the body had been taken back to Ávila, then dug up and reburied several times while people argued over where her final resting place would be, and while they were at it, each hacked off a piece of the poor woman. Her jawbone and her right foot were in Rome, part of her cheek in Madrid (Tere wondered about that since the cheek is all fat; what could possibly be left of it?), and her heart was carefully preserved in a reliquary in Alba, a nearby city. Other body parts were in Brussels, México, and Paris. There even was an article about how the glove of Thanos in the Marvel movies was based on the bejeweled metal encasement of the "incorruptible" hand of Saint Teresa.

Jesus. The poor woman's remains are spread all over the world. How can she be at rest?

Tere felt it was all quite macabre, taking pieces of her corporeal body and instilling them with meaning and supernatural power. But what of respecting the dead? Wasn't it the church-sanctioned equivalent of grave robbing? As she drank the last of her coffee, she thought about how when you were declared a saint, it became permissible, even encouraged, for everyone to take a literal piece of you. She no longer had the stomach for the pastry, so she stood, dumped it in the trash, and left the café. Tere swore she could feel her blood bubble and boil in her veins as she marched down the streets.

Anxiety increasingly flooded her system as she walked, crashing like waves into her limbs. She began to run, weaving in and out of the streets, people stepping out of the way and turning to watch her go. When it got bad like this, she needed to move her body, push it to its limits, exhaust herself so her mind was forced to turn off. She slowed to a fast walk once she got to the main plaza before stopping to lean on the statue of Santa Teresa while she caught her breath. As she gulped air, she looked up into the stone face and whispered, "I'm sorry they did that to you." This time, it didn't help either of them. Tere's mind was still galloping. At that moment a small bell rang, and she looked over to watch a kid on a bike making his way across the plaza.

Cycling.

Perhaps it was time to go back to Rodrigo's shop and rent a bike.

The store was empty of customers when she arrived, and the workshop in the back was visible from the door. Rodrigo was working on an upside-down bike on a stand when she walked in.

"Be right with you!"

She walked toward the back, and when he saw it was her, his face lit up.

"Tere! I'm so glad to see you. Come on back while I finish this."

She walked around the glass counter and stepped into the workshop. The walls were wood in this part of the building, the floors were concrete, and the room was about ten degrees cooler than the shop. There were tools on hooks all over the back wall, and the smell of rubber, machine oil, and dirt filled the air. It was rustic but shockingly organized, and just being there restored a bit of calm to her system.

As he turned the wrench, he looked up at her and smiled, a streak of grease across his high forehead. "Sorry, I'm a little dirty at the moment, or I'd give you a hug. Been restoring this baby."

"I see that." She smiled. It was an old Peugeot road bike, teal blue, with rainbow-striped stickers that wrapped around the top tube. "It's beautiful. Where did you find it?"

"Some guy on eBay. I had to drive to Salamanca to get it, but it was worth it." He pointed over to a steel counter behind her. "Can you do me a favor and hand me that box wrench?"

She grabbed it and handed it to him. Tere used to do this for Carl in his workshop, watching him repair things she had thought eternally broken, seeing wood morphed into impossibly beautiful shapes. Rodrigo wiped his palms on the rag, then pulled a pristine white leather seat from the floor behind him. "You don't use an Allen wrench for that?"

He placed the saddle on the seat post, adjusting it a bit. "Nah, they didn't use them for seats back then." He bent down, tightened the bolts, then stood to admire his work. "This beauty is from 1981."

She snorted. "So, 1981 is vintage, huh? That's the year I graduated high school."

He smiled at her. "I was three."

She picked up a rag from the counter and threw it at him. "Rub it in, why don't you?" It felt good to be joking around; the normality of it was reassuring.

Rodrigo caught the rag and finished wiping the back of his hands with it.

Tere pointed to his forehead. "You have a swipe of something up there too."

He nodded. "Thanks." Then he wiped his forehead clean. "So, I know you didn't just come here to tell me that I missed a spot."

"No, that's just a bonus. I'm actually here on business."

He straightened up, adjusting an imaginary tie with his slightly greasy hands. "Oh, I see. Well, how can I be of service, Señora Sánchez?" He flung the rag around and bowed at the waist.

Tere did what she imagined passed for a curtsey. "Well, señor, I would like to rent your finest velocipede, if you have one to spare?"

"Of course! Right this way." He gestured back toward the store and followed her as they made their way around the counter. When they reached the middle, he indicated the line of used bikes against the right-hand wall. "Choose your steed."

"And well, maybe not your 'finest,' but you get the idea." she said, already glancing over the used models, though she was having trouble focusing on just one. She was having trouble focusing in general. She just wanted to jump on any of them and take off. "Perhaps you could make a suggestion?"

He looked Tere up and down, paying special attention to her legs.

Tere didn't want to admit that the brush of his gaze caused an electric buzz over the surface of her skin; she shook it off.

"Twenty-eight-inch inseam?"

"Okay, I'm impressed. How did you do that?"

He bowed again. "It is a secret of the trade, milady."

Tere laughed. It seemed laughing was easy with Rodrigo…that and crying over vegetables.

He pulled a silver one from the center of the row, whipping it around so Tere could see it. "This is a nice one in your size. Shocks in front and back, a necessity with all the cobblestones around here." He held it out for her. "It's an older model but sturdy as hell."

"Kind of like me." She laughed, grabbing on to the handlebars.

"Try it out," he suggested, gesturing with his hand.

Tere climbed on, tested the distance of the pedals, then rode it a short way across the floor. He made a small adjustment, and it was ready. It felt so good to sit on a bike again. She hadn't ridden enough in the past year; she should have gone every day, working her grief until it was soft and malleable.

"Looks good! When are you going for a ride?"

"Right now." Tere thought that sounded rather desperate, so she added, "I need some exercise."

"Right now?"

"Yep! You got a helmet I can rent? I have a big-ass head."

He laughed. "A hard one too, I imagine."

She knocked on her skull as if to demonstrate. "And damn proud of it."

He pulled a black one off the shelf, then gently placed it on Tere's head, his face close to hers as he adjusted it, his breath carrying a hint of coffee as his calloused knuckles brushed her cheek. She'd always said she preferred a blue-jeaned man with calluses on his hands than a suited one with carpal tunnel. When the helmet hugged her head just right, he stepped back and assessed her setup. "You're ready to go. Where are you going to ride?"

"I hadn't thought that far. Any recommendations?"

He looked around the store a bit, then asked, "You want company?"

"You can just close up the shop in the middle of the day?"

He put his hands out. "Well, I mean, I will have to ignore all these clamoring customers, but you're worth it."

"I'd love some company and some guidance on routes."

"I'll get my stuff."

Rodrigo pulled a high-end but clearly oft-used mountain bike out from the back room and wheeled it through the store, that familiar ticking sound of the freewheel following him like a faithful dog. He locked up the shop, then led Tere down the hill and into the lower part of the city.

Normally, she was petrified of riding in traffic, but since it was late morning, people weren't speeding around, and she managed to remain alive, though it did little to decrease her anxiety. The route down the hill was steep and terrifying, but it kept her mind on something other than the traumatic reliquary experience, and it went quickly. He brought her to a trail that spread out from behind the train station; it had long flat sections where they were able to really let it out. The speed was exhilarating, and Tere was reminded why she used to bike so often back home. Thanks to Rodrigo, she got to see parts of the city she wouldn't have otherwise, and though they didn't have the majesty of the walls and the churches, it was beautiful in a different way: Parents walking babies in carriages, a dog tied to the handle. A woman working in her garden, oblivious to the buzz of activity along the trail that ran by her backyard fence.

Life, in all its ordinary and gorgeous glory.

She felt the anxiety begin to ebb.

They could only ride side by side for short distances before they would have to go single file for other bikes coming in the opposite direction, but to Tere it was perfect. She'd always loved the companionship of cycling with someone; it wasn't about conversation but a shared love for the outdoors, for the exhilaration of moving through the world together. Besides, she really wasn't up to talking after the morning's experience.

The two-hour ride was glorious, and though the return trip up the hill was hard work, Tere welcomed the burning feeling in her legs as she pushed on. That work did the most to refocus her body and mind; it was almost meditative. Rodrigo barely seemed out of breath when they came to a stop in front of the shop, but Tere was very winded. Once she caught her breath, she dismounted and took off her helmet. "Thank you. I needed that." She felt a small flush of dizziness but took a long sip of water, and it went away.

He was watching her as he took his keys out. "So, Tere, is everything okay?"

Wait, did he sense her dizziness? "Sure." It didn't sound at all convincing. "Why do you ask?"

He held the door open for her. "It's just, when you arrived, you seemed…out of sorts."

Rodrigo really was perceptive, but being reminded of the morning trip felt like someone just dropped a truck tire around her neck. She took a deep breath. "I went to the reliquary this morning."

"The one at Iglesia de Santa Teresa?" After she nodded, he gave a shudder as he took off his helmet. "I've never been able to go in there. Even when I was twelve and into horror and all things dark. Horror stories are make-believe, but the reliquary? That was someone's actual finger. It's just too morbid." He was shaking his head.

"It really was. I found it so disturbing." She handed him the helmet. "So, how much do I owe you?"

He handed it back. "How about you hold on to it for the rest of your stay?"

She looked over at the bike longingly. Tere got attached to vehicles easily, even naming them as if they were pets. "Really?"

"Sure! You'll need a way to get around, right? And maybe we can sneak in another ride or two?"

"I'd like that." She looked over at the bike and, with a smile, decided its name was the Silver Fox. Then she put the helmet back on and gave Rodrigo a hug, bonking him with the visor. "Thank you."

That earned her a big smile, the infectious kind. "You're welcome, amiga. Now off with you! That bike in there won't fix itself!"

"Okay, okay, I'll let you get back to it."

"Oh! Tere!" he called after her.

She turned back around.

"I almost forgot to tell you. My cousin, the priest? My mother said he's coming up for some big meeting this week. I'll text you when I know the details."

"Great! Thanks!" *This week.* That was cutting it close. If she took the chair position she would have to return to Vermont sooner rather than later, but just thinking about it made her anxious, so she tried not to.

The ride up the rest of the hill to the apartment was brutal, steep, and cobbled. She was grateful Rodrigo wasn't there to see her struggling, but when she pulled up in front of the apartment, Tere felt much better than she had before the ride. Her shoulders were no longer pulled up to her ears, and though there was still a hum of tension in her brain, she was calmer. The instant she took off her helmet, though, she had the strongest feeling of being watched. She spun around, until her eyes landed on Señor Avellaneda González Diaz standing in the center of the little park like a sentry, both he and Sancho glaring at her.

She waved, though her prevailing thought was, *What the hell is wrong with those two anyway?*

He came bustling over, his back stiff, waddling like a penguin. "A bicycle? Señora Sánchez, you're not planning to bring that inside, are you?"

"Why, yes, yes, I am. But don't worry, I won't ride it in the apartment." She smiled as she unlocked the door. Just before it closed, she heard Sancho give a quick, sharp bark.

Little bastard had to get the last word.

"In these raptures, there is no remedy. They rush upon the soul as quickly and powerfully as a mighty eagle swooping down and bearing her aloft on its wings. Without giving us a chance to think about it or plan our escape, this cloud sends us soaring. We see that we are being carried away, but we do not know where. Even though this experience is delightful, our nature is still weak, so it scares us at first. We need to cultivate a courageous spirit and hone our determination to risk everything and abandon ourselves into the Beloved's hands. Whether we like it or not, we have already been transported, so we might as well go willingly."

—Santa Teresa de Ávila,
The Life of Saint Teresa of Ávila by Herself

CHAPTER NINETEEN

After a quick shower, Tere found she couldn't sit down. She should have been physically exhausted, but anxiety had a way of ramping her up regardless. She ate some rolled-up slices of ham and cheese for lunch while standing at the kitchen counter, and after pacing the length of the apartment for ten minutes, she stormed out onto the street again. This was not a trip for relaxing, which was good since she seemed incapable of it at this point. Besides, she needed to work out the kinks in her legs. It had been too long since she'd done a substantial ride. She decided to visit the Four Posts monument Richard had recommended, which she'd seen on her way to Isabella's convent.

But she really didn't want to be alone. She texted Yolanda.

> Hey! It's Tere. Going to check out the
> Four Posts, you want to join me?

A response came right away.

> Hi! I'm on a run at the moment, but not far from
> there. I'll meet you at the traffic circle in 10 or 15.

> Perfect!

The day was bright and warm, the birds chirping loudly as they swooped from tree to tree in the small park across the street, and the plaza was filled with people coming and going from lunch, plus teens in uniforms lounging on benches in the sun like lizards. She started around the outside of the east wall, keeping to the path that hugged it. Once she passed the last hotel and started going downhill, the foot traffic all but disappeared, and she welcomed the solitude.

It felt good to keep moving; she knew from experience that the worst thing you could do after pushing yourself physically was to lie on the couch. That was when the aches crept in. Tere hadn't noticed how sedentary she'd become in the months before, rarely leaving her property. It was as if she'd been stuck in a loop, trying to find solace in the monotony of her days, trying to act as if nothing had changed. She supposed that was probably the clinical definition of depression. With this trip she was starting to feel as though she'd broken free of the loop but was now petrifyingly working without a net.

"Tere!"

The shout came from up ahead, and she saw a jogger heading toward her. "Yolanda! I'm so glad you could meet me."

They gave each other a kiss on each cheek. "I'm all sweaty, or I'd give you a hug."

She looked very fit to Tere, wearing print leggings and a crop top, her burgundy hair in a high messy bun. "I like the athleisure look on you. You run every day?"

"Psh! I wish I had the time." Yolanda stopped and leaned her hands on her thighs, breathing heavily. "What about you?"

"Me? Oh, I don't run unless there are zombies chasing me."

Yolanda peeked around Tere, looking up the path behind her. "Well, the coast is clear, so I guess we're walking."

"Unless the zombies come."

"Unless the zombies come."

Tere asked about Yolanda's week as they walked, keeping the focus off her. Tere spent enough time worrying about that, so it felt good to focus on other people's issues: Yolanda's selfish ex, the real estate market, aging. As they were walking over the bridge that crossed the river, Yolanda said in a theatrically casual voice, "So, I hear you were biking with Rodrigo Romero this morning."

Tere stopped short. "You're kidding me, right? It's been, like, an hour! And nobody even knows me here but you and that cranky guy from the first floor."

"And Rodrigo, clearly."

She nodded impatiently. "And Rodrigo."

Yolanda waved her hand for her to continue. "Yes…and?"

Tere started walking again. "It's not like that. We're friends." She could feel Yolanda staring at her. "What?"

"Nothing, I'm just surprised."

Tere pointed at her, smiling big. "Aha! I get it, *you're* interested in him." She could totally understand why and pictured them looking stunning together, with only a tiny twinge of unreasonable jealousy.

Yolanda waved her hands. "No, no. No interest. After my ex-husband, I think I'll stick to women. No, it's just…he's one of the good ones, you know?"

"Yes, he is."

She narrowed her eyes at Tere. "And I don't want you to break his heart."

"Ha! No worries there—not going to happen. He's a great guy, but I'm just not interested in being with anyone these days."

"I get that," Yolanda said as they crossed yet another traffic circle.

"I'm heading there myself; I can feel it. I think I'll welcome it because sometimes I wish I weren't interested in relationships. It's getting harder as I get older, you know? Meeting people."

"You? No way. You've got that badass, fearless style." Tere paused, then continued, "Actually, never mind. I know for a fact that fearlessness intimidates *a lot* of people."

"It's so true! Face it, as women, once we get to a certain age, we're invisible."

Tere stopped again. "We are not! The media just makes us *feel* that way."

Yolanda shrugged. "Doesn't matter why. It just is. Even in terms of work—I'm fifty-seven, and I already worry about not having enough energy to hustle like the other agents out there. And if real estate doesn't work out, at this age, I couldn't even get hired for an office job I'm grossly overqualified for and could do in my sleep."

"Really? Damn, I've been so insulated in higher education, I don't even know what it's like in the real world. Being old and being faculty doesn't seem to be an issue."

"But is it the same for women professors as it is for men? Be honest."

This got Tere thinking. She thought about having been turned down for the chair position while less-qualified men got the job, three times. And those times when she expressed an idea in a faculty meeting and no one said anything, but then twenty minutes later, a male colleague said the exact same thing, and everyone cooed over it, and bam! It had been implemented. "Well, when you put it that way… Of course, it's not the same. You're totally right." She thought for a moment. "You know, it's funny we're having this conversation now. Yesterday I was offered the job to be head of my department at the university where I work."

"Really? But that's great, no?"

"I guess so." Tere shrugged.

"You don't want it?"

"I don't know. I was overlooked for that position several times over the years, so it is tempting. If I don't take it, they'll just give it to another old white armchair academic."

"Wait, but you're white."

"Thanks for not saying I'm old. But in the U.S., I'm not really considered white since I'm Puerto Rican."

"But didn't you say your family was from here originally?"

"Well, yes." All her arguments about her Caribbean roots suddenly went out the window. She thought of the results of the DNA test she'd done that stated she was almost entirely European, only 3 percent indigenous Taino and 1 percent African. In other words, 97 percent colonizer.

"And what's an 'armchair academic'?"

"Oh, it's a term I made up. Universities are filled with professors who teach subjects in which they have no practical experience, cultures they are not part of, or languages of countries they've never been to. That sort of thing."

"What subject do you teach?"

"Well, my specialty is Latin American literature, the Caribbean, México, South America, Iberian."

"And you've been to all the countries in those regions? Talked to writers who live there?"

Tere stopped short. "Ouch."

Yolanda put her hand on her arm. "Oh my God! I'm so sorry! My mouth gets me in such trouble sometimes. I didn't mean to—"

Tere cut her off. "No, don't apologize." She looked up at Yolanda. "Holy shit. I've never thought of it like that. You are absolutely and totally right." Her head was spinning, her identity compass trying to find north. "I'm as bad as they are."

Yolanda lifted Tere's chin up so she could look in her eyes. "Oh no, you're not. Look, I haven't known you long, but I know that you think and care deeply about people and art and life. I mean, you flew across the Atlantic in order to explore and connect with your roots. I can guarantee you that none of those others would do such a thing, especially a year after losing their spouse."

Tere swallowed. No tears, just a rumble of deep feeling in her chest.

Yolanda reached up and brushed a lock of hair off her face; the gentle touch of her fingers practically knocked Tere to her knees. For a year she'd had almost no physical contact with other humans. Her friend's voice was careful and soft. "Be kind to yourself, my sister. We are always way harder on ourselves than on other people. And that's got to change."

Tere still felt a little shaken, but she hooked her arm in Yolanda's with a grateful smile, and they set off uphill again. When they passed a small strip of businesses, she could see the posts up ahead. As they got closer, she saw that the monument was composed of four columns with an open ceiling above them, a rustic stone cross sculpture in the center. When she reached the top of the rocky steps, the scenery beyond opened up, and she gasped. The entire city was spread out on top of the hill beyond, the walls white in the sun like snow crests, the bright-blue sky punctuated by small bursts of wispy clouds. "Wow. From here, with the columns around us? I could almost believe we're back in medieval times." In that exact moment, a pair of motorcycles blasted up the road behind them, mufflers rattling, throttles roaring. The two women looked at each other and said at the same time, "Almost." They laughed loud enough that the two other people there, men with vintage cameras strapped around their necks, stared at them.

Tere ignored them and stepped off the far side of the monument so she could see the view without obstruction. "Why did they build this here? For the view? I only just heard about this from a friend, so I don't know the history."

Yolanda smiled and pointed to the ground in front of them, "This is where Teresa's uncle found her and her brother trying to run away and become martyrs."

Tere gasped. "No way!" She glanced around the monument, then gauged the distance from the walls. "They got this far?"

Yolanda shrugged. "So the story goes."

They were standing in the exact same location the saint had, five hundred years earlier. Just amazing. Tere tried to picture her namesake at age seven, attempting to explain to her uncle why they needed to go, her brother Rodrigo just along for the ride. She had been subversive and strong-willed even that young. Tere liked it. And why hadn't she made the connection before that Rodrigo was also the name of Santa Teresa's brother? She'd have to ask her new friend if he was named after him.

The other visitors took their last photos, then headed down the hill, leaving Tere and Yolanda alone in that sacred place. They stood in silence, looking at the city alive within ancient walls, cars buzzing around the outside: history and modernity blending. Tere and her relative standing in the same place, so many generations apart—if time was an artificial construct, were they both there simultaneously? "The holographic universe," Tere whispered.

"What's that?"

"Oh, this view reminds me of a book I just read. It's a scientific theory that there are innumerable realities going on simultaneously."

"Wait, so the multiverse from *Spider-Man* is real?"

Tere laughed. "Yeah, kind of."

Yolanda looked at her watch and sighed. "Well, all I know is that in *this* reality, I have to head home and shower before my kids get there." She gave Tere a quick hug. "You can find your way back from here?"

"Of course! I'm so happy you were able to join me. And thank you for the truth telling. I needed that."

"It was my honor, amiga." And with a smile and a flash of impossibly white teeth, Yolanda was gone, the clean sound of her running shoes thumping the pavement providing a drumbeat to the hum of traffic.

Tere stood there alone for quite some time, just being. Then she wandered back up onto the monument and over the other side, not ready to go back to the city. She stood, looking at the unobstructed view, breathing the fresh air, and thought. She thought about the possible path Richard's call had presented and about Rodrigo's question about her plan for the future. She used to be completely predictable, never late to pick up Rowan from school, always prepared at her job, constantly putting her family's needs before her own. But as she looked off into the distance and the rolling hills surrounding the city, she realized that for the first time, she had no idea what direction she would choose next, and this trip was her first foray into an uncharted, alternate reality. Like when Santa Titi and her brother had stood here, putting all they knew at their backs in the interest of their quest.

Tere felt it then.

She could now identify the out-of-body feeling she got right before it started, followed by the slow decreasing of pressure against the soles of her feet, like the earth was letting her go. Tere looked down and saw her sneakers lift, and her arms flew out to either side, trying to grasp something, anything. She reached out to the columns behind her, but they were too far away, and she didn't know how to control her movement.

She looked up, and it hit her that there was absolutely nothing to stop her this time, only open sky, mockingly blue and bright.

That was when panic set in.

Tere twisted her body around, reaching her arms toward the monument, desperately trying to reach it, to hold on.

Her head was now level with the top.

A sob tore from her body as she reached and reached, her fingertips not even grazing the stone. There was no way she could make it in time—she was going to float off into the sky.

Alone.

Out of control.

It was her worst nightmare.

From some deep memory, the command "tuck and roll" came into her head, something from her in-line skating days, a safe thing to do when you tripped and fell. Tere started rolling, flipping her body slowly, using all the muscles of her core, unable to see through the tears in her eyes, unbridled terror wrapping its bony fingers around her heart and squeezing. She was getting dizzy, so dizzy with each rotation. Slowly she was moving closer to the monument, but she was almost even with the top; in a second, she would lose her only chance.

Flip, flip, flip.

At that point she was reaching down, the Four Posts below her, feeling as though her arms were going to loosen from their sockets. Then her fingernail scraped the stone corner, and she lurched forward and grabbed them with the tips of her fingers. She reached around with her other arm and grabbed another edge, ignoring the tearing away of two fingernails, the skin scraping against the rough stone. With shaking arms, she pulled, getting more of her fingers beneath the edge, lowering an inch, two. Holding on with one hand, she wrapped the other around the top of a column. A little lower. Her muscles were quivering, a strangled, keening sound coming from her mouth. She got the other arm fully around and shinnied down, inch by inch. She used all her lower-body strength to bring her legs under her and wrap them around the pillar. Her sneaker hit the base of the column, and she stopped, holding on with all she had, her eyes squeezed shut, fear pressing against her body like a shroud.

Please stop. Please stop. Please stop.

Then came the lowering feeling, unhurriedly, like a balloon with a slow leak, until it was hard to hang, her arms exhausted. Tere was sobbing openly now, everything weighing her down. She dropped to the ground on her butt without releasing her arms, afraid the wind would pick up and carry her off.

Then she was sitting, still half wrapped around the column, taking gulps of breaths, afraid to feel relief, terrified to let go. She looked around, worried someone had seen her—another tourist, someone in a car driving by—but also desperately wishing they had and she would have a witness to confirm that she wasn't losing her grasp on reality too.

She leaned her forehead against the stone, whispering, "I can't do this anymore. I can't do this anymore," over and over like a prayer, exhaustion flooding her body.

I can't bear this.

I'm not strong enough.

I want to go home.

But "home" wasn't just Vermont at that moment. It was her job at the college, their little familiar house, *his* garden. Home as if nothing had changed, as if Carl were making her dinner in the kitchen.

As if he weren't dead.

"Sometimes I have been able to overcome it, but the struggle has left me drained, like someone who has been in a fight with a giant. At other times it has been impossible to resist. Then it has carried away my entire soul—and sometimes my head too—and I have been powerless to hold myself back. Sometimes the experience has taken up my whole body and lifted it off the ground."

—Santa Teresa de Ávila,
The Life of Saint Teresa of Ávila by Herself

CHAPTER TWENTY

With her head down, legs shaking, and heart still racing, Tere texted feverishly as she walked back to the city. If she could have gotten on a plane right then, she would have. It was official: she'd had all she could handle.

> Richard, made up my mind on the chair position.
> Tell Hammerston I'll call him tomorrow.

She was going to "move on" in the only way she knew how. She texted Yolanda.

> Hi honey! Gotta check out early. Heading
> home for new job. I'll call you later.

She was about to text Rodrigo when she noticed she had missed a text from him. Must have been when she was fighting not to levitate into oblivion.

> My priest cousin is in town! Will meet you
> outside St. John the Baptist today at 3:15.

Tere looked at her watch. *Shit!* That had been five minutes ago. She took off running, dodging people on their afternoon stroll. Wasn't it siesta time anyway? Why were there so many people around? She really needed to go back to the apartment and book a return flight, but since Rodrigo had gone to the trouble to put her in touch, she would talk to this priest and make it the last thing she would do in Ávila. One way or another, she'd fly out the next day. She had planned to go to Saint John the Baptist later that week anyway, because unlike most of the other churches, it was original. In fact, Teresa had been baptized there. It was where the noble families of Ávila had worshipped.

Tere stopped running when she got to the Plaza Mayor so she wouldn't draw too much attention to herself but walked briskly toward the church on the other side. As she made her way around the exterior of the building, she couldn't help but take notice of its age, especially the lack of windows and limited points of entry. Built at a time when the city could be under siege at any moment, it appeared fortified like the walls that surrounded it. When she had gone almost all the way around the building, she turned a corner and came upon the entrance. It was apparent from the crowd outside that a mass was about to start, but there was an inordinate number of men in brown robes with small capes attached at their collars among the crowd.

Finding Timoteo there would be like looking for a priestly needle in a clerical haystack. Tere loitered on the outskirts, looking around at faces, when a priest next to her spoke.

"Are you Tere Sánchez?"

She turned to look at him, letting out a breath of relief. "I'm so sorry I'm late, Father. I only just got Rodrigo's text." She reached out her hand, and he shook it warmly. He was handsome, early sixties, brown hair with gray at the temples, and wearing an open and warm smile. She could see small similarities to his cousin around the eyes.

"As I'm sure you've gathered, I'm Timoteo. But I'm afraid I have to go to mass now. Would you like to join, and we can talk after?"

"Can I? I mean, it seems there's something going on. Is this a priest convention, or something?"

He had a sincere tumbling laugh, like sun-warmed river water over rocks. "Something like that. We're all in the same order but have come from all over the country for a meeting."

She gave him a grin. "So it *is* a priest convention."

"Yes, I suppose it is." He glanced down at her hands. "Señora, your fingernails…they're bleeding."

"Oh! Right." Tere shoved her hands deep into her coat pockets. "I just had a bit of an…accident at the Four Posts right before coming here."

He looked into her eyes with his priestly laser gaze, "Are you sure you're all right?"

She laughed nervously. "Oh yes, I'm fine. Thank you, though."

"Okay then." He gestured with his hand for her to go first. "Shall we go in, Señora…?"

"Tere. Just Tere."

He bowed with his head.

She smiled. "I think I will, Father, thank you."

They headed in among the crowd funneling into the main aisle of the church. She had been to a number of churches since arriving, but upon looking around, she thought this one felt different from the others: more rustic, less grandiose. There were chapels on both sides with statues of Jesus and saints, but they were made of elaborately carved wood; there was little gold in sight. The main altar was also wood, with richly carved details and an oil painting of the crucifixion at its top.

Wanting to blend in, Tere chose to sit in the last few rows, and though she got separated from Rodrigo's cousin, she was pleased to see him settle with his priest buddies in the row directly behind her. There was a couple sitting in front of her, but otherwise she was surrounded by clergymen. It was so odd to be walled in by all that restrained masculinity.

The mass sounded beautiful in Castilian, and Tere knew all the responses in Spanish, as the only time she went to church anymore was when she was visiting her family in Puerto Rico. Her parents had been bohemian artist types, and though they occasionally went to church on Sundays and on holidays, she'd never considered her household "religious," despite the fervency of the Puerto Rican side of her family.

When the priest introduced the sermon and said it was about Santa Teresa (which made sense given the number of clergy members from her order present), she felt a flicker of hope: if anyone had respect and reverence for her relative the saint, it would be them. Perhaps she would finally learn some substantive information related to her near-abandoned quest.

During the second scripture reading, she tuned out, absently watching the couple in the pew in front of her. They were in their late forties, early fifties, with grown children, she guessed. They sat next to each other but not close, both with stiff backs. The third time the man checked his phone, the woman turned slightly and threw him a look of death that must have seared off his eyelashes. Perhaps the texts were from a girlfriend, or he had been checking the scores from a sporting event. Either way, it was clear he wished to be elsewhere. He put the phone back into his coat pocket with a grunt. As the congregation stood, the woman moved her body slightly away. Tere got the distinct feeling they detested each other, and she felt empathy for both of them. She didn't believe she and Carl had held some sort of magic secret as to why their marriage had lasted so long. She attributed it to sheer luck, since they'd been so different, but she said a silent prayer of thanks that they had loved each other for so long.

She lost interest in the couple once the sermon began, and she settled in to listen attentively. However, as the priest droned on in his lackluster voice, she was disappointed to hear him go over the same life events, same stories, and once again there was no mention of the saint's levitation or the mystical aspects of her life. Such an odd omission, since these incidents were important elements in her elevation by the church to sainthood. Did they all work from the exact same script? She pictured a group of men in brown robes deciding what they would emphasize and what they would leave out "in the best interest of the people." Tere sank a bit in her seat and folded her arms across her chest like a petulant child.

She didn't take communion; they wouldn't consider her worthy of that anyway, as she hadn't been an active member of the church for most of her life. Instead, she stayed in the pew and watched the rows slowly empty, the priest blessing each one and giving them the "body and blood" of Christ. Tere realized she now had a different take on the rituals around the body of holy saints and saviors after her visit to the reliquary. At least this particular ritual was symbolic and not literal, but the connection added to the roiling in her belly that had started that morning. Had it only been that morning? Another day that felt like a lifetime.

As the mass drew to a close, despite her feelings about the individual parts of the service, Tere had to admit she missed the ceremony of it all, the "peace be with you" greetings of the people around her, the power of poetic words said in unison. She knew Nivea's hope was that one of the results of this trip would be some kind of reconciliation between Tere and the Catholic Church, as her aunt worried about her immortal soul, but it was seriously unlikely, since there were too many important points on which Tere and the church vehemently disagreed.

The mass ended, and she gathered her coat.

"So, Tere, did you enjoy the sermon?"

She looked back at Father Timoteo, who was still seated with a few of his fellow priests. She gave them a nod as they were all looking at her. "Yes, very much so, Father, though I had hoped to learn something new about Santa Teresa, and the sermon went over some well-trodden territory. That's what I wanted to discuss with you."

"Ah, but that's hard with someone who has been dead for over four hundred years. There is nothing new to learn, yes?"

Tere turned completely around and held on to the back of the pew. If they were going to have this conversation, why not now? There certainly were enough priests to weigh in if needed, and she was downright hungry to engage in discourse of this kind. "Yes, but there must be new interpretations of her scholarship, right?"

"Well, I suppose there could be, but they could never fully understand the context of her era."

"But isn't the longevity of their teachings inherent in the very definition of a 'saint'? Not to mention that she was the first woman made a doctor of the church. And her mystical experiences were what classified her for canonization and proved her closeness to God, yet there is precious little church-sanctioned scholarship that explores them. I mean, with all the research in metaphysics and quantum realities, some of her ecstasies and mystical experiences could have deeper implications, ones that go beyond simply relegating them to our limited binary understanding of the literal versus the more metaphorical interpretation, no?"

The men just stared at her then.

Tere started to think she had broken the priests when Father Timoteo leaned forward and put a hand on her forearm.

"You're a professor, aren't you?" He asked it quietly, as if giving her his condolences.

She didn't acknowledge this, just went on. "So, though as a woman, she was not allowed to 'preach,' and they were embarrassed by Teresa's clearly established role as a leader in the church, even today you extol her commitment to prayer because that fits within the accepted 'gender lines' while disregarding the exceptional outcome of her worship?"

He put his hands up in what she interpreted as a "whoa" gesture. "Now, Tere, the Catholic Church has made many strides towards gender equality. Why, in 2019, Pope Francis encouraged us to support women's rights."

"Mere platitudes, Father." Tere looked into the man's face, searching his light-brown eyes. Though she could tell he was a kind man, he was buying into the system that worked to hold half of God's people back. "With all these sermons and lectures about Santa Teresa, why does no one mention her levitations? It's as if you are all intentionally ignoring a significant piece of her experience."

The priests looked at one other. Then Father Timoteo said, with what she interpreted as a patronizing smile, "Well, because those descriptions were figurative, no?"

Finally, an honest answer she could respond to. "No! That's exactly my point. How can we possibly know that?"

"Well, because it is widely accepted that it was in her mind, a symbol of her love of God."

"'Widely accepted' does not mean 'true,' now does it?"

This time his chuckle sounded a bit nervous. "Well, no, but Teresa was a woman with deep feelings and religious conviction. Her faith is never in question, but she did have an imaginative mind."

Tere stood, her heart beating faster against her ribs. "And what does *that* mean? She was hysterical? She was making it up? It was PMS?"

The other priests chuckled at this, then went back to talking amongst themselves. Tere guessed they thought the show was over. They were wrong.

She pointed at Father Timoteo. "Look, Padre. You and your priest bros here should have more respect for the woman who founded your order. How dare you dismiss her deeply profound experiences simply because you hate women and don't believe us as capable of experiences as miraculous as men's!"

"I—I certainly don't—"

The others could only stare. Tere had broken them again.

"Santa Teresa was not constrained by gravity or by the approval of her 'betters' in the church, yet your way of showing reverence to her is to steal her bones and place them on display for tourists to ogle? Why can't you just let him rest in peace?"

Timoteo stuttered, "H-him? Steal…Tere, I think you misunderstand—"

She'd lost control of what had started as an academic discussion. She wasn't even making sense anymore. Not to mention she'd basically verbally attacked a perfectly nice cousin of Rodrigo, one of her few friends in Ávila. So many feelings were battling in her chest, it felt as if she couldn't breathe. Tere grabbed her coat, rushed out of the row and down the aisle, shame heating her face. Rodrigo had been kind enough to set up this meeting, and she'd interrogated and berated a member of his family. And at the end of that bizarre discussion, had she even been talking about Teresa anymore?

She brusquely wiped tears from her cheeks. What did it matter? She was leaving as soon as possible anyway.

"For if the will has nothing to employ it and love has no present object with which to busy itself, the soul finds itself without either support or occupation, its solitude and aridity cause it great distress and its thoughts involve it in the severest conflict."

—Santa Teresa de Ávila,
The Life of Saint Teresa of Ávila by Herself

CHAPTER TWENTY-ONE

Tere rushed out the main doors, dodged in and out among the slowly departing parishioners, turned the corner, and ran up the stairs to the upper plaza as if the devil himself were at her heels. When she got to the top, her head spun as dizziness overtook her, and her knees gave way. She grabbed on to a metal bar at the small gated side entrance, leaned her head against the ornate cast-iron door, and began to sob. *I'm just fucking everything up.* In that moment she was not only sorry she'd come to Ávila, but she also wished she had just died with Carl.

Dying was easy; being left behind was hard.

"Tere? Are you okay?"

She looked up at the familiar voice to see Juan, and she lurched toward the young man and held on tight. He was warm and tall and smelled of pine. He patted her back awkwardly, but she was just so grateful to see his kind face, grateful for his miraculous appearance just when she needed him. Eventually, she let him go. "I'm sorry, Juan. I've had a very difficult day, but I'm really glad to see you." After pulling a tissue from her coat pocket, she tried to wipe her face of tears, but they were still coming.

He was looking at her with those soulful eyes, and she knew

then for certain that he saw more than most people. He gestured back toward the entrance of the church. "Did you just come from mass?"

"I did." Tere blew her nose and worked to regain her composure. The distraction of conversation seemed to help. "Did you?"

"Oh yes, I go to this church every week."

"What did you think of the sermon?" Before he could answer, she held up her hand. "You know what? Never mind. I could really use some coffee and a pastry instead." She gave him a small smile. "Will you join me? My treat. I'd love the company."

"I—yes."

"Good." She put her arm through his. "Accompany me as I drown my sorrows in some café con leche and empty calories."

Five minutes later, they settled down at a corner table at Granier, Tere's favorite bakery in the old part of the city. She gave Juan a short summary of the conversation with Timoteo and why she had been upset. Recounting it, she was embarrassed all over again.

He thought about it for a while, then said gently, "But those things were put into place many years before Father Timoteo was even alive."

She let out a long breath. "I know. That's why I'm upset. I took out my anger on him when I was really just angry at the whole institution of the Catholic Church…" Then she remembered her slip of saying "letting *him* rest in peace." "Actually, I think I was angry at God." The last sentence fell from her lips and onto the tabletop in front of her like a cinder block; Tere imagined the weight of it making the wooden table teeter on its spindly legs.

"So, you were crying from anger?"

"Yes. I hate that I do that, but when I get really, really pissed off, it happens." With slightly shaky hands, Tere took a sip of the warming coffee. "It's stupid, huh?"

"No, not really. My mother used to do that. It would upset us when we were kids because we couldn't tell if we'd made her sad or mad."

She smiled. "Is your mother still alive?"

Juan looked at the table. "I don't know. My family is in Madrid, and I, well, I have a problem with alcohol." He looked up at her. "But I've been sober for almost two years now."

"I know, you mentioned it in your essay. That's wonderful. It's an incredibly hard thing to do."

"Do you have some experience with substance abuse in your life?"

She nodded. "My mother was an alcoholic. I grew up having to hide the car keys so she wouldn't kill us. Because my older siblings were all gone already, I basically ran the household from ages nine to twelve when she sobered up. She did the smartest thing she could have done; she'd dragged me along in her alcoholism, but she brought me with her through recovery. It saved our relationship."

"I prayed every day that my father would stop using, but unfortunately not before an overdose took him. But you read about that already."

"I'm so sorry."

"Thank you, but I believe it was God's will. I am learning that addiction is a much more common problem than people want to acknowledge. I am just grateful for my faith; it gets me through one day at a time." Tere must have made a face of some kind because Juan asked, "Do you not believe?"

"I mean, I believe in a higher power." She let out a long loud breath. "Actually, that's probably the most complicated question anyone has ever asked me, particularly today."

"I'm sorry, I didn't mean—"

Tere waved that away. "No, no, it's okay. I love complicated questions; it's literally my job. Or was. Is… Oh, whatever. Besides, it's good for me to try to articulate this." She sat back. "I believed once. I was baptized Catholic, and my Puerto Rican family is very devout. But from a young age, I had problems with some of the tenets of the church. They seemed stacked against me as a girl." She took a long sip of coffee, enjoying the sweet warmth of the milk. "I think that's why I'm so fascinated with Santa Teresa. She was so strong at a time when women were expected, even encouraged, to be weak, so driven to make a difference in an organization that not only didn't want to hear what she had to say but could have executed her for it."

Juan made the sign of the cross. "Thank God they didn't. Santa Teresa was a gift from God. She's why I came to Ávila."

"Really? Me too. You know, I'm supposedly descended from her family. The Sánchez side."

His eyes lit up. "But that's wonderful! You must be so proud of your heritage."

"Ha!" The laugh was quick but had a sharp edge. "A chain-smoking nun told me that half the town is descended from her family." Tere paused. "But I *am* proud." And in that moment, she felt it like a warming coal in her chest. "Especially since she and I share some…traits, in common."

"I can see that. You've been very kind to me."

She smiled. "Oh, that's easy. You're an exceptional person, Juan. I saw it the first time I met you. Don't let anyone tell you any different."

His face flushed and he shifted uncomfortably, but she noticed he was smiling.

"Do you really want to know why I was crying?"

He nodded.

"Something happened this morning." She flinched at the thought of the visit to the reliquary. "Those priests, the church, this city, they claim to venerate Santa Teresa, but all they do is hold her up as a pretty rose-scented statue, simply because she was a woman. And she clearly still speaks to the people even five hundred years later."

"Oh yes, she is our country's most beloved saint! She's loved throughout the world and has been for generations."

"Yet they have her mummified finger on display for people to ogle." Her skin felt too tight as she spoke.

Juan shuddered too at the mention. "I don't like to go *near* that building. It's just wrong. And those two men who work there are always trying to run me off. If I didn't volunteer at the museum, I'd keep far, far away." He ate the last bit of his almond pastry.

Tere heard the click of a puzzle piece. "Wait, you volunteer at the museum?"

"Yes, six hours a week. I clean, do some gardening, repairs—"

Tere sat bolt upright. "Gardening? You work in Teresa's garden?" Her brain was spinning, the anger turning to adrenaline.

"Yes, sometimes."

"Juan, I might have a job for you. I'll pay you fifty euros for five minutes of your time."

He pulled back, the chair legs scraping across the tile floors. "No, señora, I—"

Tere was horrified to see a scared look on his face. "Oh my God, no! It's nothing illicit or illegal. Well, maybe slightly illegal, but that will be my part, not yours."

He was fidgeting, glancing at the door.

She felt bad for scaring him. "No, it's okay, you can totally say no."

He didn't look convinced, so Tere sat back and sighed. He deserved the truth. "Okay, here's the thing, Juan. I owe something to Santa Teresa. She is part of me, of who I am, more so than I ever realized. But I think it's time the church let her rest in peace. So…I'm leaving Spain soon, heading back to Vermont and a new job, but before I go, I want…" She stopped herself. "No, I *need* to do something." She looked at his big innocent eyes and just blurted it out: "I'm going to steal the finger and bury it in her garden." She rushed to add, "But I would need your help, just for a distraction and access."

His eyebrows almost touched his hairline, his mouth hanging open. It would have been comical in any other circumstance. But she could see things turning in his brilliant head. "I owe her as well. She changed my life, saved me from my own demons." He gathered the Santa Teresa medal around his neck. "Sometimes, when I see the way people treat one another, the way they treat her remains, for that matter…well, may God forgive me"—he did the sign of the cross—"but I feel as though we've lost sight of what she was trying to teach us."

"I absolutely agree."

He looked back at her, into her eyes, as if trying to learn the true motivation for her intentions. He seemed to find what he needed. He leaned in. "I will do this, for you and for her." He lifted the medal from around his neck and kissed it. "When?"

"What time is mass this afternoon?"

"Six."

"Meet me in front, next to the Saint Teresa statue, at six fifteen." Tere shoved a fifty-euro bill into his shirt pocket.

"No, señora! I want to do this with you, and you've already done so much—" He was reaching into his pocket, but she stopped him.

"Oh no, you don't." She shoved the bill back down. "You'll find

I'm as stubborn as she was." She pointed to the medal, now on the outside of his shirt. "She would want you to have it."

And with that, the deal was struck.

"It used to give me great joy to think of my soul as a garden, and of the Lord walking in it."

—Santa Teresa de Ávila,
The Life of Saint Teresa of Ávila by Herself

CHAPTER TWENTY-TWO

As Tere rushed back to the apartment to prepare, she felt different, like an internal light had been switched on. She had been fascinated to learn of the saint's visions of being pierced in the heart by a flaming golden arrow wielded by a seraph, as depicted in Bernini's sculpture. This wound was said to bring about a love of God, a purification. It was also said that when they'd pulled apart her body, there had been a hole in the center of her heart, proving her experience and confirming her saintliness, so they'd put her heart on display too. Tere had to admit that over the previous year, she'd also felt as though her heart were on display, especially when people ran into her at the drugstore and expressed their condolences or when she broke down in the vegetable aisle while trying to buy scallions. But her heart, unlike that of her namesake's, was not blessed with incorruptibility. Was this subversive act part of what Tere was there to do? Of why she had come to Ávila? The idea had hit her not unlike an arrow when she was talking to Juan, and in that instant, she'd known what she had to do.

Back at the apartment, she changed into black clothes, though she laughed at her theatrical inclination to dress like some kind of cat burglar. She pulled back her shoulder-length hair with a scrunchie, then rolled up her sleeves so she could wrestle through the garbage and the remnants of a previous night's dinner. Yeah, she sure wasn't smelling like roses either. Tere found what she needed about halfway down and carefully wrapped it in a paper towel. She rummaged through the utensil drawer of the Airbnb and was pleased to see a wooden meat hammer, which she shoved into her backpack. In truth, she was petrified. She was a rule follower, a team player, a law-abiding damn-near-elderly woman who lived in Vermont. This plan both thrilled and scared the living shit out of her, but she knew she would not turn back.

Lastly, Tere grabbed her helmet and borrowed bike, and when she got to the door, she looked back and around the lovely apartment, wondering if she'd be spending the night there or in a Spanish jail cell. With a shrug, she pulled her helmet on, and as she went to open the door, she caught sight of her reflection in the large mirror over the credenza in the front hall. She rarely looked in the mirror, as Tere was not a vain woman, but when she gazed at the person staring back, she didn't recognize her. Helmeted and sleek, she had tired eyes, but there was a fierceness she'd not seen there before. The badass who looked back was someone she would want to be friends with, someone she would admire, and that made her smile as she locked the door and headed out into the late afternoon.

The sun was beginning its descent, spreading golden light over the walls like honey. She mounted the bike and took off down the Paseo de Rastro, hugging the path along the southern side of the walls to avoid any cars that might come down, though there wasn't much traffic on that road. Since it was late afternoon, just after siesta, there were many people languidly walking. Her mind was spinning with the plans for what lay ahead, but she wasn't so distracted that she didn't notice how glorious the afternoon was. She wondered if it was always beautiful in Ávila. It seemed that way to her.

Tere climbed off the bike when she reached the gate that led to the church, and once she'd passed through the arch, she leaned the cycle against the inside of the city wall, just to the right of the entrance so it was easily accessible. It was a risk leaving it there without a lock, but she would need it after. It was to be, in fact, her escape vehicle. But she could always pay Rodrigo back if it were stolen. Once she got out of prison, that was. She left her helmet hanging off the handlebars and attempted to tidy her hair as she walked. She had to try and look unassuming, but she could feel her heartbeat behind her face, and her hands shook slightly. Tere Sánchez was adept at many things, but clearly, thievery wasn't one of them.

Juan sat right where they had agreed to meet, his head bowed as if in prayer while Teresa the statue sat next to him, looking up toward the heavens. He was indeed a person of light, Tere was certain of that. It practically shone out of his pores. She couldn't help but wonder if people had tried to tamp his light as well and if that was why he had turned to alcohol. She might never know, but one thing was certain: Whatever happened that night, there was no way she would let him get blamed. This was all her, and she would gladly own it.

Juan lifted his head, and when he smiled, Tere could have sworn that for just a second, his eyes were glowing. He stood when she walked up.

Tere smiled back and nodded, feeling a bit like Diana Rigg in *The Avengers*. "You still want to do this?"

His eyebrows lifted. "Honestly? I've been looking forward to it since we spoke at the café. I've been wanting to get those men back since they called the cops on me the first time."

Tere waggled her finger at him like she used to with Rowan. The two boys were close in age after all. "Now, Juan, I just need a distraction. Don't do anything that will get you in trouble."

"I think the American civil rights leader John Lewis might have called this 'good trouble,' no?" He smiled big. "How long do you need?"

"Nine, ten minutes?"

"Oh, that's easy."

A thought hit her like a slap. "Oh my God! Juan! What if they have cameras?"

"Cameras?"

She nodded. "Security cameras! God, I'm such an amateur!"

Juan laughed—guffawed, really. "Have you seen that place? I think they still use a rotary phone!" He was bent over now, wiping tears from his eyes. "I assure you, there are no cameras."

She pictured the handwritten signs, the dust everywhere. "Okay, okay. I had to ask. I might *seem* tough, but I'm not sure how I would handle doing time. Which is particularly ironic since I'm about to break and enter, huh?" She smiled and gave him a high five. "Thank you, m'ijo. Watch for when I've moved into the reliquary." And then she was off, walking briskly to execute the first plan she'd made for herself in a year. Rodrigo had asked what was next for Tere Sánchez. Well, clearly her answer was trespassing, theft, and sacrilege. And she was good with that.

The old men barely glanced at her as she entered the shop's open door, their eyes glued to a soccer game that was playing on an ancient small television in the corner. She took a cursory glance at the books, as she didn't want to look as though she were on a mission. They began to argue about something to do with a play, and Tere tried to appear nonchalant as she stepped into the reliquary.

Almost immediately there was a huge crash in the store.

She spun around to see the massive rack of Teresa-related post-cards on the floor, the contents cascading across the large tiles. She saw Juan standing in the doorway. He looked her way, gave her a secret wink, then yelled in at the men.

"Come and get me, viejos!"

Oh, that scamp! But the glee in his eyes confirmed he had indeed been wanting to do that for some time.

For two men in their seventies, they rounded those cases quickly, awkwardly jump-stepping over the fallen rack, yelling and shaking their fists at Juan. Tere giggled, thanked her new friend under her breath, then rushed toward the reliquary case.

She looked behind the glass box and saw a small padlock on the latch to the case. She took the meat hammer from her backpack and whacked it off in two swings, the mouth of the lock opening as it clattered onto the tile floor. It had been loud, but from the faraway sound of yelling, she knew the men were still outside. Gently, she pried the door open and peeked in. The scent of moldy fabric, stagnant air, and dust wafted out as she held the plexiglass door wide. She was relieved it didn't smell of roses or rotting flesh, as either would have freaked her right out. Tere pulled the paper-napkin-wrapped chicken thigh bone with its clinging remnants of skin carefully from her bag, then reached around and into the case. Her hands were shaking, and she almost knocked over a lock of Saint John of the Cross's hair but managed to not disturb it. She reached for her titi's finger and froze.

God, am I actually going to touch it?

Is *this desecration?*

She looked up at the ceiling as if asking for the saint's permission, then remembered the feeling she'd had when she touched the base of the statue in the square, when she'd looked at Teresa's garden, that feeling of lightness that came on just before she levitated. How the suggestion she travel to Ávila had popped into her mind as if planted there, the certainty she'd felt when she decided she would go. Meeting Juan, the Trinidadian nun with the rosary, Rodrigo, who'd introduced her to Timoteo. All the things that had fallen into place to bring her right there, right then.

Yes, Tere was going to do it.

In fact, she might be delusional, but she felt as if Santa Teresa had called her there in part to do this very thing.

She grabbed the digit, surprised at how light it was given the weight of meaning people had put on it, and half expected some sort of miraculous feeling to overcome her. Nothing—other than abject terror at the thought of getting caught. Tere switched the emerald-and-gold ring to the chicken bone and was just placing it on the stand when she heard yelling from the other room.

Shit! Shit! Shit!

She stood the bejeweled chicken bone up as best she could, pulled her arm out of the case, and quietly closed the door. She got on her knees, swiped the lock off the floor, and placed it back with its bent shackle.

When she pulled back and fully stood up, her back ached, and she had a moment of dizziness like she had been having for years. Probably because she half expected to find a horde of police and an army of priests waiting for her in the doorway. But as she heard a string of curses and the shuffling of paper, she knew the men were just concerned about the product all over the floor. She shoved the parcel into her backpack, looked into the front of the case, and shrugged. It was nowhere near perfect, but it was going to have to do. She did a cursory reshaping of her hair—God only knew if it was covered in dust from leaning into the case or crawling on the floor—dusted off her knees, and took a deep calming breath. She stepped over to the door and peeked around the corner. The two men were standing over the rack, one with his hands on his hips, the other pulling at his hair. They hadn't caught Juan. *Thank God.*

She coughed. "Is it okay to come out now?"

The men looked up with shock. They had clearly forgotten she was there.

Tere gave them a small embarrassed smile. "I was scared by that loud noise. Is it safe?"

Their looks quickly shifted to ones of aggravation. "Yes, yes, miss. You'd better go. That boy is crazy! Who knows what he'll do next!"

They barely looked at Tere, so she doubted they would be able to identify her. An advantage, she realized, to being a woman of a certain age and, therefore, as Yolanda had pointed out, "invisible." She tiptoed out, gingerly stepping over the rack as the two men argued in increasingly louder voices. After she slipped out the shop door, she ran around the corner of the church and toward the entrance to the museum. She didn't see Juan anywhere, but she figured that was a good thing, as he was supposed to be unlocking the door to the garden.

When she walked through the entrance and up to the information booth, Tere passed the two euros for her entrance fee through the hole in the glass. The woman looked up and smiled. "Ah, you're back again, señora!"

Shit! She recognized Tere. She cleared her throat. "Yes, I'm doing some research and needed to double-check something from my notes."

"Bueno, we're closing in about forty-five minutes, but it will take me a while to balance things out, so take your time. Let me know if I can help in any way." Then she went back to looking at the monitor on the desk.

Just then, Juan appeared from inside the museum. He ignored

Tere and shoved a large ring of keys through the hole in the glass, smiling at the woman. "I'm all done for the day, Nicole."

Nicole grinned. "That was quick, Juan."

"Yeah, I just wanted to trim a bit of the ivy on the south side of the garden. I was up top looking down and noticed it didn't look right. And I want everything to be perfect for our visitors."

"You're so good to take such care with the property." She was totally flirting with the handsome young man.

Tere was just standing there frozen when Juan waved his hand in a go-ahead gesture low enough so the museum attendant couldn't see it. Ah, he was distracting her—*good*. Tere gave him a low and secret thumbs-up.

She walked briskly down the first aisle. Her heart was racing out of control, and sweat was breaking out on her forehead, but she had to admit, she hadn't felt this alive in a year. She got to the end, where the garden was tucked, and stood right at the glass.

Glancing back toward the entrance, Tere heard the flirty laugh of the attendant and knew she wouldn't be paying attention to anyone other than her bright-eyed friend.

Tere stepped over to the side where she couldn't be seen from the museum, found the door unlocked as Juan had left it, and slipped through and into the garden. The minute she stepped onto the little walkway, the green smell hit her: freshly mown grass, trimmed ivy, and budding roses. The smell of roses was clearly meant to stay with Santa Titi. The sun was lower, so Tere was able to stay in the shadow of the stone wall. But as she looked back toward the glass, she knew that though the museum was empty and she could hear the mumble of mass up above, if anyone were to come into that little alcove in the church above and look down, they would see her for certain. She had to be quick.

She took the soup spoon from her bag, dropped to her knees (she was sure the creak and pop from the joints could have been heard through the layers of plexiglass), and dug a small hole at the edge of the garden. She began to whisper to Teresa as she dug.

"I'm sorry I can't bring you to the middle of your garden, Titi, but I'm already breaking who knows how many laws. It's so quiet here, it's quite lovely. If you can get past the people with their greasy noses pressed up to the glass for ten hours a day, that is. But the soil is dark and fertile, and the grass is lush, so I think this is what you would have wanted. It's what I want for you."

The small hole was dug, and Tere took the wrapped bones from her bag, then gently held them over the hole.

"I'm sorry you've been treated so disrespectfully, and I know there are parts of you all over the world, but I wanted at least this bit of you to find peace in the very land where you were born. It is far past time for us to let our beloved dead rest."

She gently placed the bones into the hole and looked at them nested in the dark soil.

"Far past time to let our beloved dead rest," she repeated.

She gently pushed the soil over the bones, patted it down, and then looked at the small patch of dirt. "Time for me to let Carl go too."

Voices rose from inside the building.

"Shit!" The mass had clearly ended, and people were sure to wander into the side chapel; Tere would be in view.

She yanked out a handful of grass and threw it in a makeshift cover over the disturbed earth. She stumbled to her feet, and as she was taking a step, she noticed a small bush in the corner, beyond the view of the glass window. She took a deep breath.

Peonies. Deep pink peonies.

Tere looked up into the indigo-blue evening sky and whispered, "Thank you."

Then she basically threw herself through the door, her backpack catching on the latch for a terrifying moment until she was able to free it with a tearing sound. She shoved the door closed, but with the movement, she ended up smashing against the other wall, hard, and lost her balance.

A hand caught her. Tere looked up into the eyes of a man, his light eyes concerned.

"Are you okay, señora?" He made sure she was solidly on her feet.

"Oh! Yes, sorry. I felt a little faint." She looked down the hall and saw Juan holding his hands out in an "I tried to stop him" gesture. She didn't think the man had seen her digging in the garden, and she surmised he probably was a tourist, as he spoke Spanish with a German accent.

He glanced down at her hand, which, she noticed, still clutched the spoon, a few grains of dirt still clinging to it. He looked back at her face, and she smiled.

"It's my blood sugar, you know. Just need to eat something." She smiled wider, stepped away, and slowly walked toward the exit. She looked back once and saw him shaking his head at his wife, probably lamenting the weirdness of Americans.

Tere shoved the spoon into her backpack and picked up her pace as she walked toward the entrance, where a new group of visitors poured in from the recently finished mass. Tere smiled at the young woman working at the entrance, though she was busy selling tickets and warning the new arrivals of the pending closing time. Tere was anxious to get lost in the crowd. As she walked around the corner and onto the plaza, she stopped in front of the statue of Santa Teresa de Ávila. As people wandered about, snapping photos and talking in low voices, she genuflected for the first time since arriving in Ávila, bowing her head to the saint.

Rest in peace, Titi.

Then Tere stood, turned, and headed across the plaza.

She couldn't have described the sheer joy that spread through her body—from the exhilaration of the subversive act, certainly, but also from the feeling of release that she felt for her long-dead relative, for Carl, and for herself. But Tere was still aware of sounds around her and was certain that at any moment, someone would call for her to stop as the whine of sirens filled the plaza. The Silver Fox was still leaning against the wall like a faithful steed, and she allowed herself to break into a run for the last few meters. Tere pulled her helmet on haphazardly and spun the bike around, smashing it against her leg in the process. She mounted the bike as she pushed off, then rode beneath the arch and out onto the paseo. She turned right, going away from her Airbnb and its sanctuary, but she felt a need to put distance between herself and the scene of the crime.

Scene of the crime.

She laughed out loud, her head thrown back in pure abandon.

A few blocks down, Tere noticed some cyclists coming off a trail to the east. *Perfect.* She waited for the traffic to clear, crossed the road, and waved to them as she passed.

By the time her front tire hit the trail, she was giddy. Other than occasionally speeding on the Vermont interstate and smoking a few joints before marijuana was legal, she'd never done anything that remotely approached breaking the law, and she didn't think she ever would again. But this? This was a high she'd never felt before. Though that didn't come from breaking the law.

It was about being set free.

Free from holding too tight to a career that no longer served her, to an image of herself that no longer fit, to…

To Carl

He wouldn't want her to hide from the rest of her life. They had both lived loudly and quintessentially themselves, and he had loved that about her. In addition to burying Teresa's bones in that garden, she'd also buried the remnants of the wounded person she had been. She had shed the chrysalis.

Tere lifted her head and caught the scent of pine and the marsh-mallow smell of the nearby fields of yellow broom flower that carried on the breeze. She could hear a woman's voice singing a madrigal in the distance, a recording that carried the reverent echo of a church performance. She started pedaling faster, wanting to travel deeper into the countryside, closer to the earth and trees and dusty hills. Whenever she was upset in Vermont or was struggling with some-thing, she liked to take off alone on the bike trail, pedaling into the woods as fast as she could, eager to put society far behind her.

She felt her muscles warm, the fire building in her thighs and calves, the wind blowing by her cheeks with a haunting whistle. Images of the hastily packed earth over Teresa's final resting place, of Juan's wink of communion, of the city viewed from the top of the walls, and most importantly, of her beloved Carl's smile, they all ran through her mind like she was flipping through the pages of a book, the book of her life, a book of which she was increasingly proud, the pages to come unwritten, now ready to be filled. Tere felt her smile widen, the tension of her shoulders released like seeds on a spring breeze. She was light, lighter than she'd ever been in her life, tears flow-ing sideways with her growing speed, a laugh building in her chest.

It was then that Tere's feet stuttered from the pedals, and she found she could no longer reach them, that her buttocks were lifting from the seat. She looked down as the bike began to recede beneath her; the only thing that connected them was her hands gripping the handlebars. The fast-moving bike was wobbling as her weight lifted, but she raised her head and watched the trees on either side rush by and realized she was flying. She wasn't afraid this time. All she had to do was let go, and she could lift above the earth, see the countryside of her ancestors from the air, from the heavens.

She let go and raised her arms to catch the wind…

"Now comes the distress of having to return to life. Now the soul has grown wings that can bear it, and has shed its weak feathers."

—Santa Teresa de Ávila,
The Life of Saint Teresa of Ávila by Herself

CHAPTER TWENTY-THREE

Tere surfaced to consciousness as if rising from deep underwater, sounds coming in gradually: beeping and intercoms and voices.

And pain.

Damn, why do I hurt all over?

She worked to open her eyes, though they were crusty and wished to stay closed.

Bright lights, blue walls, white sheets.

Tubes running from her arms.

The hospital.

A hospital.

No, no more hospitals.

She looked around the room, and by the window, she saw Rodrigo sleeping in a chair.

What the hell is going on?

Tere might have said it aloud, as Rodrigo stirred and looked over.

"You're awake! Thank God. We were getting worried."

"'We'? Why are you here?" She knew it was a rude question to start with, but it didn't seem to faze him.

He got to his feet and stood next to the bed. "They saw the name of my shop on the rental bike and called me."

"Oh! The Silver Fox, is it okay?"

He shook his head. "I'm sorry? The Silver Fox?"

"The bike!"

"That's what you're worried about?" He laughed. "Well, the frame is okay, but it's going to need some work. But like you, I think it'll survive. Anyway, I've been here since your surgery."

She sat bolt upright but hissed as the pain flared. "Surgery? For what?"

The doctor walked in then, right on cue. Black-haired, midthirties, but with tired bespectacled eyes, he was central casting's choice for "young Castilian doctor."

"Señora Sánchez. You're awake, excellent."

"It would seem so. What the hell is going on?"

A chortle. "Your son said you were fiery."

This is just getting more surreal. "My son? He's here?" Tere figured she was shouting by then.

"No, no. But since you weren't conscious, we needed your next of kin to give consent for the surgery."

She looked from Rodrigo to the doctor. "What. Surgery?"

The doc reached down and shifted her sickly green hospital gown to show a three-inch scar on the left side of her upper chest. "The electrical systems of your heart failed. Seems you have a second-degree AV block, called a Mobitz type-two block. Your physician in Vermont confirmed you'd had prior incidents of dizziness, but when he suggested a stress test a few months back, you never scheduled it."

"Yeah, I was...busy."

"Well, the hospital here is small, so I flew in from a conference in Madrid, as we had to give you a pacemaker." He gently put the edge of her gown down and stood back to look at her, clearly satisfied with his explanation. "Any questions?"

"Wait, you mean, you went in and pierced my heart to hook it to a pacemaker?"

"Well, put simply, yes."

Tere gaped at him, her mouth open for a moment, and then she started to laugh. Hard. She felt a tightening and pain at the incision, but she couldn't stop, holding her stomach as she looked from one man to the other. Rodrigo's look was more amused than anything, while the doctor's was more concerned.

When she finally stopped and could catch her breath, she said, "You're my seraph!"

He looked at her over his glasses. "I beg your pardon?"

"Santa Teresa—an angelic being pierced her heart with a flaming arrow?"

"I assure you, Señora Sánchez, your pacemaker was installed with transvenous implantation, not a flaming arrow, and I am no seraph."

And you have no sense of humor either, sadly. She wiped the tears from her eyes, sighed, and sat back. "I have a lot of questions, actually, but the first is what happened? Last I remember I was biking on a trail outside the city walls." She left out the lawbreaking, sacrilegious parts, though they were foremost in her mind.

Rodrigo answered, "They found you quite far from the bike. You must have been going very fast when you lost consciousness."

"Lost consciousness? No, I lifted off the bike." She looked from one to the other. "I levitated." She was surprised at how easy that slipped out, probably ill-advised and sedation induced, but it was done.

The two men caught each other's eye with a look. Then the doctor began scribbling on his clipboard, and Rodrigo simply tilted his head and looked at her with his kind eyes.

The doc finished whatever he was writing and looked up at her. "Actually, Señora Sánchez, one of the symptoms of such a heart block is dizziness and disorientation. So this 'illusion' can be easily explained by the disease."

There was so much about that sentence she didn't like—"disease," "illusion"—but she didn't bother to get angry. It was just not worth it. But she really detested being in the hospital, hated the antiseptic smell, the constant beeping from somewhere. "How long are you going to keep me here?"

"You sound as if I've imprisoned you instead of saved your life." His patience was clearly wearing thin.

"I'm sorry, Doc. I just…have a negative association with hospitals. I lost my husband a year ago."

His eyes softened. "That's totally understandable. We'll see how things look in the morning, but you should be released before lunch."

"Really? That quick?"

"It's a common surgery, very straightforward."

"Good, good." Then she thought of Rowan. He'd recently lost his father, and now this? "What about my son? When did you last talk with him? Does he know I'm all right?"

He looked at his watch. "About three hours ago, to let him know the surgery was successful. The earliest flight he could get to Madrid was late tonight, so with the nine-hour time difference, he should be arriving here in about—"

"Oh no, no, no, no! That is *so* not necessary! He needs to be told I'm fine." *Jesus Christ!* There was a good chance she might be arrested once she was released. There was no way she wanted to have that happen in front of her son. That was the kind of shit you would bring up in therapy for the rest of your life: *my mother, the international relic thief.* And that was if they didn't assume he was in on it.

"Señora Sánchez, you just had a major health crisis and surgery in another country, I think—"

"Honestly, Doc? I don't care what you think." She turned to Rodrigo. "Where's my phone?" She knew she was all kinds of rude that night, but she didn't care, and she figured having her heart fail, passing out, and getting emergency surgery entitled her to some leeway. She had to stop this; no way she wanted Rowan pulled into her mess.

Rodrigo pulled the phone from the night table drawer, and she saw the crack edged across the glass in a lightning strike. He shrugged. "I was surprised it still worked."

She pulled up her favorites and dialed Rowan. He answered on the first ring.

"Mom? Mom, are you okay?" His voice cracked, and Tere's newly plugged-in heart tinged. So weird—she could actually feel the pacemaker kick in.

"Yes, yes, sweetie. I'm fine." She watched the doctor and Rodrigo whispering together by the window.

"Oh, thank God! We've been so worried! I couldn't get a flight until tonight—"

"Honey, you really don't need to come. I'm fine."

"Yeah, no, Mom. You just had heart failure six thousand miles away! I'm coming."

She took a deep breath. "Rowan, I love you, I know you care about me deeply, but I really don't need you to come. You know I prefer to be left alone when I'm sick, and I know what a hassle it is with the kids and work. Honestly, it would only make me feel worse." She played the only card she could come up with, but it was the truth.

He sighed. "I'm really not comfortable with this."

"I know, but honestly, I just need to rest—" She looked toward the doctor, and he nodded. "The doc said so, and I'd rest better if I knew you weren't dropping everything to come and sit here to watch me sleep." She looked over at Rodrigo. "Besides, I have a friend here who can help me if needed."

"A friend? Who?"

Tere brushed him off. "A cycling friend. Look, I have a few more weeks at my Airbnb. It's the perfect atmosphere to recover, right?"

"I suppose so." Another sigh. "But I—"

"Oh, gotta go! The nurse is here to take my vitals. Love you! Bye!" She pressed End, looked over at the two men, and shrugged about the fictional nurse. The truth was, she was exhausted, and she needed her sleep to recover and to prepare for what might be to come.

The next day, Rodrigo drove Tere back to the Airbnb in his tiny environmentally responsible car, which, though she appreciated, was especially rough when it bumped over the cobblestones in the older parts of the city.

"Thank God they didn't fly me to Madrid or Barcelona," she said, wincing as they hit each stone. It wasn't the incision from the surgery that hurt, more whatever had happened when she'd hit the ground. She hadn't even properly assessed the bruises yet.

"They would have, but there was no time. It was very lucky that Doctor Betancourt happened to be in Madrid at a conference. They brought him here in a helicopter."

Tere groaned. She was grateful, but she couldn't begin to imagine how much this was going to cost. She had good insurance from the university, but a helicopter? She looked down at her fresh clothes and realized something she hadn't before. "How did you get my clothes from the apartment?"

"Yolanda let me in and helped me pick some out."

"Oh my God! Yolanda! I told her I was checking out early."

"Yes, well, when she heard what happened, she assumed your plans had changed again."

She was becoming aware of how many people she had put out. "Look, Rodrigo, I wanted to apologize yesterday, but it was just so crazy."

"Apologize, for what? I can repair the bike, don't—"

She put her hand up. "It's not about the bike. It's about Timoteo." Tere's throat tightened. "I—I really didn't go there intending to argue with him. It just got out of hand."

He grinned at her. "You guys fought?"

"Well, not really 'fought.' Argued, maybe? Well, actually, I just sort of yelled at him. He didn't tell you?"

"No, I don't think he would. What did you yell at him about?"

She sighed. "Oh, about how close-minded and misogynistic the church is and about letting the dead rest... I don't even know anymore. It doesn't matter. You were kind enough to arrange for me to talk with him, and I was afraid I would lose your friendship."

Rodrigo threw his head back and laughed. "Tere, do you have any idea how many family gatherings we've had where he got into a fight with someone or another? Sometimes the man can be an asshole." He looked over at her. "In no universe would your fighting with Timoteo affect our friendship."

"Well, shit. That's a relief."

They both laughed then, though Tere's ended in a groan. Her chest was so sore.

He looked over at her. "So, what does that thing feel like?"

"The pacemaker?"

He nodded.

"Really fucking weird, actually. You can feel the little machine right through the skin."

He chuddered.

"Exactly. It's amazing, God bless modern medicine and Doctor Betancourt, but it's just kind of creepy that it's wired into my heart."

"You know what's even creepier?" Rodrigo asked.

"What?"

"That you called the doctor your seraph!"

The two of them broke out laughing so hard that he had to pull the car over until he could see through the tears.

"Don't do that again, Rodrigo. Laughing that hard hurts my incision."

When they were a block away from the apartment, the traffic stopped. Not atypical in a city, but then she noticed the flashing red and blue lights bouncing off the surrounding buildings. The buildings around the small park right in front of *her* Airbnb.

Holy. Shit.

Tere's heart was giving the new pacemaker a hefty trial run. She just prayed the police were there for something else. For some*one* else. It wasn't that she wished ill on anyone, more that she was ten clicks beyond exhausted. It had been a challenging couple of days, and all she could think about was the comfy long couch in her rented living room and a hot cup of tea. Pretty much the opposite of a cold prison cell with a toilet right there in the room.

"When are they going to let us move?" she said more to herself than to Rodrigo as she gnawed on her short nails.

"I don't know." The line of cars inched forward, and now they could see a policeman directing traffic away from her street. Rodrigo stuck his head out the window and called to the officer, "Señor!"

Tere pulled on his sleeve. "No! Don't call him over!" she whispered, but the police officer appeared in the window with a tip of his cap. Tere slunk down farther into her seat.

"What's going on up ahead?"

"I don't actually know; I was just called to divert traffic. You're going to have to go that way, sir." He pointed with his gloved hand.

"Yes! Let's go that way! Let's do what he says!" Tere begged-whispered.

"No." Rodrigo indicated her. "She just got out of the hospital, and her Airbnb is right up there. She can't really walk very far."

The policeman's eyes locked on hers.

She gave him a tight grin and a little wave, the hospital bracelet crinkling on her wrist. He was still staring at her. *This is it!* she thought. *He knows.* She was certain she was going to the hoosegow.

Finally, the officer nodded at her, pulled a whistle from his pocket, and blew. Hard.

The sound cut through Tere like a knife. "Stop that!" she yelled at him. "Why is he doing that?" she groaned to no one in particular.

Their policeman started yelling to several others who were standing at the corner of the street with her apartment on it.

Lord help me. I'll come quietly, for God's sake. Just let me have a nap once I get to my cell.

"Let them pass through! Medical emergency!" he yelled, and the other man gestured for the car to move through.

As they reached the other officers, Rodrigo leaned out his window and asked what was going on, yet again. *Must he talk to every policeman in the city?* Tere lamented.

One of them said, "Allegedly, a car hit a pedestrian right near the church. They're trying to establish the details. But you can go ahead."

Tere let out a long breath and slumped down even farther into the seat. She wasn't sure her poor robot heart could handle much more anxiety.

"To reach something good, it is useful to have gone astray."

—Santa Teresa de Ávila

CHAPTER TWENTY-FOUR

Rodrigo pulled the tiny car to a stop in front of the apartment building, put on the blinkers, and rushed around to help Tere out of the passenger seat. She was going to wave him off, as she was not overly fond of being dependent, but in truth, she hurt all over and really needed the assist.

Being on the second floor, she hadn't used the elevator in the building since she arrived, but she was grateful for it that day. Rodrigo helped her down the hall, unlocked the apartment door, and guided her in, straight to the overstuffed couch. She fell into it and let out a huge sigh. "Thank God." Just the short trip from the hospital had exhausted her, not to mention the plethora of police out front making her certain she was going to prison and/or hell. Actually, she figured the odds she was going to the latter had increased exponentially over the past few days.

Rodrigo started opening the wooden shutters, letting in the morning sun that had just cleared the oak trees in the park. Then he set about to make her a cup of tea. The police radios would blare out now and again, and though she would jump, the scare didn't last long, and Tere could still hear the birds, yet they were positively hushed compared to how they were at sunset.

He placed a cup of steaming herbal tea on the coffee table, the citrusy scent of rooibos reaching for Tere like an olfactory hug. Rodrigo also brought a throw blanket, carefully placing it on the couch next to her. "Are you hungry? Yolanda stocked your fridge with tons of groceries, drinks and—"

She put her hand on his arm. "I really do appreciate all you've done, Rodrigo. And Yolanda."

He looked at her for a moment, as if wondering whether to say whatever was on his mind. "May I ask something, Tere?"

"Why does that question make me nervous?" she joked. Kind of.

"Why didn't you want your son to come? I would imagine you would want those closest to you nearby in a situation such as this."

She might have blurted it out about the levitation in front of him, but there was no way she would talk about the theft. So she went with a partial truth. "He went through a lot when my husband died. We both did. And he's a sensitive soul, deep feeling, though he does his best to hide it. Why drag him across the world to nursemaid me? Besides, I've always healed better when left alone. Like the time I had dengue while visiting my family in Puerto Rico. All those old ladies were buzzing and circling around like gnats when I just wanted to sleep and read."

He dropped into the armchair across from the couch.

Watching him, Tere had to admit he was very handsome indeed.

"I understand that. When I broke my leg, my—"

Rodrigo didn't get to finish; there was a weird buzzing sound in the hallway.

"What the hell is that?" Tere asked, starting to get up from her seat.

He gently touched her shoulder and urged her back down. "I'll get it." Rodrigo walked into the foyer and out of sight. "It's the phone intercom. It has a camera that shows the door." He bent into the room so she could see only his upper body. "It's two men."

She bolted upright. "Are they in uniforms?"

"What?" Then there was a buzzing sound, and she jumped to her feet with a wince. "What are you doing?"

She dropped back down.

"I'm letting them in," Rodrigo called from the apartment door.

"What? Why on earth would you do that?" The door opened, and she heard men's voices coming from the entry foyer to the apartment.

Rowan. Fucking kid never did listen to her. And the other voice… *Oh no.* Tere froze when she realized who it was. "Jesus Christ, is that—?"

Rowan turned the corner, smiling at her, followed by Richard, who strode in, rushing by Rodrigo. His eyes fell on Tere and softened, though the whole thing seemed a bit theatrical to Tere. Rowan sat down next to her, throwing his six-one 220-pound frame on the couch like he was still twelve. The shift of the cushions under his sudden weight threw her a bit to the side, and she winced. Then he pulled her into a bear hug. "Mom. I'm so glad you're okay."

She breathed in his scent of bay rum cologne and laundry detergent and closed her eyes, surprised by the tears. "Me too, honey." She pushed him to arm's length so she could look at him. "But I told you that you didn't need to come!"

He dismissed this with a wave. "Psh, when have I ever done what you told me?"

"Exactly." She looked over at Richard, who was still staring at her with softened eyes. "And Richard. What are you doing here?"

He huffed. "Well, Rowan called me, and I didn't think he should be traveling alone—"

"I'm thirty-two years old," her son said incredulously.

Richard ignored him. "Besides, I'm fluent in Spanish—" His eyes fell on Rodrigo as if he'd just appeared there and hadn't just let him in. "Who is this?" he asked.

She looked around at this trio of men and sighed. *I love these guys, but I just want a nap.*

Rodrigo stood up and reached his hand out to Richard. "I tried to introduce myself at the door, but you didn't give me the chance. I'm Rodrigo Romero." He shook Rowan's hand first; they smiled warmly at each other, though warily. Richard went next, and Tere could see them gripping each other's hand like it was some kind of contest.

"Mucho gusto, Rodrigo," Richard offered in his careful Spanish. "How do you two know each other?" He gestured between them with that look on his face that he got when interrogating a PhD candidate who was defending their thesis. Or when he was dissecting an overcooked piece of steak.

"We're friends. He owns the cycling shop," Tere said from the couch, holding her head to keep her brain from bursting out her ears. Rowan was just watching them with an amused expression on his face.

The buzzing sound happened again.

"What the actual fuck?" Tere exclaimed, as Rodrigo walked back to the intercom.

He bent back into the room. "It's Juan and a nun."

Tere threw her hands up. "It's a damn circus." *Or a tribunal.* If Juan was there, that had to mean they had caught him, and he had given her up. She didn't blame him one bit; it was her idea after all, and she was actually somewhat relieved. She'd happily fess up if only she could take a short nap first. "Wait, how do you know Juan?" Tere called to Rodrigo.

"I'm letting them in," Rodrigo called from the apartment door.

"What? Why?" The nun was there because she knew. She had

been brought there, was probably the prioress of the convent or something. The idea of being confronted by a nun was scarier to Tere than the possibility of arrest and imprisonment, not to mention it happening in front of her son and overly dramatic colleague. She was in hell, she was certain.

"You? Have nuns visiting?" Richard laughed uproariously. "Who are you, and what have you done with Tere?" He actually slapped his thigh, and Tere wondered how much time murder would add to her sentence.

Rodrigo came back into the living room and shrugged at her. "You can't refuse entry to a nun."

She glared at him. "What, is that a line in the Bible or something?"

The door opened. Then there was a shuffling and rustling of fabric, and to Tere's relief, Sister Isabella, her nun cousin, whooshed into the room with Juan trailing right behind. Rodrigo and Juan did a fist bump, and everyone, the entire group of people crowded around in the living room, looked at Tere.

She cleared her throat. "Sister Isabella, not that I'm not pleased to see you, but what are you doing here?" she asked with way more politeness than she had used with the last few people.

"Why, to check on you, dear, of course." Isabella bustled over on her orthopedic shoes, the swaying brown habit brushing the edge of the coffee table. "When Juan told me you were hospitalized, I had to come." She looked over at Rowan and gasped. "Lord bless me. Is this your son, Tere?"

Rowan stood up like the polite boy he always was.

Tere gave up fighting it. "Yes. Isabella, this is my son, Rowan. Rowan, this is our cousin Sister Isabella."

The nun's hands went to her face, her eyes watery. "You are the spitting image of your abuelo! Your grandfather Jorge."

"Really?" Rowan seemed so pleased.

Then she pulled him into a big hug, grabbed a chunk of his cheek, and twisted, making cooing sounds like he was an infant. Tere felt some satisfaction at her kid having to endure that Puerto Rican old-lady ritual. She'd had enough of it for a lifetime.

When Isabella turned away to sit on Tere's other side, Rowan looked at her, put his hand to his cheek, and mouthed, "*Ouch!*"

Isabella sat down, looked up, and said, "Rodrigo, nice to see you, joven."

Tere was incredulous. "You know him too?"

"Seguro! It's a small city. How are you feeling, dear?" She put her hand on Tere's forehead, as if her heart failure were a fever that could be felt by touch. But when Tere closed her eyes and felt the nun's dry, cool hand on her skin, something lifted inside her, that feeling of being outside time and a sensation of well-being came over her. When she felt the hand taken away, she opened her eyes and looked gratefully into her cousin's smiling face. "I'm really okay, Prima."

Isabella winked at Tere. "I know you are, dear." She turned her body and indicated Juan, who was wringing his hands in nervousness, the poor thing. Tere was so sorry for dragging him into this. "That's why Juan and I are here. He—"

A banging knock sounded at the door. Aggressive and loud, like "open up, it's the police" type of aggressive. *Great.* She was going to be arrested in front of her son, her nun relative, and half the city of Ávila.

Rodrigo went to open the door once more.

In bustled Señor Avellaneda González Diaz with Sancho perched in his arms—Tere could tell by the man's jerky movements that he was all in a tizzy—followed by Yolanda, who pushed past the old man and came to stand at the side of the couch, reaching for Tere's hand.

"Amiga, how are you? What's going on?"

"Nothing, other than an unplanned visit from every single human I know in this country"—she looked to her left—"countries, plural, actually. Why?"

"I was worried something else had happened to you!"

"What? Why?"

"The Don over here." She gestured toward Avellaneda González Diaz with disgust. "He insisted I come immediately, that there was some brouhaha going on in your apartment, and I got worried."

The old man pushed forward. "Señora Sánchez, I must speak to you and Señora Cruz. I know what's on the rental agreement you signed, as it had to be run by the co-op board, and it clearly indicates that an unreasonable number of visitors is prohibited, and I must object to all this…activity!" He was waving the arm that was not busy cradling the scruffy dog (who was looking at her with his lifted lip and judgmental cloudy eyes). The old man looked at Tere. "Now, I understand that there are extenuating circumstances. However, you left me no alternative but to call Señora Cruz—"

Richard bustled forward, putting his hand on the old man's shoulder. "There really is no need for distress, señor. From here on out, her son, Rowan, and I will be taking care of Señora Sánchez—"

Tere gaped at him, certain she'd fallen into one of the alternative universes from Esmé's books.

Rodrigo stepped forward. "You know, I think that's up to Tere, Richard—"

Tere inhaled deeply and…

"Everybody out!" she yelled louder than she ever had, even louder than when she'd found Rowan carving his name into the gleaming surface of her mother's Herman Miller china cabinet.

Seven sets of eyes—eight, if you included Sancho—stared at her.

"What are you looking at? You heard me! My heart failed, they plugged it in like a goddamn iPhone, and I don't need this shit! Everybody out, except the nun and Juan!"

The four grown-ass men (five, if you counted Sancho) gawked at her, but after a pause, Yolanda stood, clapped her hands, and announced, "You heard the lady! Let's go to Barbacana and get a café con leche and let them talk, okay?" She started shooing them out.

Rowan watched it all, stood, and smiled down at his mother.

"What are you grinning about? It's bedlam."

"Ma, I have a two-year-old and a four-year-old at home. This isn't bedlam. This is entertainment."

"I'm so glad you're entertained."

He leaned over, kissed her cheek, and said, "I'll be back to check on you in an hour. Call me if you need anything." Then he grabbed Richard by the sleeve and dragged him along.

Just before the door closed, Tere heard Rodrigo call out, "Richard's buying."

Tere closed her eyes and let out a long breath, grateful for the silence. "That's so much better." After a few deep breaths, she opened them. "Okay. Have a seat, you two, and tell me what you came to say."

Juan perched on the end of the chair Rodrigo had vacated, and Isabella cleared her throat, then began. "Well, Juan is staying not far from the trail where you had your 'accident.' He seemed to know you, and I—"

He burst in. "Señora, I was not far behind you before your accident"—he gave Tere a look that told her he had not said anything about their arrangement—"and, well, Sister Isabella had mentioned she had a cousin in town from Vermont, so I put two and two together, then went to find her after they took you away since she's your family."

Isabella continued. "Yes, and on the way over here, he shared an incredible story with me." She patted Tere's leg. "He saw something I think you should hear about."

The words burst out of him, like he'd been holding them back and they were desperate to escape. "I saw you, señora, on your bicycle."

Tere's breath caught a bit. "Before the accident?"

"I saw you...floating, above the bicycle."

She gasped and put her hand over her mouth, her vision blurring. "Y-you...saw?"

He nodded. "I did. And when you let go of the handlebars, your body suddenly slumped."

Sister Isabella interjected. "We think that's when you passed out. Your heart rate went so low during the ecstasy, you lost consciousness."

Juan scooted even farther to the edge of the chair. "I've never seen anything like it! If you'd stayed awake, I think you would have flown!" His voice was animated, and his face was even more alive than it had been before. "You really are related to Santa Teresa."

Tere started crying then as the three of them looked at one another, alternately laughing and crying and laughing again. There was a witness, an actual flesh-and-blood witness. And he believed her! She hadn't thought she was crazy, but during the previous week, she had felt as though she were careening down a hill with no brakes and no sense of where she was going. In that moment things felt less out of control. She bowed her head a bit and said, "Thank you for telling me, Juan. Thank you for everything."

He nodded in response, but she didn't think he could possibly understand how much his eyewitness account meant to her. Juan had given her external verification that she was not losing her mind or hallucinating, that she really was levitating, that her period of great change had perhaps reached its zenith.

Sister Isabella smiled her evolved smile, patted both their hands, and stood with a groan. "Bueno. Well, young man, our work here is done. Let's go to Barbacana and get that Richard fellow to buy us some lunch."

Tere stood too and pulled the nun into a fierce hug, the wafting scent of lavender and bleach filling her head with feelings of home and family.

When they pulled apart, Isabella smiled at Tere, then grabbed a big chunk of her cheek and squeezed. It hurt as much as it had when she was a child but meant so much more.

Tere gave Juan a big hug too. "You're a good friend, Juan. Thank you," she whispered.

When she pulled back, he gave her a shy smile and said, "It's an honor to be your friend." Then he jumped a little. "Oh! I almost forgot!" He pulled a crumpled piece of paper from his pocket, then held it up with a huge grin. "I got in!"

"Ahhh!" She screamed and clapped and jumped like she was five, until the pain reminded her she wasn't. "I knew you would, Juan! Your application was excellent."

He shook his head. "I couldn't have done it without your help."

Tere put her palm on his cheek, like she used to with Rowan. "Congratulations, m'ijo. I know you have a bright future. And I got as much out of that as you did." She paused for a second. "Actually, that gives me an idea. Maybe I could help people like you prepare for their college applications."

"Really? We were meant to meet, señora."

Tere smiled. "Oh, we were, Juan. We absolutely were."

Isabella put her arm through the boy's then. "Okay, let's let the poor woman rest, hmm?"

She didn't walk them to the door; she didn't think anyone

expected her to. Instead she just dropped back onto the couch with a moan. She had a lot to think about, but first she was finally going to get that nap.

Just then, Sister Isabella shuffled back around the corner and said, "Oh dear, I forgot to ask. There are some wild theories around the Santa Teresa Church that the relic was replaced with a fake."

Tere froze.

"You wouldn't know anything about that, would you?"

A pause.

A wink.

Then she was gone, the door quietly closing behind her.

Tere lay down on the couch then, happy not to be trapped in a cell, and very happy that she had so many people to love.

"Remember: if you want to make progress on the path and ascend to the places you have longed for, the important thing is not to think much but to love much, and so to do whatever best awakens you to love."

—Santa Teresa de Ávila,
Interior Castle

CHAPTER TWENTY-FIVE

The next few days after Tere's surgery were blissfully quiet. Richard stayed at a nearby hotel and spent much of his day visiting museums and doing research. Rowan slept on the couch and was really good at giving Tere her space, knowing when to offer her food or drink and when to leave her alone. While she slept, he too wandered around the city at her urging.

One night, around two in the morning, Tere tossed in her sleep. She rolled over on her back and started to nod off again...

Her eyes flew open, the stucco stalactites of the ceiling were pushing into her cheeks, the light fixture digging into her hip. But instead of being frightened, she started to laugh...

"Mom!" A voice broke through her fog. "Mom! You okay?"

She opened her eyes again and saw Rowan standing over her, his hair disheveled, his face concerned. "What—what happened?"

"You were laughing in your sleep."

Tere ran her hands over her face. "I was? I—I thought I was..." She looked around, but the book lay open next to her where she'd put it as she began to fall sleep, the covers still tucked tight around her body. "I thought..." It had been a dream this time. Taking Rowan's hand, she said, "I'm fine, honey. Just a dream."

He kissed her forehead. "Okay, Ma. If you need anything, I'm in the next room."

She smiled at him as he left. Funny how their roles had switched. She was grateful he was there. But as she rolled over, she was mostly grateful to be lying in bed and not hovering beneath the ceiling.

———————

The next afternoon, she felt strong enough to get out of the house, so she took Rowan up on his offer of a walk. It was sunny and warm but with a cool breeze, crowned by that impossibly blue sky.

"You good?" Rowan asked, seeing her walking with her eyes closed.

"Hmm, yes." She looked over at him. "I just love it here."

"I do too."

"Really? That makes me so happy! Our family has deep roots here."

"I know! And the history is crazy. Makes me realize how new the U.S. really is. I mean, the forts in Puerto Rico are cool, but nothing like this." He pointed at the walls as they walked up to them. "Titi Isabella invited me to come back with Angela and the kids."

She stopped short. "What?"

"Yeah. Seems she owns a property not far from the city. I get the feeling it's quite posh."

"Hold the phone. First of all, 'Titi'?"

He laughed and pulled Tere along gently to get her to start walking again. "Yeah, given our age difference, she thought having me call her 'Cousin' was weird. She's really cool, actually."

Tere just couldn't wrap her mind around this. Not only was her son hanging out with the taciturn old nun, but she had invited him back with his wife and children. Would wonders never cease?

"Hey, have you had the yemas at this place? They're so good!" He pointed toward Granier.

"Ewww! I hate those things! They're balls of egg yolk rolled in sugar. You like them?"

"Hell yes!"

"Well, let's sit. I'll have a churro and a café con leche. You managed to find my favorite bakery."

"Oh, I can sniff them out. I think I've tried them all by now."

She couldn't even process how happy this made her, that her son appreciated the magic of their ancestral city. They sat at an outside table, enjoying their coffees and treats. The sun had gone behind the buildings, so it was starting to get a little chilly. People moved inside until Rowan and Tere were the only ones sitting at the iron tables out front.

Rowan looked around at the medieval buildings framing them on either side. "It's an incredible city, and I get how it's important to our family, but I still can't figure out why you took the urgent trip. Did you really come here to do research?"

Tere put out a finger, buying time under the pretense of chewing her pastry. She would not lie to her son, but she'd also do anything to protect him. But he already thought her somewhat dotty, so the full truth might damage their relationship. She took a sip of her coffee, then sat back into the chair. "I actually did come to do research, of a certain kind. Not for work but for myself. I don't know, Rowan. So much has changed for me over the past year."

"I hear that. Losing Dad felt like...I don't know, losing a limb or something. Ang has more experience with loss in her family. She says it's like a hole dug in the sand. In time the tide comes in and slowly refills it with sand and water, until it's whole again." He runs his finger across the carved iron of the table, sadness weighing down his eyes. "But I can't imagine the hole Dad left ever being completely filled."

"Everyone grieves differently, but I know what you mean. That's really why I came here. My grief over losing your father stopped me short. Almost as if, deep down, I believed that if I froze everything, it could stay the way it was, I could keep him with me. Sadly it doesn't work that way. Coming here has been part of how I broke free of that. It's time for me to move on."

"What do you think that will look like for you?"

Tere stared at her son. It always amazed her that her wild little boy had become such a thoughtful and intuitive man. "I'm not sure yet, but I have found a lot of clarity in this old city."

He let out a long breath. "Yeah, me too." He looked into her eyes. "I'd like to come out and see you in Vermont more regularly, by myself sometimes. I've really enjoyed spending this time with you. I mean, despite the heart failure and all."

She put her hand on his. "I've enjoyed it too, honey. I really appreciate you coming and taking care of me. And yes, the circumstances were dramatic, but I'm not sorry it happened. Sometimes you need a poke in the heart with a flaming arrow to truly wake up."

The impish one-sided grin he'd gotten from Carl appeared on his face. "Like Saint Teresa?"

She smiled back. "Kind of." Tere picked up her coffee and added mischievously, "We have more in common than you'd think."

"I'm getting that sense. Like levitating?"

Tere spit a mouthful of coffee across the table. Once she'd wiped her mouth and gathered herself together, she said, "What?"

"Titi told me."

She sputtered and coughed, unable to say anything.

He looked at her with his Sánchez hazel eyes and Carl's dark eyelashes. "It's okay, Ma. It's better than okay. It's about the most badass thing I've ever heard."

Her eyes filled. "You believe it?"

He threw his hands up, "Of course I do! Are you kidding?"

"I…I can't tell you how much that means to me, Rowan." The tears were spilling now, and she grabbed his hand.

"Mom, the only thing that got me through the year since Dad's death has been the time Ang and I have spent at the meditation center in the Bay Area. I was having trouble dealing, and it really helped. And they talk about Saint Teresa and her ecstasies all the time." He looked over at her. "I can't believe you never told me we were descended from her family. I would have come here years ago."

She sighed. "I don't know why I didn't, Rowan. Honestly, I pretty much forgot about it until this whole levitating thing started happening."

His eyes got all dreamy as he asked, "What's it like?"

"Hard to describe. And it took me a while not to be afraid of it. It's like all the things life puts on you, all the things that weigh you down, release, all at once. You're untethered, literally, and this intense feeling of well-being comes over you. Like…like you're in love with the world."

"That sounds awesome. Why do you think they started happening?"

"Isabella told me they happen at periods of great change in a person's life. I certainly had that, as we were discussing, but I actually think in my case, it was to propel me forward, to grow." She twirled her coffee cup on its saucer. "There's no bigger change we can make as humans, after all. But I'm pretty sure I won't be levitating anymore."

"Really? Why? Because of the surgery?"

"No." In her mind she pictured the patted-down dirt of the

peonies Carl had planted for her, of the resting place of Teresa's bones. "No, maybe because I finally let go…inside. That's what I think anyway. Who can know for sure about such things?" She patted his hand. "Hey, you want to go visit Teresa's garden with me?"

He downed the rest of his coffee, stood, and held his arm out for her to take. "Yeah. I went there the other day. It's really nice." They started walking, going slow, appreciating the cooling air. "But I have to say, the reliquary was a disappointment. That finger looks like a fucking chicken bone!"

The next afternoon, at Richard's urging, Tere called the dean of the university. He hadn't told Hammerston anything about her heart problems, as he was afraid it would deter them from hiring her. Of course, that would be illegal, but they would find another excuse for not giving her the job if they knew. It didn't matter because she hadn't told Richard what her answer was going to be.

"Good morning, Dr. Hammerston. It's Tere Sánchez."

"Ah! Terry, good to hear from you." He never could pronounce her name correctly, not even after dozens of years of working together, let alone call her "Doctor" in return. "I assume you're calling about the chair position of your department?"

She could picture him leaning his doughy body back in his leather chair, surrounded by his dark and imposing wood furniture, the books on his shelves not touched for dozens of years and regularly dusted by the cleaning crew whose names he didn't know. "Yes, actually. I'm—"

"Excellent. Well, I'm not surprised by your acceptance, I know you've been interested in the position for several years now."

"Fifteen, actually."

"I'm sure you understand the weight of the responsibility of running the entire English department. And that our hiring of the first woman chair in the history of the department represents our continued commitment to diversity, equity, and inclusion, so all eyes will be on you. And I think I remember hearing you're Hispanic as well, yes?"

"Um, yes. I'm Puerto Rican. If you had read any of my publications or attended even one of my lectures, you would know that."

He wasn't even listening. "Good, good. Well, we're hoping you'll be an active member of the university leadership team. I know—"

"Actually, Dean Hammerston, I'm calling to turn down the position."

He blustered, "What? Why on earth would you do that?"

"Because over this past year, I've shifted my priorities, realized what is actually important and what isn't, and I'm happy to say I'm no longer interested in participating in the crabs-in-a-bucket atmosphere you foster among your faculty. So thanks for finally offering me the position I've been overqualified for, and passed over for, for so many years, but I am officially declining."

He was still scoffing and backfiring like an old car when she pressed End. She put the phone down on the coffee table, lay back, and smiled big.

"Damn, that felt good." She'd tell Richard she'd turned it down at dinner. He wouldn't understand, and part of her still didn't, but she didn't need anyone else's approval.

"It is quite important to withdraw from all unnecessary cares and business, as far as compatible with the duties of one's state of life, in order to enter the second mansion."

—Santa Teresa de Ávila,
Interior Castle

CHAPTER TWENTY-SIX

The next ten days were gloriously quiet. Other than a few follow-up doctor visits, she lay around, read, and took daily walks with Rowan. Sometimes Richard would join them, though he would talk continuously, lecturing about whatever fountain or monument they happened to be passing. Rodrigo and Yolanda both visited often, bringing food and their lovely company. Juan had gotten a job but still came every other afternoon to make all three of them coffee and talk about life. Despite the language barrier, he and Rowan got along well, and she was pleased to see her son had a natural affinity for picking up Spanish (she was especially pleased to hear the Puerto Rican lilt when he did). Juan had even reached out to his mother. He thought he'd been witness to a miracle when Tere had levitated, and it had changed him. She didn't have the heart to tell him she didn't think it qualified under the category of miraculous. In truth, she felt Juan was the miracle.

In between time with family, both blood and found, she slept a lot. She had many dreams of Santa Teresa. In the most recent one, they were strolling around a large garden, arm in arm, the sun painting the grass with deep-honey light, the pathway stones glistening from a recent rain. The roughly woven brown wool of the saint's robe rubbed noisily against the silk of Tere's blouse, the comforting sound following their unhurried footfalls in a hypnotizing rhythm. They talked leisurely, as if they had all the time in the world, about family, life, even God. These dreams were so vivid that when Tere awoke, the licorice scent from the bright yellow fennel flowers, which spread out from beyond the garden wall, still hung in the air. Were they dreams or what the saint had called "visions"? Or perhaps they were simply a hangover from the sedatives after the surgery. Whatever they were, the dreams brought her peace and an affirmation that she was going in the right direction.

A few days before their departure, while Rowan was buying souvenirs for Ang and the kids, Tere took the opportunity to take her first solo walking sojourn back to the spot formerly known as "the scene of the crime." The weather had grown quite a bit warmer since she had arrived, and she enjoyed being in the sun as she walked the quiet midday streets. This time, when she passed through the hushed church, she paused and admired the stained glass depictions of Teresa that lined the walls, kneeled before the statue of her namesake, and lit an electric candle for Carl. She didn't want to look at the garden through glass, though, so she went back outside and peered over the stone wall that encircled the two stories like their larger counterparts did to the city.

She leaned her arms on the stones and gazed down on the neat small patch of green, the sun lighting the far corner of the garden, making the peonies glow. Tere couldn't even identify where she had dug. Juan had told her he'd gone back the next morning, when she was in the hospital, and added more grass, blending it in with the rest. He had done a beautiful job, and she was surprised at how there could be no trace of something that, for her, had been so monumental. She had buried so much into that small hole in the corner of a garden in this tiny city in Spain. That it was as if nothing had happened was surprising yet also comforting.

The night before she and Rowan were to fly out, Juan brought over Cousin Isabella, who gifted Tere a box of yemas for the flight home. Tere smiled politely, not having the heart to tell her that she detested the things. Besides, Rowan would finish the box that night, she was sure. The three of them walked to the plaza, and Juan went to the café to let them talk. When Tere glanced in a few minutes later, he was deep in conversation with Nicole, a lovely young barista who worked there. She had to smile.

Tere and her cousin settled in on one of the cast-iron and wood benches in the square.

Isabella patted her hand. "So, how are you feeling, dear?"

"Really good, actually. I get some twinges in the incision spot once in a while. Plus, the whole idea of foreign objects sewn into my body is creepy."

"Eh, you get used to it. Hips, knees—none of mine are original anymore."

"Well, between your joints and my robot heart, we have a full Sánchez cyborg." They laughed. "Thank you for spending time with Rowan and inviting him back."

Isabella gave her a dismissive wave. "No need to thank me. That boy is just delightful. You and Carl did a good job."

"I think half of it is luck of the draw, the other half genes. Of course, I was a bit surprised you told him about the levitating."

"He is way more evolved than the average person, Tere."

"I'm learning that." She was in no way objective, having raised him for thirty-two years, but it was interesting to see him through someone else's eyes. "And he's pretty taken with Spain. He wants me to come back with him and do the Camino Teresiano, get in touch with Santa Teresa by walking from her cradle to grave, her birthplace to where she died."

"Ha! Six days of walking in the hot sun? Better you than me, m'ija."

"Well, I have a few months of recovery ahead of me, but I think I'll do it after."

The sun was setting on the other side of the walls, and the sky was that bright deep blue Tere loved so much. They sat for a while in companionable silence, taking in the early evening air, kids running in zigzag across the plaza, old men playing card games with the baraja española, the Spanish deck. Tere inhaled deeply. "I'm going to miss this place."

Isabella patted her hand. "You'll be back often. I've seen it."

Tere whipped around to look at her cousin. "Wait, you've 'seen it'? What does that mean?"

"Oh, look! Let's get some roasted peanuts." Isabella stood, shuffled her way over to the cart, and ordered a bag.

"Oh no, you don't—don't change the subject," Tere yelled after her.

Isabella pushed the change back at the vendor and thanked him. After she was sitting again, sharing the piping-hot nuts, the nun finally answered. "Sometimes I see things, visions of things that haven't happened yet."

Tere stared at her. "Are you serious?" she whispered.

Isabella leaned over and said very quietly, looking around them, "Yes. I don't like to speak about it because when it first started happening, a few people started to figure out what I could do and sought to exploit it."

"Jesus." Tere tried to process this.

The nun chuckled. "Worst of all was your friend Sister Inés. She likes to bet on the ponies."

"That doesn't surprise me one bit." Tere looked over at her cousin. "Is that why you were so hard to find?"

"It's best that way. Besides, I don't like people as much as I used to."

Tere laughed. "Oh, I get that!"

"When do you start the new job?"

"I didn't take it. At first, I was scared to walk away from it, but it started to feel like going backward to me."

"Good. I was worried about you taking on a big new job right after a health scare."

"I know I could have done it; I just no longer want to."

"I can imagine that Richard fellow didn't understand that choice."

"Ha! No, no, he didn't."

"Is that why he left early?"

"Nah, he got some call from the university, some 'crisis' he had to go back and deal with. So meaningless."

"Is he your boyfriend?"

"Ewww!" Tere pulled back in disgust like a teenager. "No! We're just friends."

"Thank God. What a pompous ass."

Tere snorted.

"What about Rodrigo? Such a good man. Or that lovely Yolanda, perhaps?"

"No, all just friends. Honestly, a romantic entanglement is the last thing on my mind. I just had the most profound year and three weeks of my life. I think I need to work on myself for a while, clichéd as it might sound."

"Ah, but clichés are clichés because they are universal truths, no?"

Tere looked at Isabella. "Yeah, they are." The woman never ceased to amaze her.

"Well, m'ija. I should gather Juan from his adoring fans and head back to the convent, but first I wanted to ask, did you get the answers you were seeking when you came to our fair city?"

"Yes. Yes, I think I have."

Isabella patted her hand. "Good. You always were a smart girl." She stood up and nodded toward Juan. Then the nun bent down and kissed Tere on the forehead. "You take care of yourself, dear. And enjoy this time. Don't believe what they tell you about this stage of life. It is glorious."

"Yes, I'm beginning to realize that."

Juan smiled at Tere. "Rodrigo says to tell you he will pick you and Rowan up at nine tomorrow."

"He doesn't have to drive us all the way to Madrid, Juan. We can take the train."

Juan and Isabella threw back their heads and laughed. Tere swallowed a touch of irritation. She hadn't been good at accepting help, but she was learning.

Tere looked at her nun cousin and realized how much she was going to miss her. "Prima? You're a badass, and don't let anyone tell you any different."

"Oh, I dare them to try!" A smile. Then she put her arm in Juan's, and with the squeak of orthopedic shoes, they were gone.

Tere decided to sit there and wait until the bells rang. She wanted to hear them in the plaza one more time before she headed home.

While Rowan got them bottles of water before they boarded, Tere called Yolanda.

"Tere! You changed your mind again, and you're staying?"

"Ha! Nope, we're about to board the plane, but on that note…

that apartment you were selling when I visited you at the open house, is it still available?"

The screech from the other end of the line was so loud, Tere thought the whole waiting area at the gate could hear it. Finally, Yolanda said, "It is! It's like it was meant for you! Imagine how much fun we'll have living in the same city?"

"Wait, I'm not going to live there year-round, but I want to come a couple of times a year, maybe the whole summer? And then Rowan and his family can use it sometimes too." She also wanted to own a small piece of her ancestral city and be close to Santa Titi, but she didn't tell Yolanda that. That was hers alone.

As Yolanda talked about next steps, Tere noticed an elegant white-haired woman at the end of an adjacent row of seats. She was reading and had such a beatific look on her face that Tere couldn't help wondering what the woman was thinking about.

They announced the boarding of her flight as Rowan appeared and handed her a water, throwing their carry-ons over his shoulders. "Ma, time to board."

"Yolanda, I'm going to have to go. They're calling our flight."

"Is Rowan going back to Vermont with you?"

"Yes, he's going to help me get settled, then head back to California."

"Such a good boy and so handsome!"

Tere laughed.

"Okay, call me when you get home. Promise?"

Tere smiled into the phone, grateful. "Will do."

She tucked her phone in her pocket and slung her fanny pack across her chest, avoiding the sore side. As she turned to head toward the gate, she noticed the white-haired woman shift and wrap her slender ankle around the metal leg of the airport seating as her body lifted, then hovered several inches off the seat.

Tere froze, the flow of passengers begrudgingly adjusting as they walked.

She looked at the people around them. There was a businessman across from the woman, talking on his phone; he didn't spare her a passing glance. A twentysomething guy with a backpack sat right next to the floating woman. Didn't they see what she was doing? Tere turned to ask Rowan if he saw it, but he was already in line at the gate.

She took a step to move closer, to talk to the woman...

"Mom!"

Tere waved to Rowan, then glanced back at the woman who was now sitting normally, ankle no longer wrapped around the chair. Tere walked toward her son in a daze, so many thoughts spinning in her head.

Had this been going on around her all her life, and she never noticed?

Around everyone?

Rowan was waiting for her on the Jetway, and as she started walking down the tunnel to the plane, she realized it wasn't at all important if anyone believed, if anyone saw the woman with the white hair levitating above her seat.

All that mattered was that they were free, that they needed no wings to fly.

Reading Group Guide

1. The beginning of the story shows our main character, Tere, levitating for the first time. How does she react to this event? What would you do if you started levitating, and do you think you would handle it differently?

2. After the loss of her husband, Tere finds herself not only stricken with grief but also struggling to be the person she once was. How do Tere's roles as a wife, mother, professor, and friend evolve throughout the novel? Then, think about a loss you've experienced, and share how that might have changed you and the roles you play in your life.

3. Tere's journey begins when she makes the decision to travel to Ávila. What does she hope to find while there, and after reading the story, do you think she was successful? If you could travel anywhere in the world to find yourself, where would it be?

4. Tere is extremely proud of both her Puerto Rican and Spanish heritages, and much of the narrative focuses on her relationship with that part of her identity. What are ways in which Tere

reconnects with her culture throughout the story? Why is that important for her?

5. Tere is not only a distant descendant of Saint Teresa of Ávila but also shares her gift—levitation. Describe how Tere and Saint Teresa's lives and roles as women are similar, despite being hundreds of years apart. How did this connection between these two characters make you feel?

6. The theme of grief permeates throughout the novel. How is grief portrayed in the story? Are there any elements you found you could relate to?

7. Describe the ways mysticism and belief play roles in the story. How does Tere's belief and acceptance in her own abilities change, and how does that affect the ways she views the world and other women? Though this is a speculative piece of fiction, are there any elements of mysticism you believe in or find interesting?

8. Tere meets many people in Ávila as she seeks the answer to her levitation problem. How did each of the characters impact Tere and her character growth? Was there a secondary character you connected to the most?

9. Why does Tere bury the relic of Saint Teresa, and how was that pivotal to her overall character development? How did this event make you feel?

10. Tere is straddled between two worlds: her old life as a professor who isn't appreciated for her work, and the life of a woman

who is just now learning to spread her wings. How do these two worlds come together in the end, and what choice does Tere make for how she will live her life moving forward? Have you ever felt like you've had to make a choice like Tere's? If so, what was that experience like?

A Conversation with the Author

Tere's story is filled with grief, love, travel, and magic, and her journey is one readers won't forget. What inspired you to write this novel?

It started when the first line just came to me as I paced in my home office one summer afternoon. I have no idea where from, but it felt astonishingly "right." I sat down, and a draft of the opening scene just flowed out as if planned. I've been very interested in writing stories about women "of a certain age," when we're told we're invisible, have less to offer, when in fact there is incredible power in this era of life when you don't care what anyone else thinks. Tere reaches that point and reassesses everything, and I loved writing about her journey. Not sure where the idea for her levitation came from as it was not a conscious choice. I think deep in my brain, I think of this time of life as untethered.

You describe Ávila with such vivid detail, giving the reader an immersive experience of the landscape and culture of this town. Why is this place important to you and to this story?

My family's name, Dávila, comes from the Spanish "de Ávila" or "from Ávila," so the city has been an integral part of my identity.

It's a somewhat common name, so there are a lot of us with roots there, but one afternoon in Luquillo, Puerto Rico, my titi Georgina showed me photographs of her trip to the city, and it became a real place for me and I was determined to go. I spent a month there working on this book, and it was the first long trip I'd done solo, which was a big milestone. So many people tried to talk me out of making this trip alone at sixty, but that only made me more determined (but that suitcase was *heavy*). In between writing, I walked the streets for hours each day and fell in love with Ávila. It is steeped in history, and the people I met were just lovely. I felt at home there from the minute I stepped off the train.

Not only do we follow Tere's story, but we also learn a lot about Saint Teresa of Ávila. Why this saint?

My whole life I've been told that the Dávilas are descended from the family of Santa Teresa. I thought it was interesting, but I never connected with it. I'd read her books and did minimal research, but it wasn't until the writing of this book that I really dug in. She was a purehearted firebrand. Never took no for an answer and marched forward totally secure in her beliefs, even when threatened with execution by the Inquisition. I admire the hell out of her. Though she is well-known in name, I hope some readers might further explore her story as it is fascinating and so very inspiring. She was *way* ahead of her time, and for me, Teresa represents the best parts of the Catholic faith, but her tale is one that transcends any one religion. She was simply a fascinating, strong woman in a difficult time, so the inspiration is more human than limited to one religion.

What kind of research went into writing this novel? In general, what's your writing process like?

This book was unique for me because I spent months reading first. Books about Santa Teresa, about the Catholic Church, about mysticism, quantum physics, and getting older. I reexplored *On Death and Dying* and read numerous novels about loss. But the trip to Ávila was the part that really got the story going. Money was tight so my husband was like, "Can't you just use Google Earth to get a sense of it?" There is no substitute for walking the streets and talking to people. It was a life-changing trip for me.

What do you hope readers take away from Tere's journey?

That it is never too late to have an epiphany or to change the course of your life. In fact, as you get older, you get better, and the path becomes clearer. I hope they take away that though loss is painful, it can bring about tremendous growth. And to not allow themselves to be defined by anyone or anything—that is their task and theirs alone—and the beautiful thing about definitions is that they evolve with time.

What are some books you've read that have inspired your writing?

Like Tere, I began my readings in mysticism with the scientific part of the field. *The Holographic Universe* by Michael Talbot blew my mind. Shifted my perception of reality. My favorite book about Santa Teresa is *Teresa of Avila: The Progress of a Soul* by Cathleen Medwick. It's an excellent biography, but it also captures the essence of Teresa's work. It made me feel closer to her, even more than the saint's own books. Of course, all of Santa Teresa's writing is beautiful. I've read her books, letters, and writings several times each in English and Spanish, but they are very dense, obsequious (Medwick's book does an excellent job of explaining why), and deeply religious. But the language is gorgeous, and they are some of the most important works of Spanish literature. As for novels read for inspiration for Tere's journey, I loved Anne Tyler's *Ladder of Years* and *Matrix* by Lauren Groff, and I'm grateful to my editor for suggesting *A Man Called Ove* by Fredrik Backman. What a gorgeous and deeply felt exploration of grief.

Acknowledgments

Writing this book was an emotional and literal pilgrimage for me, and I am grateful to many people for their support in its creation.

Always first is my thanks to my agent and friend, Linda Camacho, who is unfailingly there to help and support me with the ups and downs of my writing career and talk me through the occasional anxiety freak-out. I couldn't navigate this creative life without you. And to my brilliant editor, Christa Désir, who saw the promise in a paragraph summary of this unusual story and set me loose. Her feedback through the wildly different drafts was invaluable. Thanks to Findlay McCarthy for their help early on, and Liv Turner, who jumped on this ride and provided insightful critique that helped bring out the best in Tere and the manuscript. I'm grateful to Sara Wood for the gorgeous cover and the fabulous Cristina Arreola, whose marketing and public relations prowess are unmatched in the publishing industry (I'd fight anyone who dares to argue) and who is always receptive, kind, and enthusiastic. The whole Sourcebooks staff have been so amazing. When the VP of sales, Sean Murray, told me at a breakfast in Chicago that he thought the first line of this book was the best he'd ever read, I knew I was part of a family that just *got* me, weird as I am.

To my dear friend Dawn Kurtagich, our twice-monthly writer

Zoom sessions between Vermont and Wales keep me sane and keep me going. She was in on this book since the initial idea and helped me shape the story in more ways than I can count.

My friend and fellow VCFA alum Angela Small lives at the heart of this book. The fact that we were both working on novels inspired by saints at the same time seemed predestined. This work would not exist without her wise counsel, multiple readings, and brilliant feedback. She *got* Tere Sánchez from day one and helped me stay true to her.

Thanks to Robin Ann Barron, who sat talking about what it was like to be a woman of a certain age in the Red Hen Bakery and read my really early, really rough first draft and gave me enthusiastic and encouraging feedback.

So much thanks to my friend and tattoo artist Esmé Hall, who was my guide and mentor in all things mystical. I loved that you immediately recognized that I needed to approach the world of mysticism from a scientific viewpoint and recommended many books and videos, which I consumed eagerly. You fielded weird existential texts at all hours, and I'm grateful for your wisdom, friendship, and guidance.

My dear friends and mentors Cory and August Rose, who have taught me so much about writing and life. I love that they just happened to FaceTime me as I was leaving the reliquary, and when they heard me rage about Teresa's finger and how I wanted to steal it and bury it in her garden, they yelled, "Make your character do it!" It blew the story wide open and brought me much peace.

I am so grateful to my brother, George Hagman. His read of this work from a psychoanalyst's perspective was vital in those last few weeks. He helped me understand the layers to Tere's ecstasy and also saw symbolism and meaning that I wasn't even conscious of in its pages.

My gratitude to the kind people of Ávila, Spain. I fell in love with the city during my weeks there. Particular thanks to my host, Belen González de Vega. Her lovely apartment near the square was my home away from home in the writing of the first draft. I think about it often and will be back. And Ivan Garcia at Oro Puro for the beautiful Santa Teresa flaming arrow tattoo. And to Nicole Argueta Sevilla, the lovely young woman who was so kind to me and became my friend. When I didn't know a single human in the entire country, hearing my name called in the street was enough to make me cry. It was an honor to get to know her and her beautiful daughter.

During the writing of this novel, my husband, Doug, suffered a stroke. I am eternally grateful that I didn't lose him (thank you, Santa Titi), but we went through some challenging months, and I channeled much of the pain into poor Tere. I managed to continue writing throughout, and the daily support and encouragement from him and our son, Carlos, was a godsend. These two men never falter in their belief in me and my stories, they keep me committed and on point, and I love them more than they will ever know.

And thanks to you, dear reader, for joining Tere and I on this journey. I hope you took something away from the stories of our pierced but still beating hearts. In the words of Santa Teresa, "If we have a safe, level road to walk along, why should we desire wings to fly?"

About the Author

Ann Dávila Cardinal comes from a Puerto Rican family that is indeed (she's been assured, anyway) descended from the family of Saint Teresa of Ávila. She has an MFA in fiction from Vermont College of Fine Arts and is the author of *The Storyteller's Death*, 2023 gold medal winner of an International Latino Book Award in fiction. Her young adult novels include *Five Midnights*, *Category Five*, and *Breakup from Hell*. Ann lives in Vermont with her husband, Doug, and is already making plans to return to Ávila, Spain, with her son, Carlos, to do the Camino Teresiano and walk the route of Santa Teresa's life from cradle to grave.